BRIAN FLYNN

THE CASE OF THE FAITHFUL HEART

BRIAN FLYNN was born in 1885 in Leyton, Essex. He won a scholarship to the City Of London School, and from there went into the civil service. In World War I he served as Special Constable on the Home Front, also teaching "Accountancy, Languages, Maths and Elocution to men, women, boys and girls" in the evenings, and acting in his spare time.

It was a seaside family holiday that inspired Brian Flynn to turn his hand to writing in the mid-twenties. Finding most mystery novels of the time "mediocre in the extreme", he decided to compose his own. Edith, the author's wife, encouraged its completion, and after a protracted period finding a publisher, it was eventually released in 1927 by John Hamilton in the UK and Macrae Smith in the U.S. as *The Billiard-Room Mystery*.

The author died in 1958. In all, he wrote and published 57 mysteries, the vast majority featuring the super-sleuth Antony Bathurst.

BRIAN FLYNN

THE CASE OF THE FAITHFUL HEART

With an introduction by

Steve Barge

DEAN STREET PRESS

Published by Dean Street Press 2021

Copyright © 1939 Brian Flynn

Introduction © 2021 Steve Barge

All Rights Reserved

The right of Brian Flynn to be identified as the Author of the Work has been asserted by his estate in accordance with the Copyright, Designs and Patents Act 1988.

First published in 1939 by John Long

Cover by DSP

ISBN 978 1 914150 65 4

www.deanstreetpress.co.uk

INTRODUCTION

"I believe that the primary function of the mystery story is
to entertain; to stimulate the imagination and even, at times,
to supply humour. But it pleases the connoisseur most when
it presents – and reveals – genuine mystery. To reach its full
height, it has to offer an intellectual problem for the reader
to consider, measure and solve."

Brian Flynn, *Crime Book* magazine, 1948

BRIAN Flynn began his writing career with *The Billiard Room Mystery*
in 1927, primarily at the prompting of his wife Edith who had grown
tired of hearing him say how he could write a better mystery novel
than the ones he had been reading. Four more books followed under
his original publisher, John Hamilton, before he moved to John
Long, who would go on to publish the remaining forty-eight of his
Anthony Bathurst mysteries, along with his three Sebastian Stole
titles, released under the pseudonym Charles Wogan. Some of the
early books were released in the US, and there were also a small
number of translations of his mysteries into Swedish and German.
In the article from which the above quote is taken from, Brian also
claims that there were also French and Danish translations but to
date, I have not found a single piece of evidence for their existence.
The only translations that I have been able to find evidence of are
War Es Der Zahnarzt? and *Bathurst Greift Ein* in German – *The
Mystery of the Peacock's Eye*, retitled to the less dramatic "Was It
The Dentist?", and *The Horn* becoming "Bathurst Takes Action" –
and, in Swedish, *De 22 Svarta*, a more direct translation of *The Case
of the Black Twenty-Two*. There may well be more work to be done
finding these, but tracking down all of his books written in the original English has been challenging enough!

Reprints of Brian's books were rare. Four titles were released
as paperbacks as part of John Long's Four Square Thriller range in
the late 1930s, four more re-appeared during the war from Cherry
Tree Books and Mellifont Press, albeit abridged by at least a third,
and two others that I am aware of, *Such Bright Disguises* (1941)
and *Reverse the Charges* (1943), received a paperback release as

part of John Long's Pocket Edition range in the early 1950s – these were also possibly abridged, but only by about 10%. They were the exceptions, rather than the rule, however, and it was not until 2019, when Dean Street Press released his first ten titles, that his work was generally available again.

The question still persists as to why his work disappeared from the awareness of all but the most ardent collectors. As you may expect, when a title was only released once, back in the early 1930s, finding copies of the original text is not a straightforward matter – not even Brian's estate has a copy of every title. We are particularly grateful to one particular collector for providing *The Edge of Terror*, Brian's first serial killer tale, and another for *The Ebony Stag* and *The Grim Maiden*. With these, the reader can breathe a sigh of relief as a copy of every one of Brian's books has now been located – it only took about five years . . .

One of Brian's strengths was the variety of stories that he was willing to tell. Despite, under his own name at least, never straying from involving Anthony Bathurst in his novels – technically he doesn't appear in the non-series *Tragedy at Trinket*, although he gets a name-check from the sleuth of that tale who happens to be his nephew – it is fair to say that it was rare that two consecutive books ever followed the same structure. Some stories are narrated by a Watson-esque character, although never the same person twice, and others are written by Bathurst's "chronicler". The books sometimes focus on just Bathurst and his investigation but sometimes we get to see the events occurring to the whole cast of characters. On occasion, Bathurst himself will "write" the final chapter, just to make sure his chronicler has got the details correct. The murderer may be an opportunist or they may have a convoluted (and, on occasion, a somewhat over-the-top) plan. They may be working for personal gain or as part of a criminal enterprise or society. Compare for example, *The League of Matthias* and *The Horn* – consecutive releases but were it not for Bathurst's involvement, and a similar sense of humour underlying Brian's writing, you could easily believe that they were from the pen of different writers.

Brian seems to have been determined to keep stretching himself with his writing as he continued Bathurst's adventures, and the ten books starting with *Cold Evil* show him still trying new things. Two of the books are inverted mysteries – where we know who the killer is, and we follow their attempts to commit the crime and/or escape justice and also, in some cases, the detective's attempt to bring them to justice. That description doesn't do justice to either *Black Edged* or *Such Bright Disguises*, as there is more revealed in the finale than the reader might expect . . . There is one particular innovation in *The Grim Maiden*, namely the introduction of a female officer at Scotland Yard.

Helen Repton, an officer from "the woman's side of the Yard" is recruited in that book, as Bathurst's plan require an undercover officer in a cinema. This is her first appearance, despite the text implying that Bathurst has met her before, but it is notable as the narrative spends a little time apart from Bathurst. It follows Helen Repton's investigations based on superb initiative, which generates some leads in the case. At this point in crime fiction, there have been few, if any, serious depictions of a female police detective – the primary example would be Mrs Pym from the pen of Nigel Morland, but she (not just the only female detective at the Yard, but the Assistant Deputy Commissioner no less) would seem to be something of a caricature. Helen would go on to become a semi-regular character in the series, and there are certainly hints of a romantic connection between her and Bathurst.

It is often interesting to see how crime writers tackled the Second World War in their writing. Some brought the ongoing conflict into their writing – John Rhode (and his pseudonym Miles Burton) wrote several titles set in England during the conflict, as did others such as E.C.R. Lorac, Christopher Bush, Gladys Mitchell and many others. Other writers chose not to include the War in their tales – Agatha Christie had ten books published in the war years, yet only *N or M?* uses it as a subject.

Brian only uses the war as a backdrop in one title, *Glittering Prizes*, the story of a possible plan to undermine the Empire. It illustrates the problem of writing when the outcome of the conflict was unknown – it was written presumably in 1941 – where there seems little sign of life in England of the war going on, one character states that he has fought in the conflict, but messages are sent from Nazi conspirators, ending *"Heil Hitler!"*. Brian had good reason for not wanting to write about the conflict in detail, though, as he had immediate family involved in the fighting and it is quite understandable to see writing as a distraction from that.

While Brian had until recently been all but forgotten, there are some mentions for Brian's work in some studies of the genre – Sutherland Scott in *Blood in their Ink* praises *The Mystery of the Peacock's Eye* as containing "one of the ablest pieces of misdirection" before promptly spoiling that misdirection a few pages later, and John Dickson Carr similarly spoils the ending of *The Billiard Room Mystery* in his famous essay "The Grandest Game In The World". One should also include in this list Barzun and Taylor's entry in their *Catalog of Crime* where they attempted to cover Brian by looking at a single title – the somewhat odd *Conspiracy at Angel* (1947) – and summarising it as "Straight tripe and savorless. It is doubtful, on the evidence, if any of his others would be different." Judging an author based on a single title seems desperately unfair – how many people have given up on Agatha Christie after only reading *Postern Of Fate*, for example – but at least that misjudgement is being rectified now.

Contemporary reviews of Brian's work were much more favourable, although as John Long were publishing his work for a library market, not all of his titles garnered attention. At this point in his writing career – 1938 to 1944 – a number of his books won reviews in the national press, most of which were positive. Maurice Richardson in the *Observer* commented that "Brian Flynn balances his ingredients with considerable skill" when reviewing *The Ebony Stag* and praised *Such Bright Disguises* as a "suburban horror melodrama" with an "ingenious final solution". "Suspense is well maintained until the end" in *The Case of the Faithful Heart,* and the protagonist's narration in *Black Edged* in "impressively nightmarish".

It is quite possible that Brian's harshest critic, though, was himself. In the *Crime Book* magazine, he wrote about how, when reading the current output of detective fiction "I delight in the dazzling erudition that has come to grace and decorate the craft of the *'roman policier'*." He then goes on to say "At the same time, however, I feel my own comparative unworthiness for the fire and burden of the competition." Such a feeling may well be the reason why he never made significant inroads into the social side of crime-writing, such as the Detection Club or the Crime Writers Association. Thankfully, he uses this sense of unworthiness as inspiration, concluding "The stars, though, have always been the most desired of all goals, so I allow exultation and determination to take the place of that but temporary dismay."

In Anthony Bathurst, Flynn created a sleuth that shared a number of traits with Holmes but was hardly a carbon-copy. Bathurst is a polymath and gentleman sleuth, a man of contradictions whose background is never made clear to the reader. He clearly has money, as he has his own rooms in London with a pair of servants on call and went to public school (Uppingham) and university (Oxford). He is a follower of all things that fall under the banner of sport, in particular horse racing and cricket, the latter being a sport that he could, allegedly, have represented England at. He is also a bit of a show-off, littering his speech (at times) with classical quotes, the obscurer the better, provided by the copies of the *Oxford Diction-ary of Quotations* and *Brewer's Dictionary of Phrase & Fable* that Flynn kept by his writing desk, although Bathurst generally restrains himself to only doing this with people who would appreciate it or to annoy the local constabulary. He is fond of amateur dramatics (as was Flynn, a well-regarded amateur thespian who appeared in at least one self-penned play, *Blue Murder*), having been a member of OUDS, the Oxford University Dramatic Society. General information about his background is light on the ground. His parents were Irish, but he doesn't have an accent – see *The Spiked Lion* (1933) – and his eyes are grey. Despite the fact that he is an incredibly charming and handsome individual, we learn in *The Orange Axe* that he doesn't pursue romantic relationships due to a bad experience in his first romance. We find out more about that relationship and the woman involved in *The Edge of Terror*, and soon thereafter he falls head over heels in love in *Fear and Trembling*, although we never hear of that young lady again. After that, there are eventual hints of an attraction between Helen Repton, but nothing more. That doesn't stop women falling head over heels for Bathurst – as he departs her company in *The Padded Door*, one character muses "What other man could she ever love . . . after this secret idolatry?"

As we reach the halfway point in Anthony's career, his companions have somewhat stablised, with Chief Inspector Andrew MacMorran now his near-constant junior partner in investigation. The friendship with MacMorran is a highlight (despite MacMorran always calling him "Mr. Bathurst") with the sparring between them always a delight to read. MacMorran's junior officers, notably Superintendent Hemingway and Sergeant Chatterton, are frequently recurring characters. The notion of the local constabulary calling in help from Scotland Yard enables cases to be set around the country while still maintaining the same central cast (along with a local bobby or two).

Cold Evil (1938), the twenty-first Bathurst mystery, finally pins down Bathurst's age, and we find that in *The Billiard Room Mystery* (1927), his first outing, he was a fresh-faced Bright Young Thing of twenty-two. How he can survive with his own rooms, at least two servants, and no noticeable source of income remains a mystery. One can also ask at what point in his life he travelled the world, as he has, at least, been to Bangkok at some point. It is, perhaps, best not to analyse Bathurst's past too carefully . . .

"Judging from the correspondence my books have excited it seems I have managed to achieve some measure of success, for my faithful readers comprise a circle in which high dignitaries of the Church rub shoulders with their brothers and sisters of the common touch."

For someone who wrote to entertain, such correspondence would have delighted Brian, and I wish he were around to see how many people have enjoyed the reprints of his work so far. *The Mystery of the Peacock's Eye* (1928) won Cross Examining Crime's Reprint Of The Year award for 2019, with *Tread Softly* garnering second place the following year. His family are delighted with the reactions that people have passed on, and I hope that this set of books will delight just as much.

Steve Barge

CHAPTER I
THE EXAGGERATION

IT HAS been both said and written that between what matters and what seems to matter how should one distinguish with commendable judgment? To many of us, whose lives run along the ordinary channels and down the commonplace corridors, the necessity for this choice may come but seldom. The thought is comforting. On the contrary, to others of us, a specially selected company, it may come reasonably often. Which is a thought less comforting! To a few it may come not at all. Which, however, should not be disturbing. But it came certainly once to Keith Annesley. He was in his forty-fourth year when the incident occurred. The date when it happened was the 8th day of June. It is specially marked in his diary and also—it must be admitted—in the general calendars of the civilized world. The uncivilized world, it is presumed, reserves no place in its records for the tyranny of Time and shows a complete contempt for such matters as calculated calendars.

Keith Annesley, at the time of the incident to which reference has just been made, was a moderately successful novelist and a bachelor. These conditions, separately and as a combination, afforded him a certain amount of pleasure. He lived in a comfortably sized bungalow in the country village of Blackstock, which as everybody knows is but four miles from the market town of Bridge and a mere twenty-two from the great city of London itself. In this way, it will be readily seen, Keith Annesley was able to combine competently and easily the delights of the countryside with the comparative raptures that could so frequently be obtained from regular visits to the metropolis. He was "done for" (her own description—be it noted) by a housekeeper whose name was Mrs. Fairey. She was a childless widow in the early fifties. Unhappily, the late Fairey had failed to survive an argument with a Boche at Le Cateau—the Boche had been just a trifle quicker with his bayonet. This unconsidered (on Fairey's part) trifle had made all the difference. In Mrs. Fairey's case, the name she bore was an entire misnomer, and, as Keith Annesley had said more than once to privileged friends, he was considerably relieved to think that she had not made her original appearance from the bottom of his garden. She weighed over twelve stone, you see, and, as Keith put it to his intimate cronies, he had always been appalled at anything in the nature of "upheavals".

On the morning of the particular 8th of June which has already been mentioned Keith Annesley had laboured manfully for some hours, and as a result of these labours had produced a matter of over two hundred words on the pad of foolscap in front of him. He looked at them bitterly, read them over carefully, and suddenly the bitter look on his face gave way to a smile. When read they weren't by any means as foul as he had anticipated. With a twist here and a turn there they would do. Both twist and turn were speedily accomplished. Keith Annesley nodded pleasantly to himself, gathered his papers together with a look of almost mischievous delight, and prepared, with similarly unholy joy, to put them away until his next sitting. In other words, he had reached the delightful decision that he need do no more work that morning!

He walked into his charmingly kept garden (his gardener, by the way, was both competent and cunning) by way of the french doors of the lounge and then looked at his watch. What he saw indicated there also pleased him. Within a mere matter of ten minutes the laws of the country would allow him to drink beer upon licensed premises. Good beer at that! He therefore called through the open window of the kitchen to the capacious Mrs. Fairey. The call intimated his intention.

"Very good, sir," said Mrs. Fairey with an air of resignation, and Keith Annesley went round to the front of his bungalow with a swing in his gait and stepped on to the high road that would take him firstly half a mile to the "Running Horse" (which was his primary intention), and beyond that the remaining three and a half miles to the market town of Bridge (should he so desire). Upon this present mission—it may be recorded—the former was his sole incentive. Keith Annesley strolled luxuriously down the road. The day was hot. Hot with the clear, clean benevolence of sun in our English country that belongs more to the month of June than to any other. Now that he had been released from the bondage of work Keith Annesley almost lingered in his walking. He passed the forge at the cross-roads where Dick

Richardson was swinging his hammer. Then past the row of white-washed cottages on the fringe of Blackstock and the little general shop where Mrs. Mitchell sold everything from a beetroot to a bootlace. Thus Keith Annesley came to the inn which bore bravely the sign of the "Running Horse".

Outside, there stood an ugly squat motor lorry from which rolled barrels of beer and on to which were being loaded other barrels that had served their turn and been emptied of their fragrance. Annesley walked up the square cobbled yard and turned sharp right into the bar. The bar was low-ceilinged, with oak beams and similar ancient appointments. Reliable authority ascribed the house's birth to the time of Richard II of Bordeaux. Less reputable rumour whispered that Bolingbroke himself had breakfasted there not long before Richard's imposition. Keith Annesley accepted both the authority and the rumour with interest and the good beer that the "Running Horse" dispensed with thanksgiving and charity.

Luke Weir, the landlord, greeted him from behind the bar with a hearty "Good Morning". Luke liked Annesley and Annesley returned the compliment. "One of them book-writin' fellers," commented Luke during Annesley's occasional absences, "and sometimes a bit strange to understand, but a rare good chap in spite of it." Keith Annesley walked towards his host and smilingly gave his order. Luke heard and then accepted Annesley's almost immediate invitation. The two men drank in a dignified silence. Annesley put down his tankard with a sigh of contentment. "That was good, Luke. All of it. Do you know I'm strongly tempted to have another. I am really."

Luke Weir grinned. He had heard that sentiment expressed many times in the past. "And you was never a good one for resistin' temptation." He filled Annesley's tankard again and the two men began to talk. Annesley reached to his hip pocket for his cigarette-case.

"Luke, you miserable old sinner," he said at length, "do you know—I've been thinking. I feel that I need a holiday. The urge to laze is most assuredly upon me."

"The urge to travel, sir?"

"No, Luke. You heard what I said. The urge to laze."

"Wouldn't you benefit by something more like a change, sir?" thrust in Luke Weir slyly. From under his shaggy brows he stared down at the only occupant of his bar.

Annesley laughed easily. "That's good from you, Luke. You've never done a real day's work in your life, you old fraud. No—I said 'laze', and 'laze' I mean."

"What part are you thinkin' of going, sir? At home here or abroad?"

Annesley waited to blow a smoke-ring effortlessly. "Oh—England. West Country. Definitely West Country. Coombe and tor, green meadow and lane. It's the Pick of England, Luke. There's no arguing about that. Once you've been to the West Country you're spoiled for everywhere else. This time I'm inclined towards Cornwall—the delectable Duchy."

"Yes, sir," replied an uncomprehending host. "When will you be going, sir?" he added.

"Somewhere towards the middle of the month, Luke. Don't think I can manage it before; wish I could. I've a book to finish."

Luke Weir nodded in admiration. The word "book" captivated him. Annesley looked at the time. "Time the midday paper was in from Bridge," he said.

Weir took a step backwards so that he too could see the hands of the big clock in his bar. "You're right, sir. Well past time if you ask me! It's that new boy of Caldwell's. Blast me if he don't get later with the papers every day. With no reason for it. Saucy young rat, too! Yesterday he comes into the bar here, smacks down my *Star* on the counter, and shouts, for everybody to hear, 'Here y'are, Weary.' What do you think of it? And that's what they call education. I don't hold with it, and never did, sir."

Keith Annesley smiled broadly. He had heard mine host of the "Running Horse" in this strain many times before. He leisurely selected another cigarette from his case.

Weir pursued the thread of the previous conversation. "Education so-called makes people think above their proper station. Them papers are a good twenty minutes late already. The way this boy's goin' on—we shall get 'em *after* lunch soon. Lot o' chance for you, then, if you want anything on for the first race. Next time I see him I'll give Caldwell a piece of my mind." The words had scarcely left his mouth when the door of the bar opened. That is to say it was thrust back to the accompaniment of much noise. A thin-faced boy entered. He placed two papers of those he carried, on the counter in front of the landlord of the "Running Horse". As he did so he grinned provocatively. Weir frowned at him. Then, as the boy turned, Keith Annesley noticed the announcement on the contents bill that had almost wrapped itself round the boy's knees. Instead of the customary curt headlines concerning the day's racing, he saw something, that seemed at first sight, not only to be vaguely alarming, but also to be hazily familiar. Luke Weir noticed it too. The newspaper boy went out, and Weir's eyes met Annesley's. The latter laughed lightly.

"I've often wondered how it would look in cold print," he said. "Now I know."

Weir repeated the words of the placard in wonderment. "'Death of Keith Annesley.' Gave me quite a turn with you standing there. What's the idea? Somebody's hand at a practical joke?"

Annesley, still laughing silently, shook his head. "No. Don't you know to whom that refers? It's the American Senator. The armaments magnate. He's been confused with me before this. Before I look at the paper I'll bet you what you like that it's he who's dead."

Luke Weir was still shaking his head. "Go on. I'll still say it gave me a turn. Curious how these things take you. I expect it was because you were standing there at the time. Is he any relation of yours?"

"Not that I know of. May be a sort of distant cousin. I believe that one of my grandfather's brothers went to the States many years ago, but I know nothing more than that. Actually I was over thirty before I ever heard of this fellow. Then the first time I ever did see his name it gave me a bit of a shock, I admit. Though, of course, there's no earthly reason why it should have done. Think of all the John Smiths there are knocking about." Annesley laughed again. "Damn' funny, that. That paper fellow crashing in like that."

"The man seems pretty famous at any rate," commented Weir, "for his death to give him headlines like these." He picked up the paper in a quest for more detailed knowledge.

"Oh, rather! Quite a big shot. He's been the head of a fierce armaments ramp over there for some time. The American papers have been full of him. Right in the public eye for some months now. What's it say there about him?"

Weir read the news. "'Keith Annesley, the Armaments King, died suddenly this morning at his house near Wadour, U.S.A.'" Weir cocked a sapient eye towards his listener. "Expect somebody bumped him off from the way that's put. That's about the size of it."

"Couldn't say," replied Annesley. "And I don't know that I'm very much concerned, either."

"Guess if you're not, I'm not," returned Weir, turning to greet a fresh arrival at the bar of the "Running Horse".

"No," said Keith Annesley with a chuckle. "You can class me now with Mark Twain. When I looked at that placard a few minutes ago I felt that the whole business had been—as Mark himself said—'grossly exaggerated'. Good morning, Luke. You needn't buy any black for me yet awhile. I'll see you again before I go away."

"'Morning, Mr. Annesley," saluted Weir from behind the bar.

Keith Annesley walked out of the "Running Horse" into the sunlight. When he got back to his Fairey she wondered what it was that had made him so unusually light-hearted. After all, as she said to herself, "it wasn't as though he was *going* to the 'Running Horse', he's *been* there."

That evening, Keith Annesley sat in the parlour of the "Running Horse" and joked again with Luke Weir. "It's all right," he said with a grin; "don't keep looking at me like that, I'm not a ghost, you old ass. Fill that tankard again." And Luke Weir filled it many times.

CHAPTER II
DINNER PARTY AT "HILLEARYS"

ANNESLEY was destined to remember that day for all time. For, by a coincidence, on the evening of that same day Jacqueline Hillier was found poisoned in her car. The dinner party at "Hillearys" on the evening of the 8th of June—that is to say about seven hours after the main events recorded in the previous chapter—consisted of eight people. As they were fated to play a most important part in this history their respective names were as follows. Paul Hillier, the host, his wife Jacqueline, their son and daughter Neill and Ann Hillier respectively, his brother Maurice, his brother Maurice's wife Belle, and the Vicar of Lanrebel, the Rev. Septimus Aylmer, with spouse attached. As has been stated, they were destined, in their different ways, to play important parts in the history which is to follow. Some description, therefore, of each of them may not be out of place.

Paul Hillier was a big bulky man of about fifty-five years of age. He had a heavy swarthy face, dark-brown eyes, and iron-grey hair, but despite the fact that he was aging rapidly, his mind was always alert and well-ordered. He said little or nothing, but, mostly, that trifle which he did say was to the point. He was entirely conservative in all matters and a willingly slave to the whole gamut of the conventions. Shrewd observers of him would have formed the opinion that he loved both himself and his wife a little more than either of his children. But, of course, there is always the possibility that those observers whose shrewdness we applaud might have erred in their judgment. Jacqueline Hillier, his wife, was considerably younger than her husband. In every way. If her husband's mind were alert, hers was always at least two paces ahead of it. Her eyes were dark blue and her hair, although double shaded in parts, in the main was a rich dark brown. Her eyes, besides being dark blue, were also lovely and made her almost beautiful. They certainly in themselves saved her face from the stigma of mere prettiness. And yet there was an indefinable quality in her eyes, when you caught her face in repose, that made you wonder about Jacqueline Hillier . . . wonder whether Fate had really handed her the court cards which it appeared to have done upon the surface of things.

Neill, her son, was more than a year younger than his sister Ann. He was like his mother as regards his features. He had inherited her eyes and, in addition, the Marsham nose . . . before her marriage his mother had been Jacqueline Evelyn Marsham and her father the Rev. Francis Cloud Marsham, Master of Arts of the University of Oxford. Neill's face was thin and, for his age, curiously pale. There was seldom but little blood beneath his skin, and ordinarily a deep frown pulled together the dark-brown brows over the deep-set dark-blue eyes. By inclination he was drawn more to his father than to his mother. Most of the years of his life had been spent during his father's prosperity, and he retained but little memory of the time when they had lived at a school in Sussex, and such things as a country house and landed estate were very much figments of the imagination. Neill had been to Repton for five years and was going up to Oxford at the beginning of the following October for the Michaelmas term.

Ann Hillier, his sister, was twenty and the first-born of her parents. According to the accepted standards, she was neither beautiful nor pretty, even after making allowance for the undoubted fact that Beauty, after all, lies in the eye of the beholder. But, despite these admissions, she was definitely attractive. She had a fine intellectual forehead and amazingly serene grey eyes. Her voice, too, was unusually musical, and she had to a remarkable degree her brother's quick, sensitive intelligence. This last quality, perhaps, was the main reason why she was her mother's almost inseparable companion. In fact, so constantly were they together, and so marvellously had Jacqueline worn during their term of years, that they were commonly accepted in most places to which they went as sisters or friends instead of mother and daughter.

Maurice Hillier was forty-seven—eight years younger than his brother Paul, at whose dinner table he was sitting. He was a small edition of his brother. With the same eyes and the same colouring, but spare where Paul was bulky and thinnish where Paul was comfortably covered. His eyes were more restless, though, than Paul's, and darted ceaselessly from object to object. Through Paul's help and generosity, extended to him from prosperity, he had been enabled to go on to the Stock Exchange and was doing "very nicely, thank you". He and his wife were childless, and secretly, although the fact was probably much to their credit, rather ashamed of the condition.

Belle was thin, "small-talkative", small-bodied, and small-minded. She was in the early thirties. Her redeeming feature, physically, was a head (very neat) that glinted with a sheen of coppery gold. At times she amused Jacqueline but, in her heart, Jacqueline despised her and after a short time tired of her completely. Belle Hillier, however, had a habit when she was listening to Jacqueline, in Jacqueline's finer moments, of assuming the most delightful and unshakable meekness. She would sit in her chair and listen to a sparkling Jacqueline's concise utterances, very straight and prim and with her hands clasped together in her lap. To her sister-in-law, at these moments, she always suggested an insubordinate schoolgirl being taken seriously to task for her delinquencies by a new and extremely enthusiastic headmistress.

The two remaining members of the "Hillearys" dinner party need perhaps a less detailed description than has been given to the people of the Hillier family. As has already been recorded, they were the Rev. Septimus Aylmer, Vicar of Lanrebel, and the Rev. Septimus's wife, Mildred Ramsay Aylmer. "Hillearys" and the Vicarage itself are the only houses of any real size within the village of Lanrebel, which is situated in the county of Glebeshire in the south-western corner of England. In many directions, the Rev. Septimus was an extremely fortunate man. There were reasons. He had taken a certain amount of care with regard to that. His living of Lanrebel was worth about £800 a year and his premarital love for Mildred Ramsay had been considerably stimulated by the knowledge that although she was plain (a euphemism in itself) she would bring him another comfortable income. After marriage this income assisted his fund of affection even more, and there had come a time when it might be almost truthfully but regretfully said that it had completed usurped its place. Septimus's most difficult task in his cure of Lanrebel was the taking of the evening service on the Sabbath. The rest of the week he spent in his beautiful garden or in his car, which (chauffeur drawn) took him over a considerable area of the most beautiful county in England.

Both the Rev. Septimus and his wife, Mildred Ramsay, loved to be invited to dinner at "Hillearys" even though there were occasions when the clever tongue of Jacqueline sported unmercifully with them, mainly for daughter Ann's delight. The contents of Hillier's cellar, however, gave the Rev. Septimus at all times the most gratifying compensation.

On the evening of this 8th of June Jacqueline had already given ample evidence that she was a long way from her usual self. Paul Hillier had watched her anxiously several times from his end of the table, because he was certain that she was companioned by care. Up to now, indeed, Neill and the Rev. Septimus had been the brightest lights at the table. Both Paul and Ann were affected by Jacqueline, and Belle and Maurice were content for a time to listen to Neill crossing swords with the Vicar of Lanrebel.

"Yes. The country's all very well," said Neill, "if you've plenty of cash and can get out of it at the moment just whenever you want to. Otherwise, it's cold and cruel and mentally suffocating. What do the people ever talk about? The main conversation is of flower shows, and 'turnips and tatties' almost always top the bill. I thank the Lord every day of my life that I'm going up to Oxford in the autumn. And if it hadn't been for the fact that I ran a tonsil at the wrong time I'd have been there now."

"Ah," said the Rev. Septimus, "Oxford. . . . Dear me, what a vista it conjures up for me! . . . If I could only roll back the years. Dear, dear! Dreaming spires . . . the Magdalen bridge . . . the Iffley road . . . the House . . . My dear Neill . . . if you talk any more in this strain I shall have to pray to be delivered from the sin of envy." The Vicar Lanrebel smiled a somewhat fatuous smile, drained a glass of Paul Hillier's exquisite sherry and murmured inevitably: "The kindly fruits of the earth so that in due time we may enjoy them."

Paul attempted to rally his wife. He tossed her several fragments of conversation which in the ordinary course of events she would have welcomed avidly and returned with an additional sparkle. Ann tried gallantly to support her father in his especial endeavour. But Jacqueline remained moody, almost silent, and refused to be comforted. She answered most questions in monosyllables, and Paul Hillier saw how her fingers plucked nervously from time to time at the stem of her wineglass. Towards the end of the meal, she improved a little in spirits and tendered apologies that were occasionally accompanied by smiles which lit up her face and hinted at her attractiveness.

"I'm truly sorry," she said, "but I know I've been an atrocious hostess this evening. You must all forgive me for my aloofness and I'll promise to make up for it all—" She paused abruptly and again her fingers toyed with her glass.

"Next time," prompted Mildred Aylmer with a self-conscious brightness, ". . . that's what you were going to say, isn't it, Jacqueline?"

"Next time," repeated Jacqueline Hillier almost wonderingly. . . . "Yes, that's what I did mean, I suppose. There will always be a next time. There must be, of course."

Ann detected the strange note in her mother's voice and looked towards her with increased anxiety. Mowbray, the butler, hovered behind chairs.

"I feel," said Belle Hillier, with a certain nervous tensity, "that if I play bridge this evening I shall play a positive 'blinder'. That remark is intended primarily to attract a partner."

Paul Hillier smiled and gave her the necessary sign. The guests understood and rose.

"In that case," returned the Rev. Septimus, fatuously gallant, "count on me, Mrs. Hillier. Last week, if I remember rightly, Jacqueline and Neill chastised us with whips. This evening you and I may redress the balance with a chastisement of scorpions. That is if the cards are moderately kind." He chuckled to himself with sacerdotal satisfaction, and Neill's eyelid drooped suspiciously in Ann's direction.

"Playing, Jacky?" queried Ann of her mother.

Jacqueline shook her head. "No, not tonight, Ann darling. I've a wretched head. It's utterly foul! I'd be sorry for anybody whom I partnered this evening."

Ann slipped to her mother's side and put an arm round her. "What's troubling you, little Mother?"

"Nothing, Ann. Nothing, my angel, really. Just one of my heads, that's all. I shall be all right if you leave me alone. Go into the lounge with the others. I'll join you later. Leave me to myself for just a little while longer, will you, darling?" She smiled, but Ann knew that the smile was forced for her benefit. Ann shook her head doubtfully.

"All right, Jacky, but promise me you'll come in to us before very long. It's always so dull and empty when you aren't anywhere."

Jacqueline nodded brightly. "That's a promise, Babe. I'll come in just as soon as I feel a bit better."

Ann moved off and with some reluctance joined the rest of the party in the lounge. As she entered the Rev. Septimus was still in full song.

"I always speak as I think," Ann heard him say. The wife of his bosom did not neglect the opening that he gave her.

"Yes, dear," she replied artlessly, "only much more often, my pet."

Paul called Ann over to his side. Neither he nor Neill playing. Maurice Hillier and Mrs. Aylmer were partners in opposition to Belle Hillier and the Vicar of Lanrebel.

"Mother's coming in later," Ann explained to her father. "She's got a rotten head and says that she doesn't feel up to it."

Paul Hillier frowned at the unwelcome news. Like most healthy men, he was always inclined to be just a little impatient with the mere trivial ailments of his women-folk. "Can't make out what's upset her," he muttered. "May be something she's eaten. She seemed fit enough this morning. At least I thought so."

Neill lounged up to them. "If you want me for anything I shall be in the billiard-room. I want to practise one or two special shots. Coming in, Ann?"

His sister turned. "I don't think I will, Neill, if you don't mind. Not too keen tonight. I'll stay in here in case Mother should want anything. She's not so good."

"Right-o, Ann. It doesn't matter. If you should want anything done you'll know where to find me."

Paul Hillier picked up a magazine and settled himself in his favourite arm-chair. He liked comfort more, perhaps, than most men. Ann looked at the time. "Half past eight," she said aloud.

This, then, was the disposition of the household at "Hillearys" at half past eight on the evening of the 8th of June. The fact is important.

CHAPTER III
THE FIRST BLOW FALLS

THERE is but one inn in the village of Lanrebel, which condition is surprising. It bears an uncommon name. That of the "Salvation". As also it is the only hostelry for six miles in any direction, it has been truthfully remarked more than once that it carries a happy sign. It rejoices, too, in the fact that it is a "free" house. The landlord of the "Salvation", Arthur Paske, was a man of many parts. It is true to say of him that the world had indeed been his oyster, for he had walked and talked in almost every corner of it. The East he knew in a manner and to a degree that are given to but few men. He had sung in the village choir (he was a Hampshire man), sailed before the mast, grown tobacco in Burma, tried tea in Ceylon, been in the Government service at Rangoon, and had retired at the comparatively early age of fifty-nine. To him, retirement had meant taking a pub in Glebeshire. To the "Salvation", therefore, he had brought his hard-eyed wife, Laura Paske, his son and daughter-in-law, Frank and Lysbeth, and his only daughter, Phyllis. Under their assiduous care, the "Salvation", within the space of one year, had prospered exceedingly, for Paske had mastered the Pauline art of "being all things to all men".

During the months of summer and of early autumn the twelve comfortable bedrooms of the "Salvation" were almost always full. At other times of the year there were always at least two or three visitors in residence, but on the 9th day of the June of this story Paske had once again a full house, and he rubbed his hands with pleasure every morning when he twisted the necks of the fowls determined by a cruel fate to decorate the daily menu. For Arthur Paske was an astute business man despite the many callings he had followed. He detailed to himself regularly the standing of his guests. Three authors, a painter, a motor-car "expert" (Paske dearly loved everything in the nature of a superlative), a tall athletic man who seemed to have no obvious occupation, five assorted married couples spending their usual annual holiday in the country, and finally Mr. Edmund Pereira. The last named, an American on holiday, had been at the "Salvation" now since the 26th of April. And moreover, from all obvious portents, he looked like staying several months more. For in his own words, Lanrebel was "just swell".

At a quarter past eight on the morning of this 9th day of June, Paske unbolted the big gates of his cobbled yard and looked thankfully towards the rich benison of the risen sun. He drew the big doors back and pushed the bolts into their receptive sockets, with a dominant feeling of pleasant security. Then he walked into the road and looked up at the clock of the church under the vicariate of the Rev. Septimus Aylmer. Paske compared its time with that shown by his own watch. When he saw that they agreed he nodded and smiled with satisfaction. It was important from many points of view that the clock of the parish church should be accurate. The "Salvation" stood at the junction of three roads. The road to the left led to the market town of Liskerry, the road directly facing the inn went to the popular seaside town of Laran, and the third road, which bore away to the right, dipped down and went straight to Bonallack Ferry and beyond that to the picturesque town of Frayne. As Paske stood and breathed the morning air—and the June air of Lanrebel is worth breathing—he heard the voice of the American—Pereira—immediately behind him. "Say, Captain Paske, it's a swell morning and no error. Sure, livin' here takes a load off a guy's heart."

Paske beamed with satisfaction. "Glad you like it, Mr. Pereira. Goin' to be hot too, if I'm any judge."

"Suits me," returned Pereira contentedly. "I've always prided myself that I can stand heat. Guess I'm sort of lookin' ahead, eh?" He was a short, stout man with a bull neck and very powerful shoulders. His forehead was low and his eyes rather small, but his face usually held geniality for all that, behind his normal puckered expression. As he spoke he thrust out his lower lip and peered delightedly at the landlord of the "Salvation". "You know. Captain Paske," he went on affably, "I like this little burg of yours. It's a swell place. I've been here just about six weeks now and I'm not sickenin' yet for a sight of my home town. No, sir! Not on your life! There's no sense in wantin' what you can't have. At least that's how I figure it out."

"I think you're right, Mr. Pereira. Make the best of what's in front of you and you won't go far wrong. I've always tried to do that and I can't complain. My old Dad taught me to do it."

"Complain? I'll say you can't, Mr. Paske! Well—I think I'll take my morning constitutional. Just down the drug store and back. And you won't have to drag me to the breakfast table when these legs of mine have been stretched." He waved to Paske and set off down the road that led to Frayne.

Paske went back into the inn. Most of the household staff were now up and about. Paske called to his son Frank. "Find out whether Mr. and Mrs. Baxter want to go into Laran this morning, will you, Frank, as soon you can? Tell them it's a cold lunch today. If they do want to go out I'll see about the car for them and drive them in."

"Right-o, Dad," responded Frank Paske, "I'm just going along to the garden for a picking of gooseberries. Likely I'll see Mr. Baxter out there before breakfast. He is fond of being out there in the early morning with his daily paper."

His father nodded to him and Frank Paske went into the big garage and through the farmhouse into the garden. He was a well-set-up fellow approaching thirty years of life. Not over-tall or over-big, the life he had led for years now had kept him in excellent physical condition. When his father had suddenly, and rather surprisingly, announced his intention to the Paske family that he intended to buy the "Salvation" inn and spend his remaining years there with the members of that family at his side, Frank's first reaction to the news had been one of resentment. But on second thoughts he had realized the extent to which his personal bread was buttered and he fell in with his father's new plan with as good a face as possible. The first year in the new surroundings had gone quickly, and looking back on it Frank was forced to admit that both he and Lysbeth, the young Dutch girl whom he had married just before coming to Lanrebel, had enjoyed the complete change it had afforded, and benefited in health consequently. He had pulled a basket from the garage for his gooseberry-picking, and when he had reached about half way down the garden he heard a voice hail him from the road to Frayne.

"Hey, Frank! Mr. Frank!" Shading his eyes against the morning sun, he looked over the low stone wall that bounded the kitchen garden and saw that the man who had hailed him was one of the villagers known familiarly as "Crispy" Williams. Frank Paske called back to him: "Hullo—you Crispy! What's the trouble with you so early in the morning? Too much beer last night?"

To Frank's surprise, instead of giving another answering shout, Crispy Williams bolted across the middle of the Frayne road and up the winding lane which ran at the back of the "Salvation" garden. He ran, too, as though the devil himself were at his heels with his ghostly pack. Sensing that Crispy Williams was in no ordinary mood, Frank Paske left the picking of his gooseberries and walked to the bottom of the garden. He and Crispy arrived at a given point of contact almost simultaneously. Crispy was panting now, breathless from his unusual exercise.

"Hey, Frank, but I'm gettin' too old in the tooth for quick runnin', to be sure I am. But have you heard the news, Frank? Man, but it's that terrible!"

Frank Paske shook his head in wonderment. "Crispy Williams, I haven't the ghost of an idea what it is you're talking about. How can I have? Lord, man, I haven't been out of bed much more than three-quarters of an hour. Well, don't stand there like a daft idiot— what is the news that's so terrible?"

"Mrs. Hillier," gasped Crispy Williams. "She's . . . she's . . . dead! At least that's what young Wally Treglown has just told me. I met him down the lane. He swears it's true enough."

Frank Paske put his elbows on the low stone wall that separated him from his informer. "What's that? Mrs. Hillier? Dead! It don't seem possible, Crispy. She was here at the 'Salvation' only the evening before last, along of Sir Malcolm Onslow and his wife. Regular party of 'em we had in there—playing darts in the farmers' bar. Her husband was with her. What did she die of, Crispy? There seemed nothing the matter with her then."

Crispy put his face close to Frank Paske's and almost whispered his next words. Crispy, let it be said, was not noted for the quality of his intelligence. "Young Wally says that foul play's suspected. He-hee-hee."

"Foul play!" repeated Frank Paske incredulously. "Rubbish! He's talking out of the back of his neck. And so are you. Foul play indeed! I like these rumours that get round, and no mistake. It's always the same in places like this. When did Mrs. Hillier die?"

"Why, only last night, of course. That's why I said it was sudden. There was a dinner party up at the house last night and Mrs. Hillier was found dead somewhere about midnight. That's what young Wally says."

Frank Paske seemed puzzled. "How does he come to know such a lot?"

Crispy leered at him cunningly. "Don't forget his sister's friendly with Mr. Mowbray, the butler up at 'Hillearys'. Everybody knows that."

"That's true," replied Frank Paske thoughtfully.

"There you are, you see," insisted Crispy Williams, "there's bound to be something in it."

"Doesn't follow there's any of this foul play that you're hollerin' about. Most likely an ordinary case of sudden death. Weak heart or something. Still, I'll have a word with my father about it. Perhaps he's heard something. You get along now, Crispy—otherwise you'll be late—and I'll get back to the house."

"That's all right with me, Master Frank. I shouted to you just now because I thought as how you'd like to hear the news. I be downright sorry about it myself. That Mrs. Hillier was an uncommon nice lady and she'll be missed badly in these parts. So long, Master Frank!" Crispy waved his hand and made off.

Frank Paske stood by the garden wall thinking hard for something more than a minute. It was well known in the village that Crispy's intelligence was not of the highest order, but he would hardly imagine a story of this kind. Frank turned slowly on his heel and made his way back to the house, his gooseberries still unpicked. Lysbeth, his fair-haired little Dutch wife, was busy in the kitchen, her hands moving deftly at her work. She smiled at him brightly as he passed by the window. "Where's Father?" he called out to her.

"In his den," replied his wife; "I think I heard him say he was going in there to clean his gun." Her accent gave her speech a distinct fascination. Frank moved off in the direction of his father's shed, which Paske senior had had erected on the left-hand side of the big garage as you approached it. He saw that his father was cleaning a gun, as Lysbeth had understood.

"Did you see Mr. Baxter?" his father called to him.

Frank Paske shook his head. All memory of his promised message to Baxter had gone from him, thanks to the news he'd had from Crispy Williams. "No," he replied. His father's temper was short, which fact the son knew only too well.

"Well—why the hell—"

Frank silenced him with a sharp gesture of his hand. "Just a moment, Father. Before you lead off at me, come out here for a second—do you mind?"

Paske looked puzzled. He put down his gun and stepped out of the shed. "What's to do? You look sort of scared, son. What is it?"

Frank shook his head. "Don't know altogether about being scared, Father. But what d'ye think I've just heard? Mrs. Hillier's dead!"

Paske stared at him incredulously. "Mrs. Hillier? How?"

"Found dead round about twelve o'clock last night. So I've just heard. Pretty bad news, that."

"Where did you hear that moonshine, son? You haven't been anywhere this morning. Sure you didn't dream it?"

"Crispy Williams came down to the end of the garden to tell me. I know Crispy's shortcomings, but this is different. He was on the road to Frayne and called out to me."

"Well—I'm blessed! That's bad news and no mistake. Found dead you say? How d'ye mean—found dead?"

"Don't know a thing beyond what I've told you. Except that they suspect foul play."

"Who's 'they'—the police, d'ye mean? Are they in already?"

"Suppose so. Who else could it be?"

Paske knitted his brows. "But stay a bit, Frank. I don't get all this. Where did Crispy Williams get this yarn from?"

"Young Wally Treglown. He met him up the lane."

"Wally Treglown." Paske thought over the news. Frank went on with the necessary explanation.

"You can guess the rest, can't you? Wally's sister got it from Mowbray, the Hilliers' butler."

"That's right," nodded Paske. "There's sound sense in that. They see too much of each other, those two. In the saloon here the night before last. Well, it's sad news. Mrs. Hillier was as dainty a piece as a man could drop eyes on—and would have been wherever she went and in any company. And only a couple of nights ago I was pickin' out her favourite darts for her. She always liked to throw a heavy dart, and was the real stuff on the treble nineteen. Poor girl. That's upset me properly."

"Now, don't you say that. Guess I don't like to hear that you're upset, Captain." A voice behind them caused the two Paskes to turn round. A cheerily smiling Pereira stood just behind them. His small eyes were alive with merriment.

"Just had bad news, sir," said Paske. "That's why I'm upset."

"You don't say! Now, I never figured that bad news ever came travelling to this burg. Up to now I'd been sure gladdened with the entire outfit. But spill your bad news, Captain Paske. What is it that's given you the twisting?"

Paske reiterated what Frank had just told him. Pereira nodded several times and wrinkled his fat face.

"Now—ain't that just too bad? News like that fair gives me a black honest-to-God Almighty resentment. Mrs. Hillier was always mighty nice to me, when we met in your ho-tel, Captain, and I'd like to pump lead into the yellow-hearted skate that bumped her off. That's how it goes with me!" Pereira turned adroitly, despite his bulk, and spat skilfully on the cobbled stones. He continued to speak. "A real nasty piece of work to happen in a nice tranquil little one-horse, one-eyed burg like Lanrebel. It's sort of made me feel that I could drink beer before breakfast. How long have the cops been there?"

"We don't really know anything yet, Mr. Pereira. My son had only heard the news a few minutes before you came by, and had come to tell me. It'll make a stir in these parts, I can tell you."

"Been settled here for a considerable time, I suppose, these Hilliers?"

"I believe so. Some years, at any rate. You see, I've only been here for about a year myself."

Pereira nodded as though the statement exacted admiration from him. "They're swell folks, the Hilliers. You sure don't need a telescope to see that. The few occasions that we've congregated together in your bar, Captain, have been more than sufficient to show me. As I just said to you, there's a hell-deserving skunk knocking around that I'd like to interview with the business end of my rod. Maybe one day I'll get the chance, and by the heck I'll sure take it. You never know, Captain! In the meantime, I'll get inside your trim little establishment and treat myself to breakfast. If you hear any more news concerning the tragedy, I'd esteem it as a real favour if you'd pass it on to me. You won't forget, Captain, will you? I'm sure inter-ested." Pereira turned and made his way into the breakfast room. There were several others seated there when he arrived. He took immediate advantage of the opportunity thus presented. An audience such as this made it a red-letter morning for him.

Chapter IV
INQUEST ON JACQUELINE HILLIER

THE inquest on the body of Jacqueline Hillier was held four days later at eleven o'clock in the County Hall, Liskerry. The Coroner took the usual formal identification and the members of the jury were conducted to an adjoining outhouse in order that they might view the body. The crowd, for a considerable time expectant, then began to shuffle many feet. The principal interest of the morning's proceedings was about to begin.

"Call Neill Hillier . . . You are Neill Findlay Hillier, only son of the deceased?"

"Yes."

"Will you kindly tell the members of the jury what happened to you on the evening of the 8th of June last?"

"After dinner I went into the billiard-room to amuse myself. My mother, at that time—it was about half past eight, as far as I can remember—remained behind in the dining-room; again, that is as far as I know. For some time, while I was in the billiard-room alone, I messed about with the balls. Eventually, my father joined me. We played a game of two hundred and fifty up and then three frames at snooker. When they were finished my father left me to go back to the lounge. I stayed in the billiard-room until about twenty minutes past eleven. I then felt that I had had enough and decided to return to the lounge. As I crossed the gravel drive from the billiard-room to the lounge I saw the lights of a car about ten yards, I should think, from the front gates of 'Hillearys'. That's the name of my father's house, in case some members of the jury don't know it. The car was absolutely stationary. I was puzzled at this—it seemed very strange to me—so I walked towards it. So I—er—walked towards it. When I reached it I saw that it was my father's car, and I was amazed to see that my mother was sitting in it. In the driving-seat, and with her hands clasping the wheel."

The Coroner held up his hand and made appropriate notes. Neill waited for him before proceeding. The Coroner asked a question. "You say that your mother's hands were actually clasping the wheel?"

"Yes."

"Thank you, Mr. Hillier; I thought that you said that. Go on, if you please."

"I spoke to her. She didn't answer. Then I called to her more loudly. I think that I was upset. She raised her face to mine as I looked through the window. I was the opposite side to where she was sitting. I was startled—terribly startled at what I saw there. She looked awful. She seemed to have been struck across the face by somebody or something. It was bruised, and there was blood on it. Her dress, too, was torn at the front, and her frock was muddy and looked to me as though it were grass-stained. I opened the door of the car. I saw that her wrists were scratched and torn. I took her in my arms." Here Neill Hillier stopped dead. His distress was evident. The Coroner waited in patient understanding and sympathy. Neill partly recovered, and went on. "Her eyes looked ghastly, and her breath seemed to come in choking gasps. I did not know it then—but she must have been on the point of dying as I held her there. She jerked her head backwards, as though trying to tell me something or indicate something that lay behind her. Then she spoke to me, but her words were indistinct. She said a great deal—quickly—but it was impossible for me to understand her. Just a gabble—or jabber. Suddenly she began to speak more clearly. She became coherent. She said, 'The Mile Cliff. Two . . .' Before she could finish what she wanted to say . . . she just gasped once or twice and died there in my arms."

"And then you went and called your father, I think, Mr. Hillier? Yes?"

"Yes."

"Thank you." The Coroner turned fussily to the members of the jury. He cleared his throat as he spoke to them. "Have you any questions to ask this gentleman . . . no? . . . Thank you. Mr. Neill Hillier, you may stand down. Call Mr. Paul Hillier."

The husband of the dead woman made his way to the little platform from which the witnesses were required to give evidence.

"You are Paul Hillier, the husband of the deceased?"

"Yes."

"You have heard the evidence given by the preceding witness?"

"Yes."

"You agree that your son came over to the house from the car and asked you to go back?"

Paul Hillier hesitated. "He came and asked me to go with him to the car. I obviously can't say that he came direct from the car to me. You see my point?"

"Er—no . . . I suppose you can't. Yes . . . yes. You found your wife dead . . . when you got back to the car?"

"Yes."

"Where were you when your son came for you?"

"In the dining-room. I had been in the lounge for some time. I had just left the lounge."

"And when you found that Mrs. Hillier was past help . . . you sent for Dr. Pakenham?"

"I 'phoned for him."

"Yes . . . of course, you—er—'phoned for him. And now tell me, Mr. Hillier, was there any reason, to your knowledge, why Mrs. Hillier should take her own life?"

"Certainly not. And she didn't take her own life. The idea is unthinkable. Everybody who knew her would tell you so. My poor wife was murdered. And—what's more—I'll tell you this, Mr. Coroner—"

"Please, Mr. Hillier, please! I sympathize with your . . . er . . . grief, but you must be calm and must keep to the point. Was your wife in good health?"

"Splendid. I can't remember when she last consulted a doctor. She complained of a headache that evening, it's true, but I don't consider that anything. Anybody can have an occasional headache."

"She had never threatened to commit suicide?"

"Never!" Paul Hillier's note of blunt, uncompromising emphasis rang through the County Hall.

"Thank you, Mr. Hillier. That is very clear, then. Any questions, gentlemen? No? You may stand down, Mr. Hillier. Call Dr. Pakenham."

The doctor who answered the call was young, keen-featured, lithe and lean. He stepped briskly on to the raised platform.

"You are Francis Pakenham? You are a physician, I believe?"

"Yes."

"You have a private practice at Lanrebel?"

"Yes."

"And you are also police surgeon for the district?"

"Yes. To be precise—for the district of Liskerry. Lanrebel, you understand, comes under Liskerry."

"You were called about midnight on the 8th of June last to 'Hillearys', Lanrebel, to examine the body of Jacqueline Hillier?"

"Yes. To be exact, at eight minutes to twelve. I particularly noted the time."

"Will you please tell us the result of the examination that you made?"

"I found that Mrs. Hillier was dead. The face was cut just under the right eye and she had bled profusely from the cut. The wrists also were scratched. Her clothing was torn and mud-stained. There were traces of grass on the frock. I formed the opinion that death was due to some form of poisoning." (Sensation in Court.)

The Coroner was impressed. "And you have since been able to substantiate that opinion?"

Dr. Pakenham nodded. The nod was positive.

"Yes. Deceased died from chloral poisoning." (Further sensation.)

"Was that poison, in your opinion, Dr. Pakenham, self-administered?"

"It could have been. But . . ." Dr. Pakenham showed signs of hesitation. His face looked strained.

"Yes, Doctor?" prompted the Coroner.

"Well, I'm bound to consider the external evidence of the deceased's body. I can't reasonably ignore it. The cut on the face, the injuries to the wrists, and the condition of the clothes. I have already alluded to them. In the absence of these matters, I should have given my opinion that the poison had been self-administered. As it is—well—I must admit to being doubtful."

"There was no poison found in the car, of course?"

"None."

"No empty bottle or phial?"

"None. But you must remember that I was called to the case some time after the deceased was first discovered."

"How could this poison have been taken? I mean in what form would it have been taken?"

"Let me explain something first. By chloral I mean chloral hydrate. It is a clear crystalline substance, with a sweetish taste, which dissolves rapidly in water. The usual safe dose would be from five to twenty grains. It would be taken in tablet form or in the form of syrup of chloral."

"Could a dose be forced upon a person? If that person resisted strongly, would that be possible?"

"Oh, undoubtedly. The victim could be overpowered by superior strength, as in any instance of exerted force." Here again the Coroner turned to the members of the jury. Before he spoke he blew out his cheeks.

"Are there any questions that you would like to put to Dr. Pakenham?"

An answer came on this occasion. "Yes, I should like to ask the doctor a question." The speaker was Toft, the most prosperous farmer of the Lanrebel district.

"Very well. Ask your question."

Toft stood up in his place, turned, and faced the doctor. "In your opinion, Doctor, how long was it before Mrs. Hillier's death that the dose of poison had been taken, or perhaps given?"

Pakenham's answer came at once. "Within ten minutes to a quarter of an hour."

"You are certain of that, Doctor?"

"Well—almost. As far as one can be."

"Thank you, Doctor."

The Coroner added his thanks. "Yes. Thank you, Dr. Pakenham. You may stand down. Call Charles Mowbray." The butler at "Hillearys" made his way slowly to the witness's platform. "You are Charles Mowbray?"

"Yes."

"You are engaged as butler by Mr. Paul Hillier?"

"Yes."

"You have been with him for a considerable period?"

"I was engaged a few months after Mr. Hillier came to live at Lanrebel. I have been there ever since."

"Mrs. Hillier spoke to you, I believe, after dinner on the evening of the 8th of June?"

"Yes."

"Will you tell us what the conversation was that took place between you?"

"Yes." Mowbray exuded superiority. "After dinner the guests went into the lounge for the purpose, so I understood, of playing bridge. The guests, I may say, were Mr. and Mrs. Maurice Hillier and Rev. and Mrs. Aylmer. Miss Ann Hillier and her father accompanied them. Mrs. Hillier, the . . . er . . . deceased, did not join the party. She stayed for some time in the dining-room. Miss Ann had previously informed me that the mistress had a headache. About eleven o'clock I had occasion to enter the dining-room; one of the curtains was not drawn properly, and on my way I encountered Mrs. Hillier. She told me that she had a headache, that she had endured it for some hours, and was going for a run in the car. 'To get a breath of fresh air' was her description of what she was about to do. I asked her if there was anything I could get for her, and she answered, 'No, Mowbray, don't trouble to get anything for me. It will do no good. A run out, and I shall be all right when I come back.'"

The Coroner referred somewhat ostentatiously to his papers. But the people in the Court remained perfectly quiet. Nobody stirred. Not a foot shuffled. Mowbray stood on the platform immovable. The Coroner put his question. "Did you notice how Mrs. Hillier was dressed when she spoke to you, on the occasion that you have just mentioned?"

"Just as she was, sir, when she returned."

The Coroner looked inquiringly. "When she returned? Do you allude to the time when . . ."

"I happened to be present, you see, sir, when the poor lady's dead body was carried into the house. I was close handy, naturally, in case I could be of any assistance."

"I see. That certainly answers my question, I suppose. Now, let me see—er—Mowbray, what time exactly would you say it was when Mrs. Hillier went out?"

Mowbray considered the Coroner's question. "I can tell you within a few minutes, sir. It would have been between five and ten minutes past eleven."

"You are certain of that, Mowbray?"

"Yes, sir. I can say that with certainty because I remember that the clock in the hall struck eleven just before I met the mistress on her way to the garage for the car."

"And that was the last time you saw Mrs. Hillier?"

"Yes, sir. In this life, that is."

The Coroner glanced at him somewhat severely. "That will do. You may stand down, Mowbray. Call Miss Ann Hillier."

As she walked to the stand Ann looked almost alarmingly beautiful, and certainly beautifully disdainful. Her senses were just beginning to function again after the death of Jacqueline. Her mother and she had always been close together, companions of such a kind that when her mother died Ann had reeled under the blow. Her serene grey eyes met the Coroner's courageously and unflinchingly as he began to question her.

"Will you please tell the Court, Miss Hillier, of the last conversation that you had with your mother?"

"Certainly." Ann's voice was clear and strong. She was determined not to break down in any way in front of those inquisitive, morbid sensation-seekers, most of whom had come to enjoy her mother's death. "It was about half past nine. Between half past nine, I should say, and a quarter to ten. I went to look for her." Ann hesitated for just the suspicion of a second, but forced herself bravely to continue. "She had complained of a headache earlier in the evening, and had stayed behind by herself in the dining-room when dinner was over. I went back to her to see how she was getting on, to find out whether she felt any better." Ann's fingers were clenched in her hands, and tears were on their way to her eyes. "When I found her, she was in the library."

The Coroner made an appropriate note on his pad of paper.

"She told me that her headache was a little better. She certainly seemed better and brighter than she had been when we finished dinner. Then she told me what she seems to have told Mowbray some time later. That she thought she'd have a run in the car before bedtime. That the fresh air would do her more good than anything else. Just as she was telling me that, my aunt called to me from the lounge, and I went back there to see what she wanted. I never saw my mother again alive."

Ann stopped rather abruptly. Her eyes were still fearless and her hands were steady.

"Thank you, Miss Hillier," remarked the Coroner. "I don't know whether any member of the jury would care to put a question to the witness."

"Yes." Toft, the farmer, had again given evidence of his desire to ask a question.

"Very well," conceded the Coroner.

Toft stood up. "Just two questions, Miss Hillier, that I'd like to ask you, if you wouldn't mind answering them. When your mother spoke about going for a run in the car, did the point occur at all as to your accompanying her or not?"

Ann nodded. "Yes. Not from my mother, but I asked her whether she would like me to go along with her."

"What was her reply?"

The Coroner watched Ann Hillier intently as she considered the words of her answer. "She said that it didn't matter. That she would be all right by herself."

Toft followed up. "Did she seem *anxious* to be alone?"

Ann wrinkled her brows. "No-o. I wouldn't say that she showed herself to be exactly . . . anxious. But I could see that she was desirous of being alone . . . and when I observed that . . . I didn't press my offer on her."

Toft came in again. "Now for my other question. Was it your mother's habit to take the car out late in the evening like that?"

Ann looked at the Coroner rather appealingly. He became sympathetic and superior. "I appreciate your difficulty, Miss Hillier. Answer the question to the best of your ability."

"Well . . . habit . . . she didn't do it regularly. Words are difficult. But she went out like that . . . sometimes. I can remember it. It certainly wasn't the first time she'd done such a thing. My mother was a splendid driver and could handle a car with anybody." Ann's voice wavered a little.

"I'm sorry, Miss Hillier, but when was the occasion before this? How long ago?"

More questions from Toft.

Ann thought. "I really couldn't answer that with any certainty. But I should say about ten weeks ago. I think that she's been out fairly late . . . say about three times since the better weather came."

"Thank you," returned Toft sturdily. "That's all I wished to know."

"Thank you," added the Coroner with an added touch of gallantry. "You may stand down, Miss Hillier. Call the Rev. Septimus Aylmer." (Slight sensation—the things that are Caesar's.)

The Vicar of Lanrebel walked slowly to the stand, very much in the manner that was his when he walked to the pulpit. After all, it befitted his cloth.

"You are the Vicar of Lanrebel?"

"Yes."

"Did you dine with Mr. and Mrs. Hillier at their house, 'Hillearys', on the evening of Friday last, the 8th of June?"

"Yes. I and my wife were the guests of Mr. and Mrs. Hillier. We sat down to dine about half past seven."

"What time did the meal—er—finish?"

"About half past eight. It lasted for about an hour. I am sure of that, because I looked at my watch when we adjourned."

"Would you say that Mrs. Hillier was her ordinary self during the evening?"

The Reverend Septimus Aylmer shook his head. "Not quite. You understand what I mean. Mrs. Hillier was suffering from a bad head-ache, an affliction which takes the brightness from the spirits of most of us, I suggest. I am well aware of how it affects me."

"You noticed nothing, however, beyond that?"

"No, I can't say that I did." The Vicar paused for a second. "Only . . ." Again he stopped. The Vicar knew well the value of the subtle pause.

"Yes, Mr. Aylmer?" prompted the Coroner.

"Only that I observed, during the time that we were seated at dinner—I could say, even, all the time—that Mrs. Hillier had a letter in her hand." (Major sensation in Court.)

The Coroner frowned. "Do you mean a letter in an envelope—that is to say, an unopened letter?"

The Vicar of Lanrebel shook his head. "No. There was no envelope . . . that I saw. Let me put it that she had a letter, or part of a letter, crumpled in her hand. I was sitting in such a position that I was able to notice this. Or, rather, that I was unable not to notice it."

"Was she reading this letter at all during dinner?"

"No—that I could see, that is."

"Did she make any attempt to read it?"

"No—again, to my knowledge."

The Coroner assumed an air of severity. He coughed, moved uneasily in his seat, and cleared his throat. After all, it was incumbent upon him to do his duty. "There was no unpleasantness of any kind, I take it, that you observed, Mr. Aylmer, during dinner, or later on during the evening?"

"To anybody who knew the Hillier family," replied the Vicar of Lanrebel, "such an idea is utterly ridiculous." The atmosphere of the Court became, as it were, charged with electricity. The Coroner waited for the Rev. Septimus Aylmer to amplify his denial of the suggestion. But the Rev. Septimus wasn't having any, thank you. On the other hand, he waited for the Coroner. Victory lay with the cloth! The Coroner accepted defeat as his portion, and swallowed hard. Why were certain people so definitely annoying when asked a question so extremely simple? He took a drink of water. Occasions such as these were the only times when he tasted it. Good publicity, though! Eventually he found words. "Do you feel that you can help the Court at all, Mr. Aylmer? Have you formed any opinion with regard to the poor lady's death?"

"None at all," replied the Vicar quietly. "Beyond the fact that it has been a very great shock to me, as, indeed, it has been to all of us at Lanrebel."

"Quite . . . quite! Undoubtedly . . . yes! Well—er—thank you, Vicar. No questions, I presume? No? Thank you. You may stand down. I feel that in the circumstances I must recall Mr. Paul Hillier."

Paul Hillier, recalled, looked black, angry, and forbidding. The Coroner, distressed and a trifle nervous, noticed this. He took a deep breath. "There is one more question that I am compelled to put to you, Mr. Hillier. It has arisen out of Dr. Pakenham's statement of a few moments ago. Was your wife in the habit of taking chloral?"

Paul Hillier squared his shoulders. "No, certainly not. As far as I know, she has never taken chloral in her life."

"She had not been troubled by insomnia at all?"

"Never. My wife had splendid health always. I thought that I had already made that clear to you."

"Ah . . . yes . . . I suppose that you did. Thank you, Mr. Hillier. You may stand down again. Er—thank you."

At that moment there came a stir in the room, and a uniformed policeman made his way to the rostrum upon which the Coroner was sitting. He passed a slip of paper up to the Coroner and waited for his answer. The Coroner read it with extreme gravity before bending down to the constable and conferring with him in low tones. The watchers in the Court saw the Coroner nod once—twice; in fact, several times. The policeman, his task accomplished, walked away from the Coroner's rostrum. The Coroner gathered himself together and raised his gavel. He tapped his table impressively.

"At the request of the police," he announced loudly, "the inquest will be adjourned. Advices will be sent to all of you who are concerned regarding the date and time of the Court's next sitting. Thank you, ladies and gentlemen."

The people, many of them with disappointed faces, rose from their seats and filed away. Most of them had looked forward to a surfeit of excitement. When the majority had succeeded in making their way out, a tall, lean, lithe, grey-eyed man rose in his seat and joined the rear members of the disappearing crowd.

"I wonder," he murmured to himself. And when Anthony Lotherington Bathurst admitted to a state of personal wonderment the occasion was, to say the least, significant. He walked slowly back to the inn at Lanrebel where he was staying, the inn whose sign showed to the world the word "Salvation". Arthur Paske smiled at him as he came through the doorway and walked up the cobbled yard.

"Lovely day, sir. Been into Laran?" he asked genially. Paske was always genial, except when his wife was close at hand. Anthony had noticed this.

"No," said Mr. Bathurst. "Not Laran to-day. I went along to the inquest on Mrs. Hillier at Liskerry."

"What was the verdict?" inquired Paske casually.

Anthony told him what had occurred.

Paske whistled between his teeth. "Adjournment, eh? Looks as though Crispy Williams was right after all. That there's foul play suspected. Don't you think so, Mr. Bathurst?"

"I'm inclined to agree with you, Paske," returned Mr. Bathurst. "On the whole, a rather pretty little problem."

CHAPTER V
PEREIRA CONFIDENTIAL

THE saloon lounge of the "Salvation" hummed with conversation on the evening of the inquest on Jacqueline Hillier. Paske and the stories of foreign parts that he usually told were relegated for once to the background. The three authors and the painter were forced, much against their respective grains, to talk of something other than themselves. It is observed that they took but small part in the hum of conversation. The five assorted married couples formed themselves into a sort of Benedictine circle and jabbered unceasingly concerning matters about which they knew but little. The chance callers at the "Salvation", who had also come to take the evening air, and whose cars filled the car park to every inch of its available space, talked *to*, not *at*, each other. Edmund Pereira was volubility itself. Mr. Bathurst listened to him with delicate attention. There was an "aroma" about Mr. Pereira's conversation. You could not possibly take it by large earfuls. It had to be taken like rich ambrosia, fastidiously.

It was into this company that Toft, the farmer, the man who had asked questions at the inquest, and Keith Annesley, the novelist from Blackstock in the county of Essex, in search of a holiday and rest, came almost coincidentally. Toft had driven in from "Woodruffs" (that was the name by which his farm was known) in his car, and Keith Annesley had walked down to the inn from the little Lanrebel station. He had caught the 3.15 out of Paddington, after saying good-bye to Luke Weir in the "Running Horse", and had arrived at Lanrebel about half past eight. Although he knew the place by name, this was his first visit to it. Keith Annesley almost always made a point of not catching a long-distance train in the morning. His plea was that he always liked to arrive at a place when the bar was nicely lighted, the tankards set, and the seats completely filled. Arthur Paske, proud of his latest literary capture, brought him into the lounge and introduced him to the "Salvation's" staying guests. For a reason which he would have been entirely unable to explain, Keith Annesley took the seat next to Anthony Bathurst. Neither, it must be admitted, had caught the other's name from Paske's preliminary announcement. Pereira was still talking loudly. In this particular reference the adverb is tautological.

"Nope," he said in reply to a question put to him. "I wasn't what you would rightly describe as a close acquaintance of the folk up at 'Hillearys', although we were always quite amicable together. But you must remember, ladies and gentlemen, that I have not been over-long in these parts. A matter of months only. I guess Mr. Hillier had made his pile long before he ever set eyes on 'Yours truly'. So you see that I can't give you real inside dope about 'Hillearys'." His eyes twinkled as he spoke, and he shrugged his big body with a gesture of resignation.

"Who is the orator?" asked Annesley of Bathurst. "Surely not a local prodigy?"

Anthony shook his head and passed on the desired information. A twisted look came on Annesley's face. Anthony assessed it as a clear evidence of cynicism. "I read a little of the affair in one of the London papers," said Annesley, "before I left town. The report of the case, of course, was short and extremely sketchy. I had no idea, though, that this place was so close to the scene of the tragedy. Were you down here when it happened?"

Anthony Bathurst nodded and smiled. "In me, sir, you see one of the stormy petrels of crime. I'm a human magnet. Even when I deliberately seek to avoid it, and reach a tranquil spot where the night raven should never spread his jealous wings, it runs me to earth and pins me down. It is probably my punishment for having dipped my fingers so often into the crime pie."

Annesley, hearing all this, looked at him curiously. "By Jove! I was right. You see, your face is familiar to me. I've seen it before somewhere. I'll swear . . . Would you mind telling me your name? I didn't get it when our genial host made that introductory whoopee just now. The orator, you see, was in full blast."

"I'm sorry! My name's Bathurst."

Annesley wrinkled his brows in an effort at remembrance. "Bathurst. . . . I'm certain that . . ." He looked at the tall figure of the man seated beside him, clad in a light-grey flannel suit, with the far-seeing, humorous-looking grey eyes. Revelation came immediately to Keith Annesley. "Of course! I've got it now. You're Anthony Bathurst, *the* Anthony Bathurst. No wonder your face seemed familiar to me. Good Lord—what an ass! Me, I mean, not you!"

"I apologize for the truth of all you've just said. Forget it. What's more, I'll give you a chance to get your own back." Bathurst grinned at his companion infectiously. "To my utter shame, I didn't catch your name either."

Annesley smiled sadly. "Annesley, Keith Annesley. I scribble a bit. You may have noticed my name tucked away in an obscure corner of *Tom o' Charing's Weekly*. Yes? No? Don't keep me in suspense."

Anthony played the game. "Oh yes, I've seen the name, and I'm not referring to your defunct American namesake either. You! Your own! Yours!"

"Thank you. That was most charmingly said, and takes a load from my mind. Well—what's the weather down here like? Real Glebeshire? I stayed a fortnight in Labe once, some years ago—in August. It rained every damned day, believe me. In the evenings, up rolled a mist nine times out of ten, and I quite expected to hear boys calling, 'All the classified results. Scotch matches as well.'"

"Well, to tell the truth, I haven't seen much of it to-day. As a matter of fact, I attended the inquest on Mrs. Hillier."

"Officially, do you mean?"

Anthony smiled again. "No. Just out of my blasted curiosity. I told you whenever I go away anywhere I always get a sort of 'busman's holiday'."

Annesley was interested. "Where was it—here?"

"No. At Liskerry. The County Hall. That's about six miles from here by road."

Annesley nodded. "Yes, I know Liskerry, I've been there. I was in it some five or six years ago. I suppose you had the usual collection of country yokels in solemn conclave for your jury. That's the worst of the 'Crowner's Quest' in country districts."

"This wasn't as bad as some. I must be fair. Did you notice a man come in here just about the same time as you did? A burly, thick-set fellow? I'll point him out to you. Look—he's sitting over there in the corner. Close to the table where Pereira's gone to now."

Annesley's eyes followed the direction that Mr. Bathurst had given. "Oh yes, I spotted the fellow just in front of me as I came in. Why? What's special about him?"

"Only something in relation to what you've just said. He was on to-day's jury. Put, moreover, quite a number of intelligent questions. His name's Toft, they tell me. Got a farm near here; 'Woodruffs'. About a mile and a quarter from here up the road that leads to Laran. I've passed it once or twice when I've been strolling round in the morning before breakfast. It's a biggish place that looks as though—" Mr. Bathurst broke off. Annesley noticed the break.

"Why? What's biting you?"

Anthony smiled. "Nothing very important. It just occurred to me that Toft's place, 'Woodruffs', must be about half way between here and 'Hillearys'. I hadn't thought of that before. 'Hillearys', by the way, is the name of the house where the Hilliers live."

"I know," returned Annesley. "I saw that in the newspaper reports I had in town. How did the inquest go, by the way? Anything much come out of it?"

"Shouldn't care to say."

"What was the verdict?"

"None given yet. The police asked the old man to adjourn, and he came to heel—very nicely. As per invoice."

"Do you mean that's often the case?"

"With affairs of this kind? Oh yes, quite a usual occurrence. When the show is at all sticky."

"What did you think about it yourself?"

Anthony shrugged his shoulders. "I won't deny that I'm extremely interested. It ought to be suicide. It looks so much like murder. But I have my doubts."

"If you don't mind," said Annesley quickly, "tell me all about it. It's out of my usual line, I know, and variety is good for everybody. Yes?"

"Perhaps—although I shouldn't claim, in all fairness, to have spotted very much. It's the evidence that's worrying me. Lot of straws blowing in the wind. Mrs. Hillier had a bad headache. Ordinary, you say? Perhaps. But it seems to have been an extraordinarily bad headache to take her out in the car so late in the evening. Between eleven and twelve o'clock, to be precise. Directly she returns home she dies of chloral poisoning. Husband Paul, though, says she's a complete stranger to chloral, and there's little doubt, from what I have been able to gather, that the police haven't been able to trace that she purchased any anywhere. Or, I believe, anybody else in the cast. If they had done so, ten to one it would have been put in at the inquest as evidence."

"I agree," said Annesley with a nod of the head.

"Also, there is no bottle or phial of any kind that can be found either in the car or anywhere else at hand."

"Just a minute. She might have had a number of tablets and taken them all. Loose tablets, I mean."

"Quite so," conceded Mr. Bathurst. "You've more or less repeated my own thoughts on the matter. Thoughts that have been active all the time. Then the poor lady *in extremis* spoke certain words. This came out in the boy's evidence. The son—Neill his name is. To me, as I heard them, they were very strange but, at the same time, very significant words."

Annesley leant over towards Anthony. "What were they? You've set me alight with curiosity."

"Neill Hillier said that these words—his mother's last spoken words, remember—came to him quite clearly. After many words which had been quite incoherent. 'The Mile Cliff. Two . . .' 'Two', I agree, might mean anything, but at first glance we'll take it to be numerical."

Annesley sat there, saying nothing. It seemed that he was turning the words over in his mind. "Looks to me," he said gravely, "as though the lady died game, as it were. Do you follow me, Bathurst? That she meant to give that message before she died, at any cost. Have I made myself clear to you?"

"Oh yes. And again I find myself in agreement with you. Especially as I understand that there *is* a cliff within comfortable distance of 'Hillearys', sheer almost to the water's edge, known round here as 'One Mile Cliff', which fact, I suggest, gives Mrs. Hillier's dying words not only an added significance, but also a distinctly common-sense angle."

Annesley nodded his head with a sort of slow emphasis. "Yes." This was an entirely new experience for him, as he had previously said, particularly coming to him, as it had, on the first day of his holiday. He wrinkled his brows reflectively. "What was that other word that the lady used?"

"'Two'," returned Anthony, "'to', or 'too'. As I told you, I incline myself towards the adjective of number. On the other hand, of course, I may be wrong."

Annesley broke in. "And now I agree with you again, Bathurst. I cannot see this death as self-destruction. But—is it easy to administer poison, such as this is said to have been, forcibly?"

"No. The medical bloke touched on that particular point, in answer to a question from the Coroner. But there were external injuries, remember. We must consider them and what they may mean. There is a cut under the right eye. The cut had bled. Profusely—according to the medical bloke. Also, there were scratched wrists. And torn clothing, which was also both grass- and mud-stained. Food for thought there, Annesley."

Annesley winced. "Nasty. All of it. In connection with a woman—it's—it's revolting, rather. To me. I suppose I'm not used to the contemplation even of such things."

"I haven't finished with the straws yet. Those straws that came floating to me on the wind. There was the matter of the Rev. Septimus Aylmer's testimony."

"Tell me. I can take it," contributed Annesley.

"Well, the reverend sir, who's the Vicar of the parish by the way, is rather more than ordinarily friendly with the Hilliers, and dined with them on the evening of the fatal 8th of June. Note that, Annesley. His wife accompanied him. You'll find that most of these old boys in country districts thoroughly enjoy the creatures of bread and wine, etc., that they encounter on the tables of their wealthier neighbours. Anyhow, he was roped in by the police to say his little piece at the inquest to-day. I watched the Rev. Septimus very closely all the time that he was giving his evidence. He's a wily old bird, though, and the Coroner took little change out of him, I assure you. In fact, the Rev. Septimus took most of the honours." Anthony paused for a moment or so.

"How did the affair touch him?" inquired Keith Annesley.

"That was exactly what I asked myself when he was called and took the stand. But it seems that the old boy had spotted something during dinner which nobody else in the party admits to have spotted. That Mrs. Hillier held a letter in her hand all the time during dinner. He said 'all the time', and I'm repeating his exact words."

Annesley looked mystified. "What sort of letter? Did he say any more than that?"

"No. Although the Coroner got at him over it. Septimus made the point that it wasn't in an envelope. It was a letter, or part of a letter, that she held 'crumpled' in her hand. Again, 'crumpled' was the word that he used."

Annesley noticed that Frank Paske was hovering near by. He called him over to their corner and ordered more drinks.

"The beer's excellent," remarked Anthony Bathurst, "equal to any that I've ever come across. Paske, quite a character, by the way, put me on to the Scotch ale directly I arrived, and I've certainly had no occasion to tilt at the recommendation. Interesting man, Paske. I usually call him 'Uncle Arthur'; he's travelled pretty well all over the globe. Gone places and done things."

Frank Paske took the order. He smiled at them genially through his spectacles.

"Is that the son of the house?" asked Annesley.

"Yes, he's married to a rather charming little Dutch lady, by name Lysbeth. It seems that they met at Newmarket. The Paskes lived there before they came here. She's the cook, and she's as good as the beer. You're in luck's way, coming here, Annesley."

"Strange thing, you know, that letter business," said Annesley reflectively. "The more I think of it, the more it puzzles me. I should think the police ought to be able to trace it. What's your own idea? An assignation somewhere? At One Mile Cliff?"

"It might well be that. I'm afraid, though, that we must curb our impatience and wait. Something may turn up, perhaps. It very often does."

Frank Paske arrived at the table with the replenished tankards. Annesley paid him. He smiled again, and touched his head in mock solemnity. Before he could speak, however, the voice of Edmund Pereira boomed across the room. "Hey, Frank! If I don't get more beer, and darned rapid at that, you'll find me dead of hot rage. And that won't be a pretty picture, by no means."

"All right, Mr. Pereira, I'll be coming to you right now."

"See that you do, Frank, or I'll straight away bust and spoil your carpet."

Frank Paske slipped over to the American.

Annesley couldn't keep his thoughts off the Hillier tragedy. "Tell me, Bathurst," he said quietly, "how did husband Hillier strike you? Sorry and all that if I'm too curious."

Anthony smiled. "I was waiting for you to ask me that. Well—not unfavourably. Queer bloke, though, in a way. No half-measures about him, I should say. Oh no! He told the Coroner straight that his wife had been murdered—and that was that."

"Seems to me, as a novice," put forward Annesley, "that the problem resolves itself into a matter of sorting out the various alibis. But I suppose you've looked thoroughly into most of them?"

Anthony Bathurst chuckled. "Yes, and I should say that there are several who haven't a cast-iron 'stone honker'. Husband Paul hasn't, to begin with."

"Why not? Surely he was in the house, with other people?"

"He left Master Neill to go back to the lounge, but from what I've managed to pick up, he must have altered his mind. Then there's Neill himself. He says that he stayed behind in the billiard-room. Can we be certain that he did? Then there are *'les autres'*."

"Meaning?" queried Keith Annesley.

"Paul's brother, Maurice Hillier, and Mrs. Maurice—Christian name Belle."

"Haven't heard of them before. Where do they come in? Do they live at the house too?"

"I understand not. They're just staying there. For a holiday, I presume."

"No alibis for them?"

"Don't know. Haven't heard yet. Can't get to 'em."

"I'm afraid I'm a devil for questions. You must forgive me. I'm intrigued. How did Paul Hillier make his money?"

"Didn't. One of the lucky ones. It was left him, so I'm informed. Uncle! One of the big cotton people. A rather unexpected legacy, so I hear. The uncle had two sons. Each predeceased him. Paul struck lucky. The wind—it is never an ill one for everybody—blew several thousands into his lap."

Anthony signalled to Frank Paske. He repeated Annesley's previous order to the son of the house, who moved away to carry out the order. Pereira came over to the table where Annesley and Anthony Bathurst were seated. The former watched him with a certain amount of fascination. Pereira addressed himself to Anthony as he took a third chair to the table and sat down. "Say, Mr. Bathurst" (he made the first vowel of the name long), "but I'd be mighty interested to have just a little chinwag with you. You've sort of—got me curious. I guess that you weren't at that inquest to-day because you and that little old Coroner went to the self-same academy for the sons of gentlemen when you were of tender years."

Anthony smiled, and moved his chair a little to make more comfortable room for him.

"Your guess is right, Mr. Pereira."

"I'll say it is, Mr. Bathurst. It's not so easy to pull the wool over Edmund Pereira's eyes. And now you and I can exchange confidences. For I figure it out in my own way that the police of this district may soon be barking up the wrong tree."

"So long as they merely bark, it won't matter very much, will it?" Anthony was still smiling.

"Well, we won't argue about that. I'll allow that you know as much about that as I do. Now, my opinion's this, although I wouldn't rightly call myself a swell Nat Pinkerton. Somebody at the 'Hillearys' house ain't telling the truth—not on your life, Mr. Bathurst. Trying to throw dust in the eyes of the official homicide squad. And it won't pay—not in the long run. I'm too well acquainted with nature not to know that. No, sir." He blinked like an indulgent owl at Anthony and Annesley. "What do you think about my theory yourself, Mr. Bathurst?"

Before Anthony could reply, Pereira appeared to notice for the first time the near presence of Annesley. "Say, introduce me to your friend, will you? He and I haven't yet become acquainted."

Anthony obeyed the suggestion with good grace. Pereira clasped Annesley by the hand and shook it warmly. "Say, this is a real pleasure. I'm pleased to hitch up alongside of you, sir. Any friend of Mr. Bathurst's goes with me, all the way, and then some! Now, what were we talking about when I digressed? Let me see . . ."

"You were doubting the veracity of certain members of the Hillier household," said Anthony blandly, stressing the personal pronoun.

"I was, sir! And I still am. I don't budge from that opinion. Edmund Pereira always stands by what he says. You ask the boys that over in little old Noo York, and it'll be given 'nem-con'. All the same, I'm not the only gherkin in the pickle-jar, and I should find your opinion very interesting."

Anthony moved his tankard thoughtfully before he made any reply. "I don't know how to answer you, Mr. Pereira. The main task for anybody attempting to get at the truth lies in separating the true clues from the false. The wheat from the chaff. Which means, of course, that they've all got to be thoroughly sifted and turned over before you can even start on the job—which, again, means time."

The round face of Edmund Pereira beamed satisfaction at the reply.

"Exactly, sir! Sort of sheep and goats business, you mean! Wheat and chaff, you say. I'm with you, and if I am, then I'm going to do a bit of winnowing on my own account. Yes, sir. And when Edmund Pereira gets thoroughly stuck into something—well, I guess the machinery gets going, and things happen. Frank!"

Frank Paske came up at Pereira's call. "These drinks are on me, gentlemen," said Pereira boisterously.

"I think," said Annesley, "that after this round I'll go to bed. I'm tired. I started out from my house this morning fairly early. For me—that is."

As he announced his intention, the voice of the farmer Toft could be heard coming from the other side of the room.

"Well," Anthony heard him say, "that may suit you, Freddie, but it doesn't suit me. And before this inquest is finished and done with,

I shouldn't be surprised if don't have to ask several more questions of several more people. I don't care who they are or what houses they live in, they aren't going to put anything across Josh Toft. I'm a bit too long in the tooth, for one thing."

Keith Annesley drank up his beer, rose, and said good night, but Anthony lingered for more than one reason in the lounge until well after closing-time. He heard much that interested him.

Chapter VI
FLORAL TRIBUTE

IF THE death of Jacqueline Hillier had provided Lanrebel and district with a sensation, so did the events which almost immediately followed her funeral. She was buried two days after the inquest. Jacqueline was laid to rest in the churchyard of Lanrebel, and the Rev. Septimus Aylmer, who had dined with her but a few days before, took the burial service. He read the fifteenth chapter of the Pauline epistle to the Corinthians, a trifle worse, if anything, than it is usually read in like circumstances. Paul and Neill, her husband and only son, followed her to the grave. All adult Lanrebel stood at a respectful distance. Keith Annesley informed Anthony Bathurst that he would like to go. "You've interested me," he said, advancing this view. "I feel that I should like to be there."

Anthony, who had himself been considering the matter of his own attendance, accompanied him. As far as could be seen by superficial observers, there were neither police nor incidents at the funeral. When the ceremony was over, Anthony walked back with Keith Annesley to the "Salvation", and for once in a way said very little. Pereira did not attend, and when they arrived back at the inn they found him, partnered by little fair-haired Lysbeth, playing darts against a combination consisting of father and son in the persons of Arthur and Frank Paske. Annesley went straight to his room, and Anthony wandered about more or less aimlessly for the rest of the day. There was much on his mind. From a whisper which reached him late in the afternoon, the local police were coquetting with the idea that Jacqueline had kept an assignation on the evening of her death with "somebody unknown" at One Mile Cliff. But Mr. Bathurst had his own ideas with regard to this possibility. For the time being, he decided that he would keep those ideas to himself. On the following morning, however, at breakfast, Lysbeth Paske imparted news of a somewhat surprising nature.

"Did you see the flowers yesterday, sir, at poor Mrs. Hillier's funeral?"

Anthony wondered at the reference. What was behind the question?

"I saw some, Mrs. Paske, but I don't know that I noticed any of them particularly. Why do you ask?"

She nodded her head quickly.

"Why do you ask?" he repeated.

"Well, sir, it's like this. One of the women who works here always walks through the churchyard on her way to her work of a morning. She lives up near the Liskerry road. In that little cottage by the blacksmith's forge on the corner. Coming through the churchyard gives her a short cut, you see, if she should happen to be a minute or so late. Well, sir, she says that Mrs. Hillier's grave this morning looks a fair sight."

At the receipt of this information, Anthony was stung into keen interest. "Do you mean that it's been despoiled?" he asked her.

Lysbeth shook her dainty head. Her fair hair loosened and tumbled over her forehead.

"Oh no, sir. Not anything like that. Just the reverse, in fact. Somebody's strewn it all over with lovely violets. The most beautiful that you could ever see. All kinds! Dark, and that beautiful shade they call Parma violet. There must be hundreds of blooms there—according to Mrs. Lewis's story. Quite romantic, isn't it?"

Anthony nodded his agreement, but his thoughts were fugitive. A demonstration in violet blooms! While he was thinking on these lines, Annesley came down and took his place at the breakfast table. Anthony passed on to him the news that he had just received from Lysbeth Paske. "Violets," repeated Annesley wonderingly. "I'm not well up in the language of flowers, but an idea has just struck me. Is there any special significance about the violet? I mean, has it been chosen specially for the occasion, do you think?"

Anthony Bathurst smiled, and shook his head. "I've applied a good many directions of knowledge to the science of deduction in my time, but never yet this language of flowers that you talk about. Still, it's never too late to learn. I'll have a shot at it. Let's see where it gets us."

At the first convenient moment that presented itself, Anthony beckoned to Lysbeth Paske. She came over to the breakfast table. "Concerning that little piece of information which you gave me just now, Mrs. Paske—what does the violet mean in the language of flowers? Have you any idea?"

Lysbeth nodded simply but surely. "Oh yes," she answered him, and this time her trace of accent was much more noticeable. "I have known all those things since I was a little girl at school. My sex notices them more than yours does, sir. I will tell you! In the flower language, the violet is the emblem of innocence. And also of mod-est-y." Lysbeth blushed to the roots of her flaxen hair. "It is supposed, too, to indicate the love of truth and the truth of love." Lysbeth's blush grew deeper. "That is, of course, Mr. Bathurst, if you can bring yourself to believe such things."

Annesley half smiled at the little lady's embarrassment. "That reminds me of something else," he observed rather shyly. "Didn't Aristophanes refer to Athens as 'the city of the Violet Crown'?"

"You're right there," added Anthony Bathurst. "I remember that. We find the same description in Macaulay. He calls Athens 'the Violet-crowned city'. Ion (a violet) was a representative king of Athens. You will recall that Greece in Asia Minor was known as Ionia."

Annesley followed up the point with eager enthusiasm. "Yes, and again, Swinburne. What are his lines, now? Wait half a second and they'll come to me. I know them well." He began to repeat the lines.

"Round the city brow-bound once with violets like a bride."

Anthony nodded. "Interesting—all this. A unique setting, too, for the crime mysterious."

Lysbeth Paske moved off quickly to attend to the wants of other people at another table. Edmund Pereira, twisting in his chair, seemed as loquacious as ever. Anthony could hear him holding the interest of his table companions. There could be no doubt that Pereira had personality. Anthony turned to Annesley.

"I intend doing two things to-day, Annesley. At least two things."

"Privately, do you mean, or in connection with this Hillier case?" Anthony grinned at him.

"Strange though it may appear, the answer is 'yes' to both your questions."

Annesley cracked an eggshell and looked surprised. "I don't know that I'm able to follow that. Isn't it by way of being a contradiction in terms?"

"Not altogether. You see, it's like this. I'm down here, like yourself, on a holiday. This little problem of Mrs. Hillier's death fell from the sky into my lap. It's not the first occasion that things of that kind have happened. Don't think that I wanted it for a moment. Not on your life. But all this means that I have no official connection with the case. Don't forget that. At the same time, though, Annesley, the two matters to which I intend giving my attention today will have a direct reference to it. Now do you see how things stand with me?"

Annesley nodded. "Of course. Would you regard me as appallingly inquisitive if I asked you what these plans of yours are?"

Anthony smiled back at him. He had come to like Annesley, even though he had known him for so short a time.

"Not a bit of it. To tell the truth, I'm in dire need of a confidant." He leant across the table and lowered his speaking tone. "Firstly I intend to visit Mrs. Hillier's newly made grave in Lanrebel churchyard, and, secondly, I propose to take a short walk, a walk that should be within about a mile's distance."

"I gather what you mean. You mean to walk to One Mile Cliff."

"Congratulations. Take anything you like except the big blue vase on the back shelf. That's bespoke! In other words, Annesley, you've holed in one. What are you doing?"

"I thought about getting Paske to run me out to Laran in the car. Which side of the town do you prefer? East of the river or west?"

"Well, it's all pretty. Every bit of it. In fact the entire countryside here wants a hell of a lot of whacking. Meeting anybody in Laran?"

Annesley shook his head. "No. I'm here on my own and I know nobody in Laran. But spare your sympathy. It isn't really needed. I'm an only child, a bachelor, and quite self-centred enough not to be bored with my own company."

"Don't worry! I wasn't going to gush forth in sympathy," said Anthony, finishing his coffee. "On the other hand, I was considering making you an offer. Care to listen to it?"

Annesley's eyes showed keen interest. "Tell me—what's the offer?"

"I was going to ask you whether you'd crash round with me. That is, of course, if you had nothing better to do. Don't let me drag you into anything to which you'd rather give a miss."

Annesley was almost overwhelmed. "My dear chap! There's nothing on earth I'd like better. But are you sure I shan't be in your way?"

"Certainly not. How could you be? That's O.K. then! Now I want to send a wire. Get a move on and meet me in the yard by the big gates in half an hour's time."

Annesley looked at his watch and gauged the time. "That's a bet. I'll be there on the dot."

Annesley finished his breakfast under the influence of a most pleasurable feeling. Indeed, he was surprised at his reactions. Here, on the threshold, were adventurous experiences for which he had not bargained—but everything in life was worth trying at least once! To work in joint harness with Anthony Bathurst! What a difference from the holiday plans that he had intended when he came down! He was meticulously punctual at the rendezvous. Bathurst was a matter of mere seconds behind him. It was an incredibly glorious morning, and all of Glebeshire around them was at its brilliant best. "The churchyard first," said Anthony with a whimsical grin. "We will reverse the natural order of things." They crossed the road that leads to Bonallack, and there, confronting them, was the square tower of Lanrebel church. Annesley put his hand through the big iron gate and pulled back the latch. They walked up the path, past the church itself, and then into the newer portion of the churchyard. Mrs. Hillier's grave lay in the right-hand corner on a slight slope.

"There," said Anthony, "obviously."

Flowers lay in prodigal profusion round the grave. Or, rather, around what looked like to them, as they approached, a sea of blue.

"It's a marvellous sight," said Annesley. "I've seen nothing like it ever."

They walked right up to the azure island. "Altering the words of Dr. Johnson to suit the present occasion," said Anthony, "God might have made a lovelier flower than the violet, but it is equally certain that He never did."

Annesley nodded in silence. He stood gazing down at the field of the cloth of blue.

"'The emblem of innocence', quoting the little lady of the inn."

"I wonder," returned Anthony Bathurst, "remembering how this lady died."

"You think these flowers significant?" queried Annesley.

"Decidedly," responded Anthony. "I should consider myself culpably negligent if I allowed myself to ignore them."

"And yet . . ." Annesley paused.

"And yet—what?" said Anthony.

"Well, of course . . . I'm new at the game . . . but I don't see how they can be made to fit. Into the scheme of the crime, I mean."

"Neither do I, Annesley. At the moment that is—which doesn't mean to say that I shan't before I've done with the case. Tomorrow is also a day, laddie. Don't forget that. Many a time, when the clouds have been at their darkest, I've been comforted by that thought." He stooped down to the strewn violets and took a mass of them into his hand. Annesley saw that he was examining them closely. He was intelligent enough, however, not to worry Bathurst with a battery of curious questions. He waited in patience to hear Anthony's own personal reactions. His patience was eventually rewarded. Anthony Bathurst held out to him a handful of blue bloom. "Notice anything about these, Annesley?"

Keith Annesley was puzzled. He bent down to catch the exquisite scent of them. Then he looked up again at the man who was holding them. "Only their beauty, I'm afraid. Should I notice anything beyond that? I mean—am I blind?"

Anthony smiled at Annesley's evident desire to justify himself. "Look at their condition. That was the point I was endeavouring to raise. Test it for yourself."

Annesley knitted his brows. "Condition?"

"Yes. Don't you notice anything about them?" Annesley shook his head. "I'm sorry—I'm afraid I don't."

Anthony dropped all the violet blooms which he had picked up, back on to the grave, save one, which he retained on the palm of his left hand.

"If you look at one bloom only—you may see my point better than if you gaze at them in the mass. Now take a good look at this one here. Put it on the palm of your hand. Here it is."

Annesley obeyed the injunction and looked carefully at the flower. Then he nodded as though expressing agreement. "I think I know what you mean. It's a bit . . . how can I put it? . . . let me see . . . it's a bit—flat. Something like a flower that's been pressed. You know. In a book . . . sometimes the family Bible . . . treasured memories and so on. Am I right?"

"You are. In a way, that is. But these flowers haven't been pressed or anything like that. You're only 'nearly' right. They've been crushed. That's my point."

"And what do you deduce, then, from that?"

"That the violets have been brought here by somebody, some distance. For obvious reasons, I should say. Had they been purchased locally, or even comparatively near at hand, it would have been a moderately simple matter for us to trace the purchaser. Now it's going to be a darned sight more difficult."

"Yes, I see that, of course. But the point wouldn't have occurred to me had I been here on my own. I'm certain of that. Where would you try to trace the sale?"

Anthony laughed at Annesley's eagerness. "I'm not 'in' on the case yet, as I told you at breakfast this morning. So I can't answer that question of yours. All I can do in the matter is to drop a word to the police."

"And will you?"

"Depends," returned Anthony semi-humorously. "Haven't met 'em down here yet, so I can't say." He tossed the violet bloom back on the grave and turned away. Annesley turned with him. As they did so, they saw two figures approaching them. Anthony recognized the first by reason of certain knowledge, and the second by intuition. The first was that of Edmund Pereira, the second that of the Rev. Septimus Aylmer, Vicar of Lanrebel. Mr. Bathurst decided to stay where he was for a few minutes, and motioned to Annesley to do likewise.

They stayed by the grave. The Vicar and Pereira came up to them. The latter nodded affably but made no formal introduction. Aylmer looked down at the blue blanket of bloom. Pereira cocked his head to one side and stared blankly at the grave.

"Now, gentlemen," he said, "I don't know how it gets you, but I call that nothing more than scandalous desecration. Yes, sir."

He visibly waited for the Vicar's support. But the Reverend Septimus shook a reverent head. "I don't know that I can subscribe to that. On the contrary, it seems to me . . . all of it . . . to be very beautiful. That is one aspect of the matter . . . at least. Surely you must agree with me."

But Pereira was having none of that. "Well, then, sir, with all respect, I do not. On the other hand, I find myself in absolute disagreement with you. It may be that these particular blooms here are just a pain in the neck to me. I just can't stand them. Never could. A gardenia, now—or a clove carnation . . . why, yes . . . every time. But not this patch of purple . . . no, sir. It just don't get anywhere with me. It raises my gorge."

Pereira glared at the Vicar of Lanrebel as he finished his effort.

Anthony said nothing . . . he wanted to see what the good Vicar's response to this onslaught would be. At the way events had gone Annesley seemed to be taken by surprise. But he didn't know Pereira as well as Anthony knew him. The Vicar of Lanrebel appeared to flinch a little at the American's tirade. With what appeared to be an effort he preserved his dignity.

"That may be your opinion, sir. You are entitled to hold it. I'm glad to think, however, that it is not mine." As he spoke, he looked across at Bathurst and Keith Annesley, standing on the other side of the grave. Anthony accepted the situation at which the Vicar hinted.

"Good morning, sir," he said. "My name is Bathurst. This gentleman with me is Mr. Keith Annesley. We are spending a holiday in your delightful district. Your church, I may say, is worthy of it."

The Vicar acknowledged the gesture and the compliment rather curtly. "Good morning. You must pardon my saying what I am about to say. I hope that this . . . er . . . immense . . . floral tribute to a person's . . . er . . . memory is not going to be regarded as something sensational in its . . . er . . . publicity. I have no desire that the churchyard of my parish should become a hunting-ground for curious sightseers."

Anthony raised his hat. "Good morning to you again, sir. Strange though it may seem, I assure you that I share your desire." He walked away, followed by an indignant and fuming Annesley.

"Old crab! I am glad you gave it back to him," declared the latter when they were out of earshot. "That crack was meant for us. Is it you or I who looks like a tripper?"

Anthony laughed heartily at the reminiscence. "It's true that I was annoyed for the minute by the pompous old fool . . . but I expect he means well . . . and I can quite see his point of view, on second thoughts."

"Agreed . . . but there are ways and ways."

"So that was the Rev. Septimus at close quarters, was it?" Anthony murmured almost to himself. "I hope the Coroner keeps away from his churchyard, or more fur may fly."

Annesley broke in again. "Are you going straight to this cliff place? Now?"

"I think so. Why shouldn't we? I fancy I know the way there without much trouble."

They came together out of the churchyard. Anthony manipulated the awkward latch of the gate. "Our way's towards Laran," he said. "We should pass 'Hillearys' on our way." He took Annesley through a wooden gate on the right-hand side of the road. They came to a glistening pond. "Lorvam Pond," said Mr. Bathurst. "Up there lies Lorvam village." He pointed the direction. They passed through woods, and Annesley caught, in passing, glimpses of a cream-fronted house. Anthony noticed him and nodded. "'Hillearys'," he said. "I've been this way before." He piloted Annesley past the golf course and an entirely unworthy War Memorial until they came to a curiously dismantled and broken building. Mr. Bathurst offered explanation of its condition. "Those are the remains of Red Gauntlet Fort. Goes back to the days of the Civil War. We go straight up from here to One Mile Cliff. Up you go, laddie."

They began to climb. Through three unsteady wooden gates they came to the cliff edge . . . protected by barriers, peaceful and rugged. Anthony and Keith Annesley stood at the top and looked straight down. "Good job we commenced to climb where we did. There's no straight path up . . . anywhere that I can see."

Annesley leant farther over and nodded. "As far as I can see, it's sheer. Save for that one ledge down there. Look—just there! See where I mean?"

Anthony's eyes followed the direction of Keith Annesley's pointing finger. This ledge to which Annesley had referred was about twelve feet down from the top of the cliff. Suddenly Annesley saw a curious expression come into his companion's eyes. Bathurst turned to him with a quick insistence, almost impetuous. "Give me a hand, Annesley, will you? I'm going down to that ledge. There's something there that interests me."

Anthony made instant preparation.

CHAPTER VII
THE EDGE OF CARDBOARD

"What do you want me to do?" asked Annesley. Anthony looked over the line of barbed wire and railing which formed the cliff's protection and judged the distance. "On second thoughts, I think I can manage on my own. I certainly am going down. Stay here to lend me a hand should I want it as I'm coming back." He put his leg over the protective railing and safely negotiated the wire. Keith Annesley followed suit and stood by him. The strip of grass on which they stood was narrow in the extreme. Anthony dug his fingers and toes well in and slowly lowered himself towards the ledge below. Keith Annesley watched him anxiously. Anthony wriggled slowly and carefully down until he stood perched precariously on the ledge. Now Annesley could only just discern the top of his head. Then he managed to see Mr. Bathurst kneel down dangerously on the grass and busy himself with something that appeared to be in front of him. This was all that he could see. He waited in patience for Anthony to return. Eventually he heard Anthony calling to him. "I'm coming up again now, Annesley. Stand by to give me a hand when I ask you."

Annesley waited for Anthony to appear again. He could hear him coming—slowly and with great care. Suddenly he saw Bathurst's outstretched fingers. Lying flat on the edge of the cliff, he stretched out his hand and gripped them. With Annesley's help, thus given, Anthony hauled himself up again. He brushed the knees of his trousers and his elbows. Annesley waited before he questioned. "What was it that you went after?"

Anthony held his handkerchief carefully. "Scraps of burned paper. I spotted them from up here; one was blown on the wind just at the moment I happened to be looking down. There's one fairly large piece. The other pieces, though, are very tiny. Look at them for yourself." Anthony shook the pieces from the handkerchief on to the palm of his hand. There were nine pieces of thickish paper burned brown. The wind on some previous occasion had obviously caught them in flight and blown them against the side of the cliff, where they had lodged in some of the thicker and coarser tufts of grass. One of these pieces that Anthony had recovered, however, was different from the other eight. It was not of the same ordinary paper. The texture was extremely thick and much stouter. Also, it had been burned scarcely at all, probably because it was more difficult to burn it.

"What do you think of this?" Anthony asked his companion.

"Cardboard of some kind," replied Keith Annesley.

"I agree. Anything more than that?"

"Negatively—yes. It's part of—not a postcard."

"Why not?"

"It seems to me it's too thick to have been torn off a postcard."

"I agree with you again. A good quality Christmas card would you say? Would that fill the bill?"

"No, I don't think so. Too thick again." Annesley turned it over and carefully examined it. There was something which looked like a dark grey line extending towards the edge of it. Something in shape which looked like part of a loop. "It's had writing on it." It was Annesley who advanced the opinion. "Something written in pencil. Not in ink."

"I think you're right again. That dark grey streak, something like a wave, that the flames have scarcely touched at all, seems to have somehow the stroke of a pencil."

"To me," said Annesley again, "it's as much like the lid of a box as anything. Something like . . . say . . . the lid of a box that new shoes are put in when you bring 'em away from the shop."

Anthony smiled. "We disagree at last. The surface of those box lids is . . . smooth. You know what I mean. A sort of glossy surface. This is a rougher surface and crinkled. Serrated, rather. Look at it here. See my point?"

Annesley nodded. "Yes, I follow you."

Anthony took out his magnifying-glass. Under its effect, the grey looped streak looked like a scrawled undulation. He examined it closely. Turning the glass first this way and then that, after a time he handed it over to Annesley. "Have a look at it under this."

Annesley did as he was requested. "Well?" inquired Mr. Bathurst after a moment or so, "what do you make of it? Anything definite come to you?"

Annesley shook his head. "Just a pencilled scrawl, I'm afraid. I can't make anything satisfactory out of it. Can you?"

"I think that I can. It looks to me like a scrawled or scribbled 'hea'. Three letters. H.E.A."

Annesley continued to look at the fragment of cardboard. "H.E.A," he repeated after Bathurst. "Such as part of the word 'heard', eh? Is that it?"

"That's the idea. 'Heard' will do as well as any word to point my suggestion. Any word with 'hea' forming part of it."

Annesley began to nod slowly. "Ye-es, I get you. I see what you mean. It's certainly a feasible proposition." Anthony stepped back to the road over the protective barrier which railed off the cliff-edge. Annesley did likewise. As he did so, he handed the cardboard fragment back to Anthony. The latter carefully placed it, together with the eight other tiny burnt paper flakes, between the leaves of his diary. "What kind of a night was the night of the 8th of June? Down here?" The question was Annesley's.

"Glorious! No June night that ever was, was ever better."

"That's hardly how it was where I live. I'm in Essex—getting on for thirty miles out of London. I remember it. I drank beer in a pub."

"Why did you ask?" said Mr. Bathurst.

"I was thinking of Mrs. Hillier's suspected assignation at this cliff place. Of course, if it were a lovely night as you say, that makes the idea, I think, a trifle more likely."

"Only—perhaps."

"Why do you say that? Seems to me it's sound enough."

"Well, barring the absolutely abnormal, any night of an ordinary English June shouldn't be too bad for that sort of joke, should it?"

"I see. I suppose not. Now I come to consider it intelligently. Well, where do we go from here?"

Anthony smiled at Annesley's eagerness. Then he slowly shook his head. "There are many places I'd like to go to, which, I'm afraid, are barred to me. Also there are several people I could bear to chat with. All sorts and conditions. But in all probability the pleasure will be denied me for the reason that I shan't get the opportunity."

Annesley nodded. "Yes. I can appreciate your position. Situated as you are here. Did you say several people?"

"Well—the three Hilliers to begin with. Call them the primary Hilliers. Husband Paul and the two children Ann and Neill. Then there's another gentleman—Mowbray, the butler. To say nothing of the secondary Hilliers. The brother, plus his partner in the married state. But there you are—I'm on the fringe of the affair only—and unless something extremely extraordinary happens—on that fringe I shall probably be compelled to remain."

Annesley smiled. "In the meantime I suppose you are actuated simply by—"

"Call it indecent curiosity, Annesley, and you won't be far out. I'm the stormy petrel of murder, Annesley, as I mentioned to you last night. Come and see what the 'Salvation' has to offer us in the way of lunch and liquid refreshment." Keith Annesley accepted the position and followed Anthony along the path by which they had come. There were moments when he judged silence to be the epitome of discretion. And this was certainly one of them.

Chapter VIII
ANN HILLIER MOVES

It was about an hour after lunch at the "Salvation" had finished when the unusual occurred. Mr. Bathurst was taken by surprise. When this surprise came to him he was seated in a deck-chair in the garden. Seated is a euphemism. His deck-chair was situated about a hundred yards from the two tennis courts of which the "Salvation" boasted. It must be admitted that Anthony was much more than half asleep in the sultry haze of June heat when through his heavy-lidded eyes he saw Paske the elder making a short cut across the grass towards him. Anthony gave no sign that he had observed the approach of Paske. Paske came straight up and halted in front of Mr. Bathurst's deck-chair. Also he coughed. "Mr. Bathurst," he said—"sir."

Anthony murmured a reply. "I won't say that I'm at your service, Paske. You are too old a hand to be deceived, and I should be the last person in the world to attempt the deception. But tell me the worst." Anthony lolled a long leg lazily in front of him.

Paske kept a very straight face. It was his pride that he could always do so. "A young lady wishes to see you, sir."

"A young lady? But I don't know any—down here, that is. What's her name, Paske?"

"Miss Hillier, sir. Miss Ann Hillier."

Paske's statement galvanized Anthony into life. He sat up in his chair. "What's that? Ann Hillier—here! I say! Where exactly is she, Paske?"

"Outside the 'Salvation', sir—she's come in a car."

"And you say she's asked for me?"

"Yes, sir. I thought it was strange, myself." Not a muscle of Paske's face moved.

"Oh, you did, did you, Paske? Well, in that case I must see her at once if it's only to annoy you." Anthony strode across the grass at an alarming pace for so hot an afternoon. Paske was lengths behind as he followed.

Anthony soon discovered that his host's version of the affair was correct. Outside the "Salvation" was a Bentley. Inside the Bentley sat a girl whom Anthony recognized at once as Ann Hillier . . . the girl whom he had previously seen in the County Hall, Liskerry. Anthony, of course, was hatless. He raised a hand, therefore, in dutiful salutation. The girl leant back a little and spoke to him through the window of the car.

"Please forgive me troubling you, Mr. Bathurst. I know perfectly well that it's frightful cheek on my part. I don't even know you . . .

or anything like that, but I do so want to talk to you for just a few minutes. Please say that I may."

Anthony smiled at her as he bent down to speak. "Only too pleased. Where shall it be, Miss Hillier?"

"Could you—would you—jump into the car now and let me drive you somewhere? We could talk as we went along. I assure you that I'm quite a competent driver and that you'll be perfectly safe in my hands." She opened the door to him in invitation. "Can I persuade you?" she urged.

"Miss Hillier," said Mr. Bathurst, "you have conquered already . . . I place myself unreservedly in your hands." He went round to the other side of the car, got in and took the seat beside her. "All the same, you know," he added, "you have me completely guessing."

Ann Hillier started the car and went straight ahead to take the road to Bonallack Ferry. "I'm afraid this is all very improper, and—er—unconventional. I just had to see you. I feel sure, though, that you will understand."

"But just tell me this, Miss Hillier . . . How did you know that I was here?"

"My brother Neill saw you and recognized you at Liskerry at the inquest on my mother." She stopped suddenly, as though the mere expression of the words had hurt her.

Anthony was careful to say nothing that might add to her embarrassment. He awaited her further explanation.

"You see, it's like this. Neill saw you in Court the day when Claude Merivale was tried for the murder of his wife. Campbell Patrick is a friend of my father's. You were pointed out to Neill. He told me yesterday that he recognized you at once. Well . . . I've been wondering ever since why you are here, and whether, being here, you will help me. Have I such a priceless cheek?"

"The first answer is 'holiday-making'. The second is 'Yes, if I can'—but how can I? The third—well, my dear young lady—"

She checked the pace of the car and flashed another smile at him. "What a shame to spoil your holiday. But it's about Jacqueline, my mother." As she spoke, her face became hard and set.

"Go on, I'm listening," prompted Anthony.

"First of all, Mr. Bathurst, I am certain that my mother was murdered."

Anthony still waited for her.

"And I want help, Mr. Bathurst. Badly! I haven't asked you to come with me now to talk intelligent nothings. I want your help." She half turned in her seat and looked at him with eyes that seemed to grow larger and larger every moment. "Be sweet," she said, "and help me."

"It may well be, Miss Hillier, that you have an exaggerated opinion of my powers. But tell me all that you know."

She shook her head as she adroitly swung the car round a sharp corner. "I know nothing," she said, "except my own mother. That's the trouble."

"I'll be very quiet. Tell me all that you feel the desire to tell me."

She was silent for what seemed like a long time. Anthony could see that she was endeavouring to arrange her thoughts. Ann Hillier looked straight ahead of her. There was a steadfastness in the grey eyes. "Promise me that you won't judge me as only a woman. Or even as only a girl. So many men do that. They delight in doing it. If you do, you'll be wrong, because most of my friends would give me credit for quite a lot of intelligence, and, without being conceited, I don't think they'd be wrong. I'll tell you first of all about my family. I mean by that, our immediate family at 'Hillearys'. Just the four of us. Only three now." There was no grief in the last sentence.

Anthony nodded in sympathy. Ann Hillier went on.

"We have been different from the majority of families. I am sure of that. In our domestic relationships, I mean. We all liked each other. I think that I can justly say that. But—it's difficult to explain properly. You see, I want you to understand. To understand perfectly—I mean. Don't think that there were two camps in the house or anything like that . . . because there weren't. Or that we lived in a house divided against itself . . . because we didn't. But it was like this . . . Jacqueline and I were absolute pals . . . always together . . . and Neill and Paul are tremendous pals still . . . you see what I'm trying to tell you . . . Jacqueline and I simply adored each other . . . Paul and Neill always crash in together . . . and she and I . . . and they . . . probably loved each other more than the others . . . Oh hell—what am I saying? Anyway, you see what I mean, don't you, Mr. Bathurst?"

Anthony nodded sympathetically. "I think I do, Miss Hillier. Go on as you're doing and tell me just what you want to tell me. As I asked you just now. In your own way and just as the mood takes you. I'll try not to interrupt you."

Mr. Bathurst leant back in his seat and waited for her. Ann began to drive fiercely again. He saw from a signpost by which the car flashed that they had come to within two miles of Bonallack Ferry.

"Thank you," she replied simply. "Well . . . it's because I knew Jacqueline so well—so intimately—that I'm positive she was murdered. I can't visualize the bare possibility of . . . anything else . . . having happened." She paused for a bare second. "For the last two months Jacqueline and I have been abroad. We've been in France for a little holiday. We came back just a week before the . . . evening of the dinner. We went at Easter and spent April and May over there. It was lovely. All of it. The spring flowers . . . and everything. We toured . . . all over the place. We had a perfectly lovely time. There wasn't a cloud on Jacqueline's horizon . . . all the time she was as happy as any woman could be—that I'll swear." She backed quickly as a car approached them in the narrowness of the lane. "I've driven with her, drunk with her, dined with her, danced with her till the small hours of the morning . . . been her constant companion . . . lived practically every single second with her . . . and I'll swear again that she had neither worry nor anxiety. Think of us not as mother and daughter but as two sisters. Are you getting a better picture of her?"

Anthony nodded silently.

"And these two months, Mr. Bathurst, mark you, were the last two months of her life! April and May. They weren't last year or the year before, they were almost now. Surely . . . if Jacqueline had been contemplating anything . . . dreadful . . . I should have seen some sign of it."

"It would appear so . . . unless . . ."

"Unless—unless what, Mr. Bathurst? Tell me—please."

"Well . . . unless the trouble . . . whatever it may have been . . . didn't come along until after your return from abroad. That's common sense, isn't it?"

"But how could it have, Mr. Bathurst? We came back here on the first of June. She was absolutely splendid. High-spirited and full of the memories of the marvellous time that we'd had. Since we have been home . . . we've met nobody . . . and absolutely nothing has happened. Everything has been as . . . tranquil . . . as it could have been. There's Bonallack Ferry," she suddenly pointed. "Shall we go across in the car and back to Lanrebel by Frayne and St. Flame? Do you mind?"

"Not at all, Miss Hillier. Count me as in your hands until you deliver me again to the 'Salvation'."

Ann ran the car on to the flat-decked ferry-boat and for a time they talked commonplaces. In the streets of Frayne, running downhill, Ann at once harked back.

"Well," she said almost ominously, "you can remember where I was. That we were back from the Continent and Jacqueline hadn't a care in the world. That's how she was when we got back from France."

"Go on telling me about her," said Anthony.

"About Jacqueline? I want to. She was a marvellous woman. She would have been forty-one next month. She looked about twenty-five." Ann stuck out a stubborn jaw. "May sound ridiculous. But it's true. She and I, more often than not, were taken for friends." She shook her head. "Not sisters. I mean not mistaken for sisters. We weren't very much alike."

They were almost through Frayne by now. The road to St. Flame lay just ahead. Ann continued. "She was terribly sophisticated . . . that may sound a foolish statement about a woman of her age . . . my own mother. But she gave me the impression—had given it, I think, ever since I've been old enough to notice these things—that she had always been the same. I could almost describe her as 'hard-boiled'."

Here it was that Anthony made his first interruption. "You see where this is leading to, Miss Hillier, don't you?"

"Where?" she asked him instantly.

"To another question. I'm afraid an inevitable one. What had occurred to her in her early life . . . to make her as you say she was?"

Ann's face hardened at his words. "Do you really think that? That there had been something?"

Anthony paused for a moment before he replied to her. "I'm beginning to think so," he said quietly.

"Why?" she asked. "Why . . . exactly?"

"Well—to account for this unusual sophistication that you describe. You have just stated that she had been like it ever since you can remember. See what I mean?"

"But what could it have been?"

"I should say . . . without any direct knowledge . . . either a great tragedy in her early life, or perhaps a terrific love affair. Have you ever heard of either in connection with her?"

Ann shook her head emphatically. "Never. Either from her or from my father. But that proves nothing, does it?"

"No," said Mr. Bathurst. "Nothing."

Ann drove on in silence for some moments.

"Miss Hillier," said Anthony suddenly, "going back to the various statements that came out at the inquest—to the Rev. Aylmer's in particular—I have been wondering if you have any comments to make on it."

Ann frowned. "You mean about the letter that mother is supposed to have had during dinner?"

"Yes."

"I know nothing of it. I knew nothing of it. Absolutely nothing! If Jacqueline did have a letter that day, I didn't know about it. Of one thing I'm certain, though. That letter didn't come by the morning post. Because if it had, I'm certain that I should have seen it. Especially when I know that I was down to breakfast before Jacqueline was."

Anthony listened to her and considered matters. "There is still another possibility. Miss Hillier."

"What do you mean, Mr. Bathurst?"

"That it didn't come through the ordinary channels of the post."

Ann knitted her pretty brows. "But surely . . ."

Anthony interrupted. "I was thinking of a letter that *might* have been delivered to your mother by hand."

Ann frowned again. "That would mean, then, that it came from somebody . . . near at hand. Wouldn't it?" she urged.

"It certainly points that way."

"I can't understand that, Mr. Bathurst. I can't believe it either. Not with Jacqueline."

"Don't overlook the fact that she mightn't have been expecting it. Collusion—at which I take it you're hinting—isn't a *sine qua non*."

"No. That's so," she said thoughtfully.

"Strange that if Aylmer saw it—you didn't. During dinner, I mean."

Ann remained thoughtful. "There's this about it. Mr. Aylmer was sitting in a better position for seeing what Jacqueline had in her hand than I was. Which might explain it."

Anthony came at her again with yet another question. "When you were in France with your mother, Miss Hillier, she received, as far as you know, no unusual correspondence, I suppose?"

Ann disposed of the question as soon as it had been asked. "None. I can answer that without the slightest hesitation. More often than not, I saw the post that came for us before Jacqueline did. So that I've no help for you in that direction, Mr. Bathurst."

Anthony became as thoughtful as Ann herself had been. An idea came to him. He would ask another question. "Miss Hillier," he said gravely, "have you by any chance visited your mother's grave to-day? Forgive me if the question causes you unnecessary pain."

Ann turned a startled face towards him. "No. Why do you ask? What do you mean?"

"You have not heard of anything . . . in connection with it?"

Her face, as she stared at him, held many emotions. "I've been out in the car nearly all day. I went out directly after we finished breakfast this morning and I've scarcely spoken to any of them at home. But tell me—you frighten me! What has happened?"

Anthony sought appropriate words of explanation. "Nothing that should cause you any anxiety."

"Then, what do you mean, Mr. Bathurst? Please tell me."

"Since your mother was buried, an extraordinary tribute has been paid to her memory. Her grave now is a mass of violets. I've seen nothing like it ever before. Their massed beauty is remarkable. But . . . well, it's difficult for me to describe all my feelings with regard to it . . . the gesture seems to me to be so unique . . . that I'm at a loss to find a satisfactory explanation." He watched Ann Hillier's face closely for her reactions.

"Violets?" she repeated wonderingly. "A mass of violets? But what a remarkable thing. . . . I cannot understand it, either; it . . . amazes me."

"It amazed me. It amazed me twice. Firstly when I was told of it, secondly when I saw it. And the second amazement transcended the first. It's so utterly unlike anything that I have ever seen. The grave is covered with them."

"Who could have done it?" Ann almost whispered the words to herself.

Mr. Bathurst let her know that he had heard them. "Do you suspect anybody, Miss Hillier? Search your mind thoroughly."

She shook her head. "No, I don't. It's all so difficult. I mean . . . it's all so sensational, isn't it? You know—theatrical. Would anybody who . . ." She paused. By certain landmarks that they were passing, Anthony knew that they were nearing Lanrebel again. He waited for her to finish. She turned to him. "Mr. Bathurst . . . the idea that has come to me may be ludicrous . . . but do you think that the violets could have been put on Jacqueline's grave by the person who murdered her?"

Anthony looked straight ahead of him. "I feel bound to say that it's a possibility I have considered, Miss Hillier. Although there is nothing to support such a fantastic theory. As I said before . . . it's such an extraordinary procedure that one can't meet it with ordinary weapons. That's how I feel about it."

"If you feel like that, with all your experience, you will understand so much the better how I feel. I'm not puzzled. I need a stronger word than that. I'm just utterly bewildered."

"Tell me something else, Miss Hillier, before we part company. Had your mother been photographed recently?"

Ann furrowed her brows. "Do you mean—specially photographed? Not as one of a group or anything like that?"

"No. Say a photograph of herself—taken fairly recently."

"No. I'm sure of it." Ann was decisive.

"Thank you. Was there any photograph in her possession that she valued more than any other?"

Ann's reply was prompt. "If there were, I never knew of it."

"Thank you again. Now a third inquiry. Is there any photograph missing from your home? *Any* photograph? Of an individual or of a group . . . or even of anything or anybody? I regret that I'm so indefinite. I can't avoid the condition. I'm attempting to explain something to my own satisfaction."

Ann took some time over her reply to Mr. Bathurst's last question. When she answered, she spoke slowly. "To my knowledge, no photograph of any kind is missing from 'Hillearys'."

"Thank you, then, for the third time, Miss Hillier. And there's the blessed sign of the unblessed 'Salvation'. Need I say how thoroughly I've enjoyed the drive?"

"I am glad. It was cheek my asking you—really. And you will help me?"

"If I can. Don't hesitate to call on me again, should you ever fancy that I might be of assistance."

Ann stopped the car outside the "Salvation". Anthony alighted. Her eyes were steady and purposeful. "I must arrange that you come to 'Hillearys'," she said. "I shall have to think of something. An excuse to bring you there."

"It would help, undoubtedly," replied Mr. Bathurst. "Good-bye, Miss Hillier."

Ann held out her hand.

"*Au 'voir*, Mr. Bathurst."

CHAPTER IX
AT "HILLEARYS"

IT MUST be admitted that Ann Hillier was as good as her word. Soon after ten o'clock on the following morning she drove her car again to the "Salvation". Anthony Bathurst was with Pereira and Keith Annesley when her message was brought to him. He excused himself to his two companions and went out into the road to speak to Ann Hillier. The morning was glorious. Anthony bore the benison of the sun on his face and neck with a sense of exultant gratitude. She smiled at him gratefully, her hands on the wheel. "Could you . . . possibly . . . come up to the house now . . . or are you most frightfully engaged somewhere else? Because if you can come along now I've worked the oracle for you with Paul. That's Father."

"You've wasted no time."

"I didn't intend to. I believe in striking when the iron's hot. Paul's in one of his better moods this morning. So I cashed in on it at once.

Told him you were here and what I wanted. And that's that. Don't you think I've done well?"

Anthony was acutely conscious of her attractiveness. Something that she had said, however, interested him more than anything else. He sought information, inasmuch as the time was opportune. "One of his better moods?" he questioned, repeating the words she had just used.

She nodded brightly. "Mmm! You want me to interpret? Well, he's nervy . . . gets on edge . . . and worries terribly. I don't mean about Jacky particularly . . . he's always been like it . . . used to drive a car, but he's scared stiff now and won't look at a steering-wheel. . . . Well, there you are, and this morning he's a bit better than most. Got the idea, Mr. Bathurst?"

Anthony returned her smile. "I think so, Miss Hillier."

"And you'll come along with me?"

"Yes," Anthony nodded. "I'll come along with you, since you've asked me so nicely."

Her face expressed her gratitude. She beckoned to him. Anthony took the seat at her side. "Tell me," he said, "who's at the house now of those who were there on the eighth?"

"Everybody bar old Sep. Aylmer and his wife, moody Mildred. Old cow! One dose of them goes a hell of a long way—take it from me. Mr. Bathurst." Her voice changed. "By the way—I've seen the violets. I went up to the churchyard yesterday—after I said goodbye to you. They're so lovely—they almost took my breath away. I could scarcely sleep last night for thinking of them. They're so absolutely wonderful."

"You can make no suggestion concerning them?"

Ann shook her head. "I wish I could. I just can't. My brain's been in a whirl ever since I saw them. It all worries me. Look! There's 'Hillearys'."

Ann drove the car up the approach at a fast pace. "You must see Paul first. Wouldn't do to upset his majesty. You have to mind your step with Paul. He'll be in his den, I expect. You string along with me." Anthony followed his companion through a doorway, down a spacious corridor, until they reached another dark-coloured door outside which she halted. Anthony could already see the magnificence of the garden. Colour was everywhere. Ann made a sign. Anthony understood its significance. She knocked at the door and a rather heavy voice replied at once . . . "Come in." Ann beckoned to Anthony and he accepted the invitation. As he stepped into the room, Mr. Bathurst saw Paul Hillier for the second time. Ann, with unwonted nervousness, precipitated the introduction. Paul Hillier rose from his desk and held out his hand to Anthony. Anthony noticed at once that at close quarters his voice held a combination of suavity and strength.

"Ann, my daughter, has told me about you, Mr. Bathurst. Let me say at once that you are very welcome at my house."

Mr. Bathurst replied suitably. Hillier's face was worn as that of a man who has borne great suffering and conquered the agony by sheer force of character and personality. Ann placed a chair for Anthony. Paul Hillier gestured to her to stay, and sat down again.

"I have been thinking things over, Ann," he said, "since you broached the subject to me this morning. I am not clear on one or two points, Mr. Bathurst. Perhaps you will be good enough to enlighten me."

Again Mr. Bathurst responded suitably.

"I see. But first of all I want to make sure of this. Are you here, Mr. Bathurst . . . in the district I mean . . . in connection with the death of my wife?"

"No, Mr. Hillier, I happen to be staying at the 'Salvation'. Just for a few days' holiday. I felt that I had earned them. The time was convenient and I wasn't over busy. So I took them. For my entanglement in your sorrow . . . you must blame Miss Ann here." Hillier looked relieved at the statement. Anthony went on. "After all, my connection with the Yard is only semi-official at the worst of times. I'm afraid that I've only myself to blame with regard to that."

"In that case, Mr. Bathurst, I should be obliged if you would undertake to investigate the affair of my wife's death. My daughter Ann made the suggestion in the first place. Now that I know better how you stand with regard to the official police I am prepared to accept Ann's idea. What do you say? Will you undertake the task?"

Anthony felt that the stars in their courses were once again proving too much for him. If the expression on Hillier's face were almost enough to persuade him, that on Ann Hillier's would undoubtedly have clinched matters. Mr. Bathurst surrendered to his fate with resignation.

"Very well, Mr. Hillier. In the circumstances I'll do all that I can to help you."

Hillier rose and shook Anthony Bathurst by the hand. "Thank you. Now where would you like to start? Is there anything . . . ?"

Anthony shook his head. "I think I know everything there is to be known concerning Mrs. Hillier's death. With reference, that is, to the circumstances of her death. I was present at the inquest at Liskerry."

Hillier looked up in surprise. His face changed a little.

"I was not aware of that, Mr. Bathurst."

Anthony nodded. "Yes. I was there the whole time. For no reason beyond the individual whim. But I'm extremely interested, Mr. Hillier, in one or two matters that have taken place since Mrs. Hillier's death. In connection with one of these I should value your opinion. I refer to the curious tribute that has been paid to your wife's memory. You have seen the grave, Mr. Hillier . . . since the funeral, I take it?"

For a moment, Hillier made no reply. Anthony's words seemed to have shocked him. He put his two hands to his head. Anthony watched him. Ann watched her father too. Eventually Hillier lifted his face to speak. "I have seen the grave, Mr. Bathurst, so that I know to what you refer. Beyond that I can say nothing. I am as puzzled at the incident as you. I have, however, asked myself certain questions. I was bound to in the circumstances. Is it perhaps a tribute from the entire district to a lady who was loved by all? Given anonymously . . . on account of its unusualness? Frankly, Mr. Bathurst, I don't know. I cannot supply the answer."

In this atmosphere Anthony found himself wishing that Ann were not with them. Certain questions were raising themselves in his mind. He decided to hold them back for the time being.

"Arising out of the inquest proceedings, Mr. Hillier, may I put this to you? You stated, when you were being questioned by the Coroner, that you felt certain Mrs. Hillier was murdered."

"I did—and I'm still of the same opinion."

"Equally frankly, then, will you—is there anybody whom you suspect as having been likely to cause your wife harm?"

Hillier's answer was emphatic. "Nobody. I wish there were. It might make matters easier for me. That's the strange part about it."

Before Anthony could frame a suitable reply, he heard somebody whistling outside the door. Hillier frowned at the nature of the interruption. He glanced towards the door. The door opened and a young man entered, to pause irresolutely on the threshold. Anthony recognized him immediately as Neill Hillier. "Oh, I say . . . I'm sorry! I didn't know that you had anybody here."

Ann's eyes looked daggers at him.

"It's all right, Neill," Paul Hillier spoke quietly to his son. "You may come in. Close the door, will you? This is my son, Mr. Bathurst. Neill—Mr. Anthony Bathurst."

Anthony saw that Neill Hillier's face was flushed.

"Oh—how d'ye do? Wasn't aware that we were going to be thus honoured."

Anthony noticed his blue eyes and the delicately featured nose. He judged (and his judgment was sound) that Neill Hillier was like his mother. Paul Hillier heard the significant note in his son's voice. "Mr. Bathurst is here at my request, Neill. In case you're labouring under a wrong impression."

"Oh, really! I didn't know that you and Ann had fixed things. Seems I wasn't consulted." He eyed Anthony. "Well, if you're dying to ask me any questions you'd better go ahead at once."

Anthony smiled disarmingly. "I don't think I need—really. You see—I happened to hear the evidence that you gave at the County Hall. I retain a clear memory of it."

"Good. That's a relief, then. I positively loathe saying the same things over and over again. Especially when it touches a matter like the death of one's own mother. I was the last to see her alive, remember. It will take me a long time to forget that fact." He turned to his father. "There's nothing you want me for, is there? In that case, then, I'll clear out and leave you to your discussions."

"Very well, Neill. That will suit me."

Neill Hillier gestured a parting salutation which rather ostentatiously included Mr. Bathurst and walked from the room.

Paul Hillier spoke. "He's nervy and unsettled. Not himself by any means. It's not to be wondered at, I suppose, considering all that he's gone through."

Anthony concurred. Since the interruption, Paul Hillier seemed strangely ill at ease. "Well," he began again, "if you'll let me know what you . . ."

Anthony came in to help him. "Leave me for half an hour to the devices and desires of my own heart. For one thing, I'd like to get the lie of the land. I'll come back and see you again before I go."

"Thank you. Ann will take you round. I'm sure there's nothing she'd like better." Paul Hillier waved them to the door.

"I would like," said Anthony, "to see the various rooms and then the situation of the garage."

"Come with me," said Ann Hillier. "I'll take you."

CHAPTER X
NEILL HILLIER MOVES

ANTHONY Bathurst and Keith Annesley walked along the road between Lanrebel and Laran. It was three days since his visit to "Hillearys" when Ann Hillier had acted as his guide. When they came to the cross-roads at the top of the hill a powerful car flashed by them.

"Pereira," said Annesley. "Our friend Pereira is enjoying the beauties of the Glebeshire countryside." There was emphasized censure in his voice. The mention of Pereira seemed to remind Annesley of the death of Jacqueline Hillier. He gave the reminiscence to Anthony Bathurst. It was accompanied by a question. Mr. Bathurst was frank and concealed nothing. He told Annesley of the contacts he had recently made with Ann Hillier.

"So you went up to the house?"

"Yes. Three days ago. I saw the two Hilliers, father and son. Also the brother. That is to say Paul Hillier's brother, and the brother's wife. But I couldn't get in touch with the butler, Mowbray. I hope to do that on a later occasion. I saw the rooms that were referred to at the inquest and I saw the car in which Mrs. Hillier died. Then I poked round the garage. All this under Miss Ann's supervision and benediction and, I ought to tell you, at Hillier's serious request. Unhappily, though, I picked up nothing, Annesley. Absolutely nothing! Not a stitch, shred, or fragment."

Annesley expressed sympathy. "That's bad luck! Although I'm absolutely new at the game, I think that I can understand how you feel. That your personal reputation's at stake. I feel, too, because of that, that I should like to be able to help you."

"That's good of you. Well—your chance may come. In affairs of this kind, you never know."

They turned into the road that leads to Plant. "Tell me, Bathurst," said Annesley, "do you yourself feel certain that Mrs. Hillier was murdered?"

Anthony hesitated over his reply. "No," he answered eventually, "I am not certain. If she were murdered, I've come up against a blank wall. That means less than nothing, though. I've been in the same position many times before—so I'm not worried about it. That experience has taught me not only to wait, but also how to wait. At the same time, though, I'm willing to admit that this problem is different from any that I've previously tackled."

Annesley's interest increased. "That's interesting. In what particular direction?"

"The circumstances of the death and, more than that, perhaps, the complete absence of any reasonable motive."

Annesley nodded agreement. "Yes. I can see your difficulty. Are you still considering the possibility of suicide?"

"Oh yes. I must. At the present moment that's much more than a consideration to me. But I must confess it doesn't satisfy me altogether. I wish it did. You see—it's at variance with my intelligence. When that condition comes along it generally serves as a warning to me. From such warnings I have often profited."

Annesley nodded again. "Hallo," he exclaimed as he looked ahead of him. "Here's friend Pereira coming back. He certainly flogs that car of his." Pereira streaked by again.

"It can take it, Annesley. I've rarely seen a better bus. American make, of course. Now, where was I?"

"Warnings," prompted Keith Annesley.

"Ah yes. Let's look at the problem in this way. It would be feasible, I think, to search for a possible motive amongst the people who were at dinner with Jacqueline Hillier on the evening that she died. Whom have we?"

Annesley gave back the answer. "Paul and Neill Hillier. The brother and his wife—I can't remember their names. The Vicar and his wife. That's the lot, isn't it? Oh—and the daughter. Your friend, Miss Ann."

"Yes. We may regard that list of yours, I think, as comprehensive. Perhaps, though, we ought to add to it the name of Mowbray the butler."

"Pretty hard going, all those," commented Annesley.

"Sticky undoubtedly. Not much in that lot, is there? Suppose we start with Paul?" Anthony smiled as he put the question.

"Husband? Should put him out of it. Normally speaking."

"Don't agree. Any husband may have a motive to murder any wife. With the complement also the case. People living together—you know! Still, in the absence of any direct evidence to the contrary, we must assume that Paul and Jacqueline were quite happy together."

"Somehow I don't seem so sure."

"Why not?"

"Just a hunch. What about the children?"

"As far as I know, no trouble anywhere. All more or less attached to each other. Ann and her mother especially. Much more than an average attachment. Any hunches coming from there, Annesley?"

Annesley was amused at Bathurst's question. It was so typical of the man. "None. Children and their reactions take me out of my mental depth. I've had no experience of them. So we come to the brother and the brother's wife."

"I saw them both when I was up at the house. Formed favourable impressions in each instance. I should say from what I saw of them that Maurice is about ten years junior to Paul. Smaller physically, and perhaps smaller in every way. Couldn't and can't see him as the murderer of his sister-in-law. Not even if he wished to murder her. But, of course, with regard to that I may be hopelessly wrong. You follow what I mean? There's Laran, Annesley, nestling down there by the sea. This is the best view that you can possibly get of it. The river bridges add to its attractiveness, don't you think? They give the place an 'up the river' appearance. Don't you agree?"

Annesley looked at the prospect that spread in front of him and assented. Anthony returned to his familiar argument.

"Now—Mrs. Brother-in-law. From the late Mrs. Hillier's standpoint, that is. What about her?" He answered his own question. "Although I'm not so sure about her. I think that she and her husband are well matched. He's so small. She's petite. Much younger than Maurice himself. Fifteen years at least I should think."

"Clever?"

"Don't think so. Difficult to tell, perhaps, from one encounter." Anthony hesitated. "I should assess her as intelligent."

"Mrs. Hillier was poisoned." Annesley stressed the last word.

Anthony turned and looked at him curiously. "Meaning exactly, Annesley?"

"Well, I may be wrong, of course, but I'm always inclined to class poisoning as a feminine method of murder rather than as a masculine. Don't know why, but it generally appeals to me in that way."

"You imply by that that in your opinion a woman is more likely to poison her victim than a man? Based on Lucretia Borgia, perhaps?"

"I do."

"Don't know that the history of crime over any length of period will support you. I can recall Palmer, Crippen, Neill Cream, Chapman and Armstrong without even pausing to remember."

"And I can retort with Maybrick, Major, Bryant, Mrs. Thompson with her powdered glass, and . . ."

Anthony shook his head. "I think I know why you think as you do—but there's nothing in it. Of that I feel certain."

Annesley shrugged his shoulders at Anthony Bathurst's somewhat summary dismissal of his opinion. "Well, I'll give way to you on the psychology of crime. It's been your job longer than it's been mine. All the same, I know perfectly well what I mean."

Anthony smiled. "I know you do. I said so just now. But I can't see Belle Hillier filling the poison picture."

"So that by elimination we're left with the Vicar of Lanrebel and his wife. Doesn't seem very hopeful, does it?"

"It does not. I told you that when we started."

"Never mind. Let's stick to our guns. What about the reverend gentleman? Nothing doing?"

Again Anthony hesitated. "Not exactly, perhaps, but we can say almost. Certainly nothing to cause any suspicion."

"So that brings us back to where we started from. The odds are on suicide."

"Yes, I agree with you there. Because I can't see a motive anywhere. Not the faintest sign of one. Which brings me once again to the question of the violets."

"Just a moment. There was the letter that Aylmer saw in Mrs. Hillier's hands at dinner. That seems to me to precede the violets not only in time, perhaps, but also in importance. Am I right—or wrong?"

"You can't compare the two incidents. That's what you're doing . . . or, at least, are inclined to do. They belong to different categories. I haven't overlooked your letter point . . . don't think that."

"You rate it as of less importance than the matter of the violets?"

"Frankly, Annesley, I do. For this reason. Letters *may* be just ordinary. That letter which Aylmer says he saw in Mrs. Hillier's hands may have been nothing more sinister than an invitation to a bridge party somewhere, which Mrs. Hillier, having recently received it, hadn't had time to mention to anybody. The massed violets, however, are very much another story. They are extraordinary. They are unusual. They are so entirely abnormal and unexplained. And they are so much all those adjectives that one continues to wonder about them. Have you followed me all the way, Annesley?"

"Yes, all the way. Putting it as you have done, I cannot help agreeing with you. So I take it from what you've said that you are concentrating on the violets."

"I know one thing about them already, Annesley. That I previously suspected."

"What's that?"

"They weren't purchased locally. I can tell you that for a certainty. I've made inquiries in Lanrebel, Laran, Liskerry, Frayne, Bonallack, St. Flame, and in the surrounding district. Question therefore that raises itself, where *were* they bought?"

Annesley nodded. "That's decidedly interesting."

"As well as being disconcerting. The District inquiry was a comparatively easy matter. The Rest of England ditto will be a horse of a very different colour."

"An almost impossible one, I should say. Still, you might strike lucky. You know your own business best, I suppose."

"If there is a criminal lurking in the offing, Annesley, I'm inclined to the opinion that he is an unusually clever one. He covers his tracks so well. The loose ends which as a rule stick out in various places in affairs of this kind are conspicuous so far by their absence. Well—what shall our programme be to-day, Annesley? Shall we lunch in Laran and make a day of it and get back to the 'Salvation' for dinner or ride back there now?"

Annesley thought it over. "Where can we lunch here? Know anywhere decent?"

"What do you say to crab sandwiches and beer? I can take you to a place where each is of the best."

"How far from here?"

"Not more than three hundred yards from where we stand."

"That's O.K. with me, then. I'm content to rely on your judgment. What's the name of this earthly paradise?"

"It's an ancient smuggling-house and rejoices in the name of 'The Merry Mariners'. Follow me! I'll lead you to it."

Annesley discovered within half an hour the truth of Mr. Bathurst's eulogy of the house. The fresh crab was excellent and the sandwiches well made. The beer was in the same class. The afternoon went all too quickly. The deck-chairs on the beach were supremely comfortable. The sun was gloriously hot. The air was magnificent. Annesley surrendered himself to the mood of the moment and slept. Anthony Bathurst lay back in his deck-chair and lazed. The difference should be noted. The acuteness of the Hillier problem receded. At six o'clock Mr. Bathurst leant over and prodded his companion in the ribs. "'"The time has come", the Walrus said . . .'"

Annesley blinked at the reminder and loathed the idea of immediate effort.

"It may sound incredible, but it's gone six," said Anthony, grinning at Annesley's lassitude. "Time to make a move—are you fit?"

"Do we walk back?" questioned Annesley.

"A walk is most certainly indicated, especially for you in that condition. Otherwise—where will that appetite be?"

"As a tyrant," murmured Annesley, "you would gain high marks. As a despot . . . Oh, well—I like the efficient in everything. Get going."

They made the Parade again and sauntered in their own time back to the "Salvation". Annesley agreed that it was worth the effort. Old man Paske came to meet them at the door of the lounge.

"Mr. Bathurst," said Paske quietly and before Anthony could speak, "I'm sorry that you haven't been here during the afternoon. Mr. Neill Hillier wanted to see you very urgently. I'm putting that in his own words, Mr. Bathurst. He came down here just after lunch."

Annesley could see that Bathurst was annoyed at having missed the encounter. "That's bad luck, Paske. Mr. Annesley and I walked in to Laran and spent the day there. Had I known that I was likely to be wanted . . ."

"I wasn't aware," remarked Paske pointedly, "that you and Mr. Neill were acquainted. Had I known that . . ."

"We weren't," replied Anthony drily—"until a day or so ago. Did he leave any message for me—or arrange to come back again?"

"No, sir," returned Paske. "I told him that I would tell you that he had called, and he seemed satisfied. From his manner, though, when he went away, I shall be most surprised if he does not return. Perhaps this evening, sir."

"Thank you, Paske. As far as I know I shall be in all the evening. So that if Mr. Hillier calls you'll know what to tell him."

Paske nodded and turned aside.

"I'll see you in the dining-room, Annesley, in about twenty minutes from now." Mr. Bathurst and Keith Annesley went to their respective bedrooms. Arthur Paske stood and watched them.

The dinner that evening was good. The various guests within the walls of the "Salvation" responded to it in their varying ways. But no message came to Anthony Bathurst from Neill Hillier. After a time Anthony and Keith Annesley and some others adjourned to the lounge. Frank Paske came in there on their heels with his inevitable tray for orders. Orders were given to him. Annesley picked up a magazine. Mr. Bathurst stood by the window. He observed the condition of the weather. "There's a change coming," he remarked, "unless I'm a very bad judge. It's going to blow quite a lot during the night. 'Heaven help the poor sailors'," he quoted semi-whimsically. Arthur Paske, loitering at the door of the lounge, overheard the remark and spoke eagerly.

"There was a gale warning on the six o'clock radio, sir. We often get 'em in these parts, following upon sunshine such as we've had the last two days. The warning that was given didn't surprise me at all."

Thus prompted, the general conversation turned to wind and weather. Anthony left the lounge and stood for a while at the main door of the "Salvation". From here he commanded sight of three roads. After a time Annesley joined him. The wind was increasing in force. At times it was frightening. The trees swayed to it in a gaunt and giant unison. The sky showed the menace of clouds. Dark copper-coloured clouds that held threats and almost sinister menace. Anthony thought over things. If Neill Hillier came to him to-night the errand must indeed be judged important. Anthony returned to the lounge with Keith Annesley. Rain fell suddenly on the window. Anthony still waited patiently.

Slowly the hours passed. Neill Hillier did not come to the "Salvation" inn. At half past eleven Annesley retired for the night. At midnight, two hours after the house had closed, Mr. Bathurst came to a decision and himself went to bed. As he ascended the stairs, a heavy gust of wind sent a burst of rain rattling on the window that faced him at the top of the staircase. Away in the distance there came the heavy rumble of thunder, and Anthony knew that the storm fury was gradually closing in on them. As he opened his bedroom door he heard a car drive into the yard of the "Salvation". He saw the momentary flash of its lights on the window. "Somebody been out late," thought Anthony. Another crackle of thunder interrupted his train of thought. Much nearer this time! Two seconds later the storm broke.

CHAPTER XI

THE SECOND BLOW FALLS

IT HAPPENED that night that Mr. Bathurst looked at his watch as he got into bed. The action was unusual. He remembers the time well.

It was twelve minutes past twelve. He thinks that despite the fury of the storm he must have dozed for about an hour. Suddenly, and with his mind in confusion, he found himself sitting bolt upright in his bed. The reasons for the occurrence were these. There were shouts outside the "Salvation" and a bold hammering on the big wooden doors. The man who shouted was afraid. Afraid and anxious. The note in his voice that attracted Anthony's attention shrilled high and clear above the noise of the storm. Slowly . . . or so it seemed to Anthony . . . there came stirrings inside the inn. Heavy dragging feet could be heard going down the staircase to the place from which came the disturbing noise. Voices were raised and the bolts drawn back. Anthony sat up and listened eagerly. Then came the scraping of feet over stone and vague murmurings. His attentive ears were confused. The wind had dropped a little. Anthony took a chance and slid out of bed. He went to the door of his bedroom and listened. A door banged to in the wind. This added noise seemed an unnecessary aggravation. Anthony could hear Paske's voice. There was a high, raucous tone about it, as though Paske were rattled over something. It was full of querulous annoyance. He heard Paske say, "There's God's curse on the place. It's a judgment on me. It serves me right. And you, Laura, you go straight back to bed. This is no place for you—or any woman. D'ye hear me? You can do no good. Go on, now—at once—or I'll put my hand across you! Frank, you come here and give Sergeant Spiers and me a hand, will you?"

Anthony came to an immediate decision. He must get downstairs at once. What had happened? A cold fear clutched at his heart. A fear that was vague and foreboding as well as cold. He hastily threw on a coat and trousers and went down to the commotion below. When he had descended the stairs the big entrance doors of the inn had been bolted again and the storm shut out. Anthony looked round him. There were voices in the lounge. He attempted to identify them. Paske's, Frank Paske's, and a sharp voice which Anthony in this tone had not heard before. He frowned to himself as he rapped at the door. He was uncertain as to how . . . The medley of voices ceased at his knocking. Steps crossed the room and somebody opened the door to him. Paske's face stared at him in the doorway. Annoyance was written all over it. "May I come in?" said Anthony. "I heard the knocking . . . it woke me up . . . you see, and I wondered . . . perhaps I can help—"

A sharp voice cut in. "Who's there, Paske?"

"One of the gentlemen staying here, Sergeant—Mr. Bathurst."

"Tell him to clear out. And sharp at that. This is no place for curiosity or for the company of interfering busy-bodies."

"Just a moment, Sergeant Spiers. I realize, of course, how right you are, but possibly this may affect your decision. It's up to you to refuse, I know, but you may be able to stretch a point."

The uniformed man glanced sharply at the card which Mr. Bathurst had handed to him. His face changed at once. "Oh, in that case—come in, sir; I'm sorry. I didn't know it was you."

Anthony noticed at once how wet his clothes were.

There was a curious patch near the right shoulder. He followed Sergeant Spiers into the lounge. He saw that Paske and Frank Paske were standing by the big settee that backed the wall which was against the passage.

On the settee, flabbily helpless on the soft comfort of the cushions, sprawled a body. Inert. Motionless. Spiers gave Frank Paske a curt order. "Lock that door, Frank! At once! Else we shall have other people poking their noses in." He caught Anthony's eye. "I beg your pardon, sir—but you know what I mean."

Mr. Bathurst did not trouble to answer. He had seen the body on the settee. The face was white and upturned. It was familiar to him, and he knew now why Neill Hillier had not come that night to the "Salvation" inn at the time when he had been expected.

Jacqueline Hillier! Neill Hillier!

<h1 style="text-align:center">CHAPTER XII</h1>
<h2 style="text-align:center">MORE MYSTERY</h2>

"WHERE was he found?" asked Anthony quietly.

"About a hundred yards from the Laran crossroads," answered Sergeant Spiers.

"By you?"

"Yes. I was going the rounds. My ordinary duty. He was lying in the ditch at the side of the road."

"How was he killed?"

"Struck down from behind. By a heavy blunt instrument, in my opinion. Taken by surprise I should say. His head's all smashed in at the back. Pretty gruesome."

"You picked him up and brought him along here?"

"That's it. In case there was just a chance. This is the nearest place of abode. When I picked him up I thought he might be still living."

Anthony made a calculation. "You found him, then, about a quarter of an hour ago?"

Spiers nodded.

Anthony went on. "And the place where you found him would be between here and his own house?"

Spiers nodded again. "Yes, of course! But what could have brought him out on a night like this? That's the question I've been asking myself all the way along. I carried him, you see."

Anthony heard the Sergeant's question but kept his own counsel. "What about a doctor?" he queried.

"Mr. Paske has already 'phoned for Dr. Lambert. He's got to come in from Plant." Spiers looked at his watch. "Dr. Lambert should be here within another ten minutes."

"Rotten job," commented Frank Paske tersely. "Dragged out of bed on a filthy night like this is to look at a . . . I've seen his head at the back. It's ghastly." Frank, as he spoke, shivered.

"For the love of Mike, Frank, bring in some whisky," said his father. "From what I can see of things, there isn't one of us here who couldn't do with a drop."

Anthony was thinking hard. He turned to Sergeant Spiers. "I'll tell you what I'm thinking, Sergeant. Funny place to murder anybody! On the public highway. Don't you think so yourself?"

Spiers was quick with his reply. "On most nights, yes, sir. To-night, no, sir! Indubitably—no!" The Sergeant was puffed and pompous.

"Dark and lonely, you mean?"

"All that, sir, and since the storm started—as black as your hat. And the number of people who've been abroad to-night, sir—well, you could count 'em on the fingers of one hand. I know, because I've been travelling the roads."

"I suppose so. In that case, then—"

Paske interrupted with a touch of impatience. He had been at the window, listening. He turned, grey-faced.

"There's a car! Listen! It's stopping here. It's Dr. Lambert. Let him in, will you, Frank?"

Frank Paske went out through the lounge after unlocking the door and wrestled with the big double doors. For the second time that morning Anthony heard the bolts being pulled back, then Lambert's heavy, booming voice, and strange clucking noises which the man thought fit to make with his tongue against his teeth.

"Young Hillier, you say. Tut . . . tut . . . that's bad . . . nasty. Your father's 'phone call fairly knocked me over . . . I could very well have done without this job . . . I can tell you. Still—talking won't get us anywhere. Where is he?"

Anthony heard Frank Paske say, "Come this way, Doctor," and saw the door of the lounge open. Dr. Lambert floated into the room something like a big pink air balloon that has been blown out to a perilous size. Spiers explained matters and indicated Mr. Bathurst's presence. Lambert gave a short sharp nod, mouthed an entirely unintelligible something, and swayed restlessly over to the settee and its burden.

"H'm, h'm!" he grunted several times before silence came. Anthony waited patiently for whatever Lambert chose to say. At length Lambert spoke. "Poor young fellow. After his mother, too. The Irish would say that she called him to her. Seems there's a fate on the family. Death instantaneous. Bad fracture of the skull." He became technically professional. "Parietal bone . . . upper portion of occipital bone and squamous part of temporal bone—all badly injured. Whoever got him meant making a downright job of it. H'm—dashed nasty business."

"How long would you say he had been dead, Doctor?" Mr. Bathurst's question came quietly.

Lambert wrinkled his nose in strange, ugly creases. "H'm. How long? Difficult to say. Well . . . let me see. The time now is . . . ." He looked at his watch. "Not less than four hours. Killed, I should say, somewhere between nine and ten. Yes, that's it . . . say four hours."

Anthony heard the doctor give his opinion. So Neill Hillier had intended to come to him that night. After all, he had actually started out . . . and been struck down on the way. He addressed a pertinent question to Spiers. "Which side of the road was he lying, Sergeant, when you found him?"

"The left-hand, sir, as you come this way. I suppose a car couldn't have . . ."

Mr. Bathurst shook his head with decision. "No. It wasn't a car. You can dismiss the idea. Look at his clothes. And his body. Only his head has suffered. Isn't that so, Dr. Lambert?"

The doctor went to the settee again and busied himself with the body. As they saw him loosen much of the dead man's clothing, Lambert suddenly turned to Sergeant Spiers. "Did you carry him here, Sergeant?"

"Yes, Doctor. I felt that I must get help. I wasn't absolutely sure when I picked him up that he was dead. It was so damned dark. I've marked the spot, of course, where he was lying. There's a clump of foxgloves just by it."

Lambert spoke to Anthony Bathurst. "Re your car question. As far as I can tell, there are no other injuries, so I agree with you."

"Thank you, Doctor." Anthony turned to Spiers. "He was bareheaded, I take it, Sergeant, when you found him?"

Spiers nodded. "There was no sign that I could see of any hat or cap near him."

Frank Paske broke in: "There wouldn't be. Don't worry about that. Mr. Neill seldom wore a hat. You'd always see him bare-headed. Or almost always."

"Nice job to tell his father," put in Paske senior. "Two of 'em in less than a fortnight, quoting the doctor's words. It's a bad business."

Anthony did what Dr. Lambert had done a few moments previously. He went to the side of the settee and looked down at the body. When he returned to the middle of the room again his face was white and set. "That's a terrible head wound, Doctor. I've never seen a worse one. He must have been struck with terrific force."

"He was, undoubtedly. By an unusually powerful man wielding an unusually heavy instrument. Once the blow crashed home it was all over with him. As I told you—death was instantaneous." Dr. Lambert mopped his forehead with his handkerchief.

Anthony nodded. "I agree. And that makes a satisfactory feature about it. It narrows the field of our inquiry. All the same, I'm worried. It seems to me that there's something wrong about it all. Something that none of us understands. Each of these two Hillier deaths is so strange! Mrs. Hillier drives out in a car late at night, and then drives back to her house to die. This boy, her son, walks out in dirty weather for a reason known to himself, and, presumably, one other, and meets his death, as I said just now, on the public highway." Mr. Bathurst stopped in his narration and shook his head. He had, however, made an impression upon his hearers. Arthur Paske, for one, had expressed his agreement with Mr. Bathurst's conclusions with a series of nods. Dr. Lambert, for his part, broke in on a different note.

"I'm afraid that Mr. Bathurst is taking me somewhat out of my depth. My concern is to tell you that the man is dead and the reason why he died. Within limits, of course. Well—I've done that, which means that for me there's no more to be said." Lambert puffed out his pink cheeks again in an effort, possibly, to assist his explanation. Spiers accepted the position as Lambert had outlined it.

"Very good, sir. I'll make the usual arrangements with regard to the body. And you'll make your report as well, Doctor."

"That's the idea, Sergeant. You carry on as required, and I'll come down again in the morning, or, to be more correct, later on to-day. Well—I may as well hop into my little bus again and get back to bed. And the sooner the better, as far as I'm concerned." He turned to the rest of the company. "I'll wish you all a very good morning, gentle-men; I wish we had met in more pleasant circumstances. I expect that I shall be seeing most of you again." He waved to them cheer-ily as Frank Paske saw him out. As he went, Anthony Bathurst put a question to Sergeant Spiers. "Have you been at work at all on the first Hillier death, Sergeant?"

"Yes, Mr. Bathurst. I'm acting under Inspector Rockingham of Liskerry. If I may ask you the question, sir—what was your point with regard to that?"

"I was wondering why Dr. Lambert came along here just now. I understood that Dr. Pakenham was the official doctor for the police, and also that he lived close at hand here in Lanrebel."

Arthur Paske answered, although the question had been addressed to Sergeant Spiers. "I 'phoned for Dr. Lambert, Mr. Bathurst. You see, I happened to know that Dr. Pakenham was away for a few days. He was in here one evening towards the end of last week. As a matter of fact, he comes in pretty regularly. He told me he was off for a fortnight. When I had to 'phone just now, I remembered that and to save time got straight through to Dr. Lambert. He's the nearest doctor when Dr. Pakenham's not available, and always deputizes for him when required.

Spiers corroborated Paske's statement. "That's perfectly true, Mr. Bathurst. It's all in order. Dr. Pakenham's been a bit off colour since this Hillier business started. He's taking a fortnight's leave."

"I see," said Anthony. "That explains a little matter which was puzzling me. Thank you." He was about to put a further question to Spiers, when he checked himself. For a reason. He realized that he had no official connection with the case and depended upon Spiers' sympathetic consideration, and therefore could not embarrass the Sergeant. The man so far had certainly treated him with extreme courtesy, and he must remember that fact, from every point of view. What he wanted to do he must do alone. The time to communicate any vital findings might well come later. Even if it didn't, no harm would have been done.

Frank Paske returned after seeing Dr. Lambert off the premises. He grimaced. "Bit of a pig, old Lambert. At least, that's my opinion. Very different from Dr. Pakenham. He's a gentleman all the way through. The Hilliers wouldn't have had him for their regular doctor if he hadn't have been. Well, Sergeant, what do you want us to do now?"

Spiers commenced a series of orders. Anthony judged that the time was opportune for his exit. "As I can't do anything to help, gentlemen, I think I'll hit the hay again. Thank you for all your kindness, Sergeant. I appreciate all that you've done. If you should want me for anything, you know where to find me."

"Very good, Mr. Bathurst," returned Sergeant Spiers. "I'll remember that." With that parting remark from the Sergeant, Anthony retired to his bedroom and his bed.

But, it must be admitted, not to sleep!

CHAPTER XIII
THE DITCH

IF DR. Pakenham had intended being away for a fortnight, that intention must have gone by the board. For as Anthony Bathurst and Annesley later on that day walked up the road that started from the "Salvation" and made its way towards "Hillearys" a car passed them and Mr. Bathurst was able to see that the driver was Dr. Pakenham himself.

"I am taking you, Annesley—with your agreement, of course—" he said to his companion, "to the place where young Hillier's body was found. Spiers has described the spot to me and has told me exactly how to find it. Although I'm not so sure now that I needed his information."

"How do you mean?" demanded Keith Annesley curiously.

"Why, if I'm not mistaken, that car which has just passed us is on a similar errand to ourselves." Anthony pointed up the road.

Annesley's curiosity was but increased. "Again—what makes you think that?"

"The man driving that car is Dr. Pakenham. The Divisional Surgeon of Police, and, in addition, the family doctor of the Hilliers. Yesterday—he was away. To-day—as you see—he's back. I deduce that the murder of Neill Hillier has accelerated Dr. Pakenham's return. That's why, too, I think we shall find him at the place to which we are going."

"On the other hand, we may not."

"I'd bet on it, Annesley. Anyhow, we shan't be kept in suspense very long."

"From what you told me, Pakenham's a Lanrebel doctor. Besides being the police doctor, he practises in the district. So that there might be nothing beyond the ordinary in his being on this road just now."

"There might not be, Annesley, as you say. But he's come back from his holiday in too much of a hurry for me to alter my opinion. When we reach the top of this rise we shall have the answer to our rather trivial problem." Anthony smiled. The two men walked some distance in silence. At length they came to the crest which Anthony had mentioned. He extended a triumphant finger. "Behold, Annesley—the attendant car of Dr. Pakenham."

Annesley looked ahead and saw a car drawn up by the roadside. "There's a patch of foxglove there, Annesley. I'll present you with that piece of information before we get there."

"I don't see your doctor anywhere along there," said Keith Annesley, "chance it! Do you?"

Anthony shaded his eyes with his hand. "He's there all right. The car hides him. I fancy that he'll still be there when we arrive."

Annesley surveyed the country around them. "What frightful havoc these summer storms do cause. Just look at it all round, wherever the eye can travel."

Anthony let his eyes roam. Beaten foliage, ruined bloom, scattered leaves, and broken boughs were discernible almost everywhere. "Yes, Annesley. Nature has her way when she intends having it. She's relentless. Nothing can stand against her. You and I were lucky last night. We were indoors and could watch it. That makes a deal of difference. I expect we should have thought about it very differently had we been out in it." As Anthony finished his sentence, Annesley caught sight of a figure standing between the car and the side of the road.

"There's your doctor friend," he said. "You were right. As you said, the car was hiding him."

"Don't call him friend. I've never spoken to him in my life. I saw him at the inquest on Mrs. Hillier. That's the sum total of my acquaintance with him."

They had come now to within a few yards of the stationary car. Anthony again made demands on Annesley's attention. "See that clump of foxgloves growing on the bank? The Sergeant told me about them when I asked him to describe the place where Neill Hillier's body was found. Come on. I'll do most of the talking." Anthony went straight up to Dr. Pakenham. "Good morning, Doctor. A sad business, this."

Annesley saw a tall, lean, clean-shaven, smartly dressed man. He judged his age to be a little under thirty and thought that he should have been a sailor. His eyes were quick . . . almost restless. He frowned slightly as Anthony Bathurst addressed him.

"Er . . . yes. But I don't think that I . . ." He paused as abruptly as he had commenced to speak. Anthony bridged the difficulty.

"My name is Bathurst—Anthony Bathurst. I happen to be stopping with the Paskes at the 'Salvation' inn down the hill there. I was there with Sergeant Spiers when young Hillier's body was brought in . . . early this morning. This is Mr. Keith Annesley . . . the novelist. He is staying at the 'Salvation' also. Oh—Annesley . . . this is Dr. Pakenham, the Divisional Surgeon."

The frown on Pakenham's face grew bigger. "You know my name? I wasn't aware that we had ever—"

Anthony intervened. "I was at the County Hall, Liskerry, the other day . . . at the opening of the inquest on Mrs. Hillier. I heard you give your evidence. That's how I recognized you when your car drove by us just now. I realized that we were bound to pass by you. Annesley and I were walking."

"Oh . . . I understand." The doctor nodded to himself.

Anthony deliberately walked across the ditch. "So this is where Spiers found the body—eh?" He looked up the road and then down it—in the direction from which he and Annesley had just come. "Pretty lonely spot, too. At the best of times. It's not difficult to imagine what it was like last night. How far are we here from 'Hillearys'?"

Pakenham answered without hesitation. "About a quarter of a mile. 'Hillearys' is across there." He pointed across the road . . . rather vaguely. "But you should know, Mr. Bathurst. I understand that you've—"

He checked himself suddenly. Anthony waited for him. "Mr. Bathurst," he proceeded, "it would be idle for me to pretend that I don't recognize your name . . . and its usual connection. May I ask if you are at all in on this case . . . that is, specially?"

Anthony smiled at the question. "You may, Doctor. And the answer is 'No'. You can regard me in this instance as a purely private investigator. I trust that it will make no difference to . . . well . . . shall we say . . . our relations?"

Pakenham pursed his lips. "Oh . . . by all means, certainly not. I came along here because . . . when I heard the news of young Neill—I thought I'd like to have a look at the place where he was found. I got in touch with Spiers and he put me wise. What do you make of it?"

Anthony shook his head. "Nothing. Nothing at all! What is there? A ditch, a grassy verge, and a tarmac road. And according to your professional colleague, Dr. Lambert, from Plant, somebody cracked the boy's head from behind—almost exactly as an eggshell might be cracked under a mammoth spoon. I've seen the wound . . . so you see I'm inclined to believe Lambert."

Pakenham nodded, stooped, and peered at the ditch.

"And he rolled down into here. Rather surprising that Spiers spotted him."

"In a way, I suppose it is. But the ditch is shallow." Anthony began to speak slowly, as though he were carefully weighing every word. "There was grass on Mrs. Hillier's clothing when she died in her car. There was grass on that dead boy's clothes when Spiers brought him to the 'Salvation' this morning. Curious, that."

It occurred to Annesley that Pakenham was watching Anthony rather anxiously. The latter turned to the doctor.

"Tell me, Doctor. Something I could bear to know. I'm going back to the evidence that you gave at Liskerry. If Mrs. Hillier destroyed herself. . . . it's an utter impossibility for Neill Hillier to have done so . . . isn't it?"

Pakenham hesitated, although there was nothing furtive or stealthy about the hesitation. "Neill Hillier was murdered. That's self-evident I should say. He couldn't possibly have killed himself . . . from what Sergeant Spiers and you yourself have told me. But you mentioned the inquest on his mother." Pakenham stopped again, and his eyes held a far-away look. Mr. Bathurst waited patiently for what was to come. "You will remember, if you heard all my evidence at the inquest, that I stated that Jacqueline Hillier died from chloral poisoning. That is certain. I mean by that—that you need have no doubt about it. But there is also something that I did not say. And as you are who you are . . ." Again Doctor Pakenham showed signs of hesitation. Again Anthony Bathurst waited for him to go on. "I did not say that something—because I didn't happen to be asked about it. There was really no reason, I suppose, why I should have been asked. It was scarcely in the Coroner's province to ask it. Considering the nature of the evidence that I was giving. About having been called to Mrs. Hillier dead in the car, I mean. But, had I been asked by anybody, I should have said that, in my opinion, Mrs. Hillier was the very last person in the world whom I should have expected to commit suicide."

Pakenham stopped abruptly. To Annesley, listening, it seemed that he had said rather more than he had intended to say. That his words had run away with him.

"Why do you say that?" asked Anthony quietly. "Did you know her particularly well?"

"I had the honour to be the Hilliers' doctor. Not that I was ever wanted much in my professional capacity. But I saw a good deal of the family, naturally, and came in contact with her continually. Socially as well as professionally. I'll take my oath that Jacqueline Hillier was as sane as any woman that ever breathed. A good deal saner than most. I wouldn't use the cliché 'in love with life' with regard to her, because it wouldn't be true or adequate. There was something much more intense about her than that particular phrase even suggests. In fact she always gave me a most vivid impression that—not only was she living her life to the utmost, but with a definite and set purpose behind it all."

"Excuse my butting in," contributed Annesley eagerly, "but I've been listening and I've grown interested. What do you mean exactly, Doctor, by what you have just said? I scribble a bit, you know, and I'm usually on the lookout, I suppose, for such matters as psychologies and reactions. They help me in my rather feeble attempts to build up character."

Dr. Pakenham seemed to understand him. "Well—let me put it to you like this. Jacqueline Hillier always gave me the idea that she had a definite task to perform . . . in her life . . . before she died. A task that she had not yet performed . . . or even begun to perform. Something that she *knew* she was to be called upon to do . . . that she had dedicated herself to do, and which she was quietly waiting to do. And because of these things . . . I can't contemplate the possibility even . . . of her having killed herself and in that way abandoning her duty."

"She had married," urged Anthony Bathurst in a tone that suggested opposition. "She had given her husband children. To one of these children she was, I understand, most unusually attached. I suggest by these remarks that she had given certain hostages to fortune."

Pakenham shook his head. "I can see that you haven't thoroughly understood me. My *point*! What I allude to was in her eyes. You could see it in her eyes. It was always there. You couldn't miss it. I'm a poor hand at explaining things, I expect, but I know only too well, myself, what I'm trying to tell you. The best word that I can think of is 'dedicated'! Jacqueline was dedicated to something. To a mission or a cause. And I'm dead certain that she would never have surrendered while she had a heart in her body."

Annesley nodded. "I understand you perfectly, Doctor. As far as I am concerned, you have made yourself perfectly clear."

Anthony came in again. "And suppose I admit your contention, Doctor? How do you know that when she died, her mission had not been fulfilled? The task not completed? The dedication not consummated? They are fair questions, I think."

"I don't absolutely know it, of course. Your questions are such that only one person could possibly answer them with any certainty. That person was Mrs. Hillier herself. All the same, I don't see how her mission, or what I choose to call her mission, *could* have been fulfilled."

Anthony persisted with his point. "You will forgive me, I'm sure, Dr. Pakenham, if I raise difficulties. But if you don't know what Mrs. Hillier's mission was, which you admit to be the case, how can you say that the unfortunate lady didn't fulfil it?"

Pakenham shrugged his shoulders. "Well, you must make ordinary allowances, especially when you come to consider the circumstances. I don't know, of course. I can only judge from what I see . . . and hear, and think. How could it have been? In what way had Mrs. Hillier's life altered, for example? What had she done? Who had come into her life that hadn't been in it before? What new contacts had she made? There are three points for you which must illustrate my meaning. If I had the time I could doubtless think of many others. But those three will do for my purpose."

"Just a moment, Doctor. I can even take up the cudgels against you with regard to one of the points that you have actually nominated. You asked in what way had Mrs. Hillier's life altered. By that, you mean, I take it, her normal, everyday life. Let me point out to you that Mrs. Hillier had recently spent as long as two months abroad. In France, to be precise. From Easter to the end of May. These months were almost the last two months of her life. You see my drift, Dr. Pakenham?"

Pakenham shook his head with a hint of impatience. "Those two months were merely an ordinary holiday, which she spent with Ann Hillier, her daughter. Why attempt to invest them with an importance that wasn't theirs by right?"

Anthony shook his head. "I don't think I am. I'm only pointing out to you that there was a recent period during which something might have happened. Again, let us examine the evidence given at the inquest on Mrs. Hillier by the Vicar of Lanrebel, the Rev. Septimus Aylmer. The worthy Vicar referred to a letter, or paper of some kind, which Mrs. Hillier had in her hands during the time that she spent at dinner on that last evening of her life."

"What of that? A letter? Possibly quite an ordinary letter. It signifies absolutely nothing. As likely as not old Aylmer imagined it." Doctor Pakenham dismissed the suggestion contemptuously.

Anthony shook his head again. "I'm afraid, Doctor, that I can't dismiss either the journey abroad or the letter of Mrs. Hillier as lightly as you would have me. You may be right. On the other hand, I may be right. There is nothing positive about either position. We will leave it at that. And of course many thanks for your attention, Doctor. I'm afraid that I must have kept you here longer than you intended to stay."

Pakenham nodded. "That's all right. Only too pleased to be of any assistance. Only too pleased. Well, I'll wish you good morning."

He got into his car and waved to them as he drove off. Annesley turned to Anthony. "Well . . . and what do you make of all that?"

Anthony was watching the car as it travelled into the distance. "I am not so sure, Annesley. Doubtless you observed that Dr. Pakenham knows a great deal about the Hillier family. Far more than I anticipated he knew. And I don't know either that I'm particularly anxious for my next interview with Mr. Paul Hillier."

"Don't see why," returned Annesley. But Mr. Bathurst merely shook his head and smiled.

CHAPTER XIV
BREAKFAST AT "WOODRUFFS"

JOSHUA Toft sat at his breakfast in the spacious, stone-flagged kitchen of his farm "Woodruffs". His wife, a woman with mean, anxious eyes, was seated opposite to him. If anything, her eyes on this particular morning were more anxiety-laden than usual. There was a look on her husband's face which disturbed her. Having been married to him for thirty-one years, she knew to a nicety what almost every look of his betokened. Mr. Toft, as he ate and drank, had the morning paper propped in front of him. His face was set and hard as he read. Mrs. Toft ventured upon a remark which was as commonplace as most of the remarks that had come from her during those same thirty-one years of wedlock. "Anything in the paper, Joshua?"

"Ay, lass. I should just say there is an' all." He did not suppose for a moment that Mrs. Toft would be content with that morsel of information. That was all he felt like saying at the moment. Mrs. Toft, of course, immediately came for more.

"I meant anything out of the ordinary, Joshua. You might have known that, I should think." As she spoke, the thin meagreness of her face became accentuated. Toft looked across at her churlishly. Her spare angularity had never pleased him. This morning it irritated and annoyed him much more than ordinarily. But he controlled himself and the measure of his reply.

"Ay! Well out of the ordinary. When I tell you what it is, you'll get the shock of your life."

Amelia Toft shook her bird-like head and blinked her little eyes. "That's impossible, Joshua, I've had that already. I had it when you told me about poor Mrs. Hillier the other day."

"Oh—you think so, do you?" Joshua Toft's tone held a nasty, sneering note. The irritation which he was feeling manifested itself in the tone of his voice. He continued: "Well—you're wrong. You're due for a surprise. The shock you had at hearing of Mrs. Hillier's death don't count with this new one." Joshua Toft paused for effect and moistened his lips. "There's been a murder."

"A murder—how d'ye mean—a murder?"

"Just what I said. You know what a murder is, don't you? Nothing more, nothing less. And one for me to go on the jury again. Foreman, again, too, I expect." Mrs. Toft put her cup quietly into her saucer.

"Joshua, what dreadful things you say! You don't never mean that there's been a murder in Lanrebel?"

"I do! Here in Lanrebel. And last night at that. I nearly said another murder. Here you are, Amelia. Look for yourself. There it is in the Stop Press column." Toft deliberately withheld names from the wife of his bosom. Mrs. Toft took the newspaper from her husband with trembling fingers. Her eyes took in the meaning of the paragraph which Joshua Toft had pointed out to her. She read the lines quickly. Her brain kept pace with her eyes and she understood.

"Mr. Neill!" she gasped. "Murdered! Oh, I can't believe it! Who would want to murder young Mr. Neill? Such a well-behaved young fellow."

"More than want to," growled Toft, "who *has* murdered him! That's more to the point, I should think."

Amelia Toft handed back the newspaper with a shaking hand. "It's terrible! I shan't want to live in the place if this sort of thing is going on. First his mother—now Mr. Neill. There's a curse been put on Lanrebel."

"Rubbish," interposed Toft with scant regard for the woman's feelings, "no curse at all. That's stuff and nonsense. Plain villainy call it, and you'll be nearer the mark. These things are due to the wickedness of men—not to the interference of goblins and spooks. That's just old wives' talk! The villainy must be traced and punished. And if I'm foreman of the jury again, which I've no doubt will be the case, I'll promise you that it shall be." He took up the newspaper again and made further comment. "His body was found in a ditch near the crossroads. With extensive head injuries. Believed to have been the victim of an attack from behind. He was taken to the 'Salvation' inn by Sergeant Spiers in the hope that life was not yet extinct, and afterwards examined by Dr. Lambert from Plant. When the doctor saw him, however, he was beyond all help, having been dead for some hours." Toft rose from the breakfast table and thrust his hands into the front pockets of his riding-breeches. "Dammit all, I was not satisfied at the inquest on Mrs. Hillier. Satisfied? I was a long way from being satisfied, I can tell you. That car ride late at night! I didn't like the sound of it. I *don't* like it. Why did she mention the Mile Cliff? Why was she so keen to be alone when she drove out? Tell me that, Amelia! Didn't I question young Ann Hillier with regard to her mother's habits? I've thought over her answers a good many times since that inquest day. And let me tell you—I am certainly not satisfied! No, sir!"

Toft lurched towards his seat and sat down again. Amelia Toft knew from experience that Toft, once he put a hand to the plough, did not lightly withdraw it.

"Tell me what you think then, Joshua," she urged with sleek encouragement.

"What I think!" He stared at her in something akin to incredulity. "What I *think*! Why, I think that Mrs. Hillier was murdered as well—which means both of 'em. That's what I think! That's what I've been trying to tell you. In other words, first the mother, then the only son, Neill."

Mrs. Toft demurred. "You've always been one for sensation, Joshua. Ever since I've known you. You know you have. Who would want to injure any of the Hilliers—let alone murder them? It's ridiculous!"

Toft glowered at her. "Oh, ridiculous, is it? How do you know? What do you know of the Hilliers' private life? What do I know of it? What does anybody know of it? Outside their own family. Are *you* told when Hillier has a row with his wife? Or with his son? Are these things ever public property? Do they publish them in the local paper? Charity begins at home, I know, but do other people know when I have a row with you?"

"As a rule," returned his wife with a surprising show of courage, "I should think that a good many must! Judging by the way you shout and holler at me."

"Rubbish! All families have their share of skeletons, and there's no reason why the Hillier family should be an exception to the rule."

Mrs. Toft shrugged spare shoulders. She realized that argumentatively it was time for her to call a halt. Toft looked at her curiously as though he were assessing her from a certain definite point of view. Before he could speak again, however, she put a question to him. "According to that paper, young Mr. Neill must have been struck down during the evening some time. What time did you come back from the 'Salvation'?"

Toft thought. "I left there about half past nine. The clock on the kitchen mantelpiece was ten to ten when I got in. I should have left there before if it hadn't been such a dirty night. I had those Milk Board accounts to do. But why?"

"I was just wondering if you happened to see anybody knocking about between here and the inn. You must have come along about the time of the murder."

Toft's face was hard as he replied to her. "I wasn't lookin' round tryin' to see people. What do you take me for? I was gettin' home. It was a night you wouldn't turn a dog out even though you harboured a grudge against it. All the time I was makin' my way home I was cussin' myself for bein' such a fool as to go out in the first place. Beer's beer—but a night like that . . ." Toft indignantly justified himself.

Mrs. Toft stared wide-eyed out of the window. Her husband's annoyance increased. "Well?" he demanded—"did you hear what I said to you?"

She nodded mechanically. "Yes, Joshua. I heard what you said. I can see what you mean and I realize how you must have been feeling."

"Good. That's just as well. It's a comfort to me, I must say."

But Amelia was in an unusual mood that morning. Instead of the meek surrender to him that was her wont, she seemed to have discovered resources of hitherto unsuspected spirit.

"There is no call for you to show temper, Joshua. Or to speak to me sarcastic. I asked you a civil enough question, and there was no call for you to have bitten my head off." She compressed her prim lips.

For the second time that morning, Toft looked at her curiously. The wordy warfare had not gone its accustomed way. He judged it politic to alter his tactics. He went back, therefore, to his previous activity of Amelia assessment. What he had seen evidently satisfied him. He leant over the breakfast table towards his wife with a show of unusual confidence. "Look here—I'll tell you something, Amelia! Something that's been on my mind for some little time now. So far I've kept it to myself. But you'll have to promise me that you'll hold it! Keep it to yourself and not chow it over with the first old hen you meet down the road when you go out. Promise?"

Amelia Toft was savouring the enjoyment of sweet triumph. For once she had stood up to the domineering Joshua and withdrawn from the encounter with "honours easy". She intended to hold on to the triumph a little longer. "I like your style! I do indeed! You and your 'old hens'. I suppose I'm an old hen myself directly my back's turned. Well—well—well. How times do change, to be sure! And the men with them. I can mind the day when I was—"

"Oh, shut up and forget it! I'm talkin' seriously. You don't seem to realize it. Mixin' up matters of murder with your petty jealousies. Are you goin' to listen to me or aren't you? If you are—promise me what I just asked you."

"Oh, all right, I promise! What is this wonderful piece of news?"

Joshua Toft appeared to make a calculation. "When was it that Mrs. Hillier and the daughter returned from that foreign holiday trip they had not so long ago?"

"They came back about the beginning of June. The first week. I can remember that well. She had only been back about a week when she died. But what's all this got to do with my promising not to talk? I don't understand."

"You will if you wait patiently," he retorted grimly.

"Well, then, get on with it. Don't be so long-winded," she snapped back.

"On the evening of the 2nd of June, leastways I think it was the 2nd of June from what you've just said, I came out of the 'Salvation' a little earlier than usual. I should say from memory that the time was about twenty past nine. I took my usual way back here. It was a lovely night, too. When I came to the crossroads, and before I took the turning here to 'Woodruffs', I saw a car standing in the shade of the hedge by the crossroads. Of course it was getting towards dusk, and I couldn't see the number, but from the shape and the colour of it I'd go bail that it was Mrs. Hillier's car. I know that car too well to mistake it. Well, there was I 'stomping' up the road, wondering what the blazes could keep Mrs. Hillier's car there like that at that time of night, when something caught my eye and made me look all the more." Toft timed his pause to a nicety. His wife's curiosity and natural sense of scandal were by now thoroughly aroused.

"What was it, Joshua? Tell me!"

Toft lowered his voice to an appropriate tone. "I saw a man come up. He came up and stood by the car. Whoever was inside the car must have spoken to him. Because he stood there for some little time. Then—mind you, Amelia—he got in the car. A moment or so later the car moved off. It would be going in the direction of 'Hillearys', too. Now, lass—what do you think of all that?"

"Who was the man? Don't keep it from me, Joshua. I've a right to know."

Toft shook his head. "Search me, Mother, I didn't recognize him. It was too dusky like at that hour of the evening."

"What was he like?"

"I couldn't rightly say."

She sought values. "Was he tall or short?"

"Tall. Leastways—above the average."

"Stout?"

"No—not stout. I should say on the slim side."

"Young or old?"

"Couldn't say. Shan't guess at it."

"Joshua—do you suspect anybody?"

"Nobody. Not a soul. Honest, lass."

Amelia Toft came to grips with her lord and master. "And why have you kept all this to yourself for so long? Fair scatty—it seems to me, keeping a thing like that on your chest. And you on that inquest jury, too. I'm that surprised at you, Joshua, I can't understand you."

Toft was defensive. "Do I want to make a fool of myself? To go out of my way to do it? What was there in it—that I could prove—anyway? It might well be as innocent as possible. I don't know for rights who either of the two people were. Now do I? Look at it for yourself."

"But you don't think it was innocent—for all your fine talk! Otherwise you wouldn't have blabbed it to me now."

Toft replied to this last indictment slowly and gravely. "This death of young Master Neill seems to have made a difference. To me and to what I think. That's how I'm seeing things now."

His statement sobered her. Her shrewishness suddenly departed. "I can see how you feel, Joshua. You mean it's all got bigger and more important than it seemed to be at the start. Yes—I see what you mean. I think you're right." She nodded her head as she finished the sentence.

Toft rose and patted her on the shoulder. "Good for you, Mother. I knew you would understand. Point is now—what can we do about it? To put things right I mean, and get at the truth."

"That we can't tell—yet. But a chance may come our way all the same. You never know when a chance like that is coming. All you can do is to be ready when it does come."

"Trust me for that, lass," returned Joshua with challenge on his face. Amelia's eyes glistened with admiration as she looked up at him. She knew from experience that when her husband put his hand to a job of work he seldom removed it until the time was ripe. Joshua Toft filled a pipe slowly. Then he moved slowly off to the first of his day's duties.

Chapter XV
ANN IS IMPATIENT

Anthony Lotherington Bathurst sat in the library at "Hillearys". He looked at his watch for the third time since his entrance. When Ann Hillier entered, he rose to greet her. "You sent for me, Miss Hillier. I am at your service."

"Didn't you intend to come, then, even if I hadn't 'phoned you?"

He held her finger-tips for the fraction of a second before she waved him back to the comfort of his chair.

"Frankly, no," he replied.

She frowned. Her face, already white and strained with her newer sadness, seemed to take on an even heavier burden. "And why, Mr. Bathurst?"

"I have no good news for you. And you, since our last meeting, have met another sorrow. I would prefer to come bringing help than bringing the mere recital of empty effort."

She winced as she took a seat at his side. "You have been to the inquest on . . . Neill?"

Anthony nodded quietly. "Yes."

"There is nothing?" The tone almost held entreaty.

"Nothing, Miss Hillier."

"You have no . . . idea . . . about anything . . . yet?" Her eyes searched his face.

Anthony hesitated, but for seconds only. "I would not say that. I have, perhaps, the glimmering of an idea."

"About Mother . . . or Neill?"

"About your brother. It is so entirely nebulous, though, at the moment, that it would be almost valueless for me to discuss it with you. Indeed, I had much rather not."

"I see. I won't worry you about it, then. The inquest on my brother was adjourned, I suppose?"

"Yes. Similarly to the previous one. I expected that to happen. The police were responsible for the adjournment, of course."

"I am thankful I was spared this second one to-day. If you only knew how thankful. I don't think I could have faced it coming so quickly on top of the other one."

"What was it you wanted me for—specially?"

She was eminently candid. "Nothing. Special, that is. I just wanted to know if you had made any progress. My father, you see . . . since Neill died . . . has been almost beside himself."

"I understand."

"He absolutely worshipped Neill. As I told you before, the bond between them was not ordinary." She smiled a wan smile. "More like the silver cord. You know what I mean—the other way round."

Anthony Bathurst gestured his understanding. He decided upon a bold course. "About your mother, Miss Hillier. You will remember how frankly and intimately we talked of her, you and I, that afternoon you drove me to Frayne and back. I should like to ask you something else about her. May I?"

"You may, Mr. Bathurst. What is it?"

"Would you agree with the opinion that your mother was dedicated to a purpose? That she felt, as it were, that she was living for the consummation of something—and that when that consummation was effected the need and reason behind her living were gone and that she had fulfilled her purpose?"

Ann thought hard over his words. "I think I know what you mean. Let me consider it for a moment." There was a pause. "Yes, I do think that's possible. Although I've never before had it put to me quite in the way that you put it."

"Thank you. I shall remember that. It may help me considerably before the end of the case is reached. Now another question, Miss Hillier. And please forgive me for asking it. Indeed, I've hesitated about asking it. I take it that your mother had no romantic attachment at the time of her death?"

Ann regarded him critically. "None, Mr. Bathurst. You can be absolutely sure of that. I am certain that I should have known if there had been one. Please get the idea out of your head."

"Now let me put it like this, then. I'll alter the terms slightly. Were there any admirers near at hand? Or even—an admirer? A persistent admirer?"

Ann puckered her brows. "That is not quite the same thing, is it?"

"No. I don't mean it to be. I altered my terms purposely. I am glad that you have appreciated the difference so quickly."

When Ann replied, her words came slowly. "There was no admirer, no persistent admirer, to use your own words, whom my mother encouraged."

Anthony stuck to his guns. "Although it may need two people to make what I meant by a romantic attachment, one alone may make an admirer."

"Isn't that rather difficult for me to answer? For how can one tell? I mean—to be absolutely certain about it. Jacqueline was popular. Very popular. She had personality. She was vivid—always so alive. She liked men better than women. Men liked her. But to pick one out of them, as you're asking me to, as a special case, as it were—no, I don't think that I'm justified in doing that."

"There was nobody, then, whom you could reasonably—well, shall we say—tease her about? You know what I mean?"

"I don't think there was. Seriously, that is."

Anthony felt keen disappointment. Because of that, he decided to come to closer grips with her. "How do you, then, explain the words spoken by her just before she died? According to your brother, they were, if you remember, 'The Mile Cliff. Two'."

Ann Hillier shook her head dubiously. "I have thought over that until my brain has simply refused to think any longer, Mr. Bathurst. All I can say with regard to it is this. That she had been able to drive the car as far as that—and no farther. Because of something terrible that happened to her when she arrived there."

"You told me before that you were certain she was murdered. Was the murder casual—something that happened with tragic unexpectedness, or by deliberate contact? No—I've put that badly. Let me alter it. Was she killed by somebody whom she met accidentally? Or by someone whom she had expected and gone out to meet? Had, in fact, driven out designedly to meet? In other words—was the murder the result of an assignation?"

Ann Hillier was plainly disturbed. With her reply, when it did come, she plunged. "I'm certain that she *hadn't* an assignation! Jacqueline would never have kept a thing like that from me. I'm positive of it."

Anthony cut in again. "Suppose we forget the ordinarily accepted meaning round the word 'assignation'. It almost always, I suppose, has attached to it the romantic significance. That assignations are lovers' meetings. Look at it more in the terms of an appointment. An appointment which, for all we know, might have been eminently straightforward and utterly aboveboard. How about it *then*? Do you still refuse to accept its likelihood?"

Ann nodded emphatically. "Yes, I do. If Jacqueline went out to meet anybody that night deliberately, I'm sure that she would have told me something about it. She wouldn't have kept me completely in the dark."

"You see where that brings you then, don't you?"

"How do you mean exactly, Mr. Bathurst?"

"Just this. That taking you on your own terms, your mother must have been murdered by a *casual* contact. That is so, isn't it?"

Ann looked dubious again. "I suppose so. Looking at it in that way."

"It must be so. You can't argue against it. Now, then! If she met her death in that way—what was the motive?"

"I don't know. I can't think."

Anthony proceeded to follow up his point. "It wasn't robbery, was it? That fact is certain. We know it. I haven't heard the slightest suggestion that anything of value was taken from your mother."

"No," she half whispered. "Nothing."

"What, then, remains which may be regarded as coming within the realm of motive? Revenge? That's a feeling which could not have been harboured by a stranger. Wanton brutality? The odds against that possibility, you will admit, are tremendous. Sadists and wandering sex maniacs, thank goodness, are few and far between. There isn't much left for us, is there? Just one single possibility, perhaps."

"What is that?" almost gasped Ann Hillier.

"This," replied Mr. Bathurst with slow deliberation. "That somebody whom your mother did not know was forced to silence her, on account of certain knowledge which she may have possessed. Knowledge which in potential use was detrimental to his own safety." Mr. Bathurst finished with a shake of the head. "But the odds against that having happened are almost as high as they were against those other contingencies I mentioned just now. You see, I am unable to forget that your mother *chose* to go out. Now you work out for yourself what the chances are. For your mother to go out in her car at that time during the evening, and meet by accident a person whom she did not know, but who desired her death for the reason that I have just indicated—"

Ann Hillier put her hand on Anthony's arm. It was trembling. "Don't go on, Mr. Bathurst. Please. It upsets me. What you say sounds so plausible. So—logical . . . and almost unanswerable. It overwhelms me. All the same . . ." She paused.

Anthony spoke to her quietly. "Have I convinced you, Miss Hillier?"

"No," she replied, with a show of something like petulance. "No. There's always the unknown quantity, the odd chance. We don't know what it was in this case—yet. I believe that Jacky was murdered. And I don't believe that she took the car out to meet somebody. I'm sorry, Mr. Bathurst, but there it is. Forgive me and put it down to my feminine obstinacy. But you won't upset my opinion."

Anthony smiled sadly. He was thinking, "Why is she so convinced? What makes her so certain? Sophisticated as they make 'em. And essentially of her generation." He *said*, though, "I am glad that you said 'feminine obstinacy'. I find that easier to contend with than something you might have said."

"What is that?" Her eyes were hard and her mouth was set.

"Feminine intuition," he returned.

Ann shrugged her shoulders. She attempted to make it clear to him that she was not specially pleased. He thought again, "Cool as blazes. And just taken troubles as hard as any girl has ever taken . . . one right on top of the other. Amazing." He retraced his conversational steps.

"I always find that I can make allowances for the more feminine femininities. Such as the one we mentioned. 'Obstinacy'. But there's no arguing with such things as intuition. They're a law unto themselves."

Ann relaxed a little and let a half-smile play round the corners of her mouth. It was there, however, but momentarily. The hard sadness returned. Suddenly she turned and addressed Anthony. "You've asked me a lot of questions, Mr. Bathurst. About my own views on the . . . case. And I've answered them to the best of my ability. What about reversing the position? Let me ask you one . . . or more than one."

"Go ahead, Miss Hillier. I'll do my best for you."

"Do *you* think my mother went to meet anybody on the night she died?"

He nodded. "I'm afraid that I do, Miss Hillier."

"Deliberately?"

"Yes. Quite deliberately. But nobody you know."

"Nobody I know?"

"No. Up to now you have not met him. Although you have no doubt seen him."

Ann looked puzzled. "And Neill?"

Anthony was evasive. "On that my mind is open. I don't know how to answer you. I would rather that you didn't press me."

Ann accepted the inevitable. She changed the subject. "I am sorry that my father is out. I will tell him that you called. With regard to

Mowbray, I'll do what you've asked me. Although I want to avoid as much as possible gratuitous agonies of soul. I'll confess something to you. I was delicate and even nervous as a young child. But I outgrew each of these conditions and I have deliberately schooled myself to be self-reliant. I don't quite know why I am telling you these things. I think it's because there's a feeling in me, deep down somewhere, that you ought to be made aware of them." She held out her hand to him. "Good-bye till next time, Mr. Bathurst."

"Good-bye, Miss Hillier. Till next time, then."

Ann watched him as he walked up the drive. She watched him from the window until he was out of sight. Then she found a chair and sat on it, twisting her hand-kerchief in her hands.

Chapter XVI
SECOND FLORAL TRIBUTE

The Hillier Murders Case, as the more sensational news-papers had named it, had been in the hands of Detective-Inspector Rockingham of Liskerry for just over a week, when a new sensation came to the district. Rockingham had received orders to take over, for the main reason that the powers that be at Headquarters were becoming restive. Sergeants Whitehead and Spiers, the officers from whom he had officially taken over, had achieved but little since the adjournments of the two inquests upon Jacqueline and Neill Hillier. Both Whitehead and Spiers for most jobs were efficient officers. Their industry, however, was more remarkable than their powers of imagination. They surrendered the reins of responsibility to Rockingham with some regrets, possibly, but on the whole the regrets were submerged beneath feelings of relief. The burly figure of Detective-Inspector Rockingham, therefore, became a familiar sight in the streets of Lanrebel and the surrounding district, and he mingled, true to police tradition, with the company of mourners and sightseers at Neill Hillier's funeral.

Anthony Bathurst passed him on several occasions without making himself known to him. Keith Annesley, the novelist from the county of Essex, whose holiday-time at Lanrebel was growing short, and who had already stayed there longer than had been his original intention, was the companion of Mr. Bathurst on one of these occasions. As Rockingham passed them, Anthony called attention to him. "The other police 'wallahs' have been superseded. Evidently they weren't pleasing enough to the blokes at the top what count. Poor devils, sorry for them. There, but for the Grace of God, went A.L.B. or even Mr. Keith Annesley. Solemn fact. Good job I'm not a married man with a couple of kids to go to bed hungry."

Annesley nodded. "They've been stood down, you mean, for not making enough headway?"

"As you say, laddie. Want of official faith in two good sergeants, Whitehead and Spiers. Those were their monikers."

Annesley smiled and quoted certain lines.

> "Unfaith in aught is want of faith in all.
> It is the little rift within the lute
> That by and by will make the music mute,
> And, ever widening, slowly silence all."

"As you say, Annesley. Hefty official rift within ponderous official lute. That was from 'Vivien's Song', wasn't it?"

"Er—I'm not quite sure. It seemed to fit the occasion, I thought."

"Oh—admittedly. But, joking apart, it must be a pretty lousy job being a country copper let loose on a case of this kind. Nothing to get his rustic teeth into."

"You've awakened all my sympathy, Bathurst," said Annesley. He went on to exclaim immediately, "As a matter of fact, I think it must have been lying right at the surface of me, waiting to be brought to life. I'll tell you why exactly. You weren't in the lounge at the 'Salvation' last night, were you?"

Anthony shook his head. "No. I was interested in two trees in two different fields. Call it a voyage of arboreal exploration. But why do you ask? What happened in the aforesaid lounge?"

"Oh—we were all talking. In just an ordinary conversation. The Paskes and their women were in there, and Pereira—and the general talk drifted to the Hillier murders. That is if it required any particular drift inclination. We'd all had almost enough of it—the men I mean—particularly young Frank Paske—when Pereira started his verbal pyrotechnics. I expect you've heard some of 'em before. By

Jove, was he violent? Vocabulary absolutely lurid. Called utter scorn and contempt on the entire police forces of Great Britain and Ireland. Beg pardon—Eire. Demanded high Heaven as his witness to their blazing incompetence and stark boneheadedness. That last, by the way, was one of the words that Mr. P. actually used. He kept on, too, a proper rort—for a good twenty minutes. If you can reasonably employ the adjective."

Anthony grinned at his exuberance. "Why not almost '*un mauvais quart l'heure*'? At least, that's how it appeals to me from your description of it." This jocular note of Mr. Bathurst's, however, vanished as quickly as it had been born. "But tell me, Annesley, what was Pereira's main point with regard to the police? I'm rather interested."

"Nothing in particular. It was just a general strafe. The usual gibes and jeers at their methods and at where you can always find the police. Selling tickets for their sports, football matches, race meetings, and on traffic control—but never where they're really wanted. You know the idea, you must have heard it thousands of time before. Proper man-in-the-street-and-keep-the-rates-down stuff."

Mr. Bathurst nodded his agreement. "I know what you mean, Annesley. But all the same, I'm just a little mystified at Pereira's particular censure. I don't see how any intelligent man can deliberately pick on this Hillier case as a reasonable one for police strafing. I think it's much more a 'pity the poor police' problem. There's precious little knocking about in the way of clues that I've been able to see."

"I agree, but Pereira's chief argument was that in a village like Lanrebel, crime detection, especially when it comes to big stuff like murder, should be a comparatively simple matter. The field of inquiry is so small. In a big city, he said, it was a very different matter. There—you could understand the difficulties of the police and make allowances for them. But in a cockle-shell like Lanrebel—"

Annesley's gesture as he broke off was an eloquent conclusion.

"Well, I don't agree with him," said Anthony. "What he maintains doesn't follow as a matter of course at all. Murder detection may be mathematical to an extent, but you must have certain values given you when you begin to assemble the two sides of your equation. If you're minus almost everything in the nature of a value—Hello! Who's thus running on so hot a morning? He must have unusually strong reasons for such violent exercise!"

Annesley looked ahead down the road. A man came running towards them, his hands outstretched in extraordinary fashion. "I've the fancy," said Keith Annesley quietly, "that he's trying to attract our attention. Judging by the way his hands are moving. He *is* waving, isn't he? What do you think yourself?"

Anthony gazed in the direction of the oncoming figure. "I agree with you, Annesley. It looks to me, now that I can see him more clearly, as though our courier is either badly scared or violently excited. Either condition may give us food for thought. Don't forget, my dear fellow, that vital clues sometimes come like manna. From Heaven above."

Annesley was caustic. "This bloke doesn't look much like an angel—chance it!" The man's shouts grew louder. His arms waved more wildly. By now Anthony was able to identify him for Keith Annesley's benefit.

"The gentleman who approaches is popularly known as Crispy Williams. He is by way of being a popular figure amongst the villagers. I owe my knowledge of his nickname to young Frank Paske. He pointed him out to me the other day."

The two men stopped in the middle of the road. The runner began to swerve. His excitement was proving too much for him. His arms dropped, and as he came to Anthony Bathurst and Annesley he began to call out. Anthony was able to distinguish words: "Up in the churchyard, masters, Master Neill's grave. A brave sight. I see the car. I see the car leave." Crispy halted in the road. His breath came in quick, short gasps. Anthony caught him by the sleeve and steadied him.

"Now, now, Crispy," he said. "What's all the fuss about? What's the matter with you? Anybody would think you'd seen a ghost."

Crispy Williams shook his head vacantly. He began to collect himself. "No. Not a ghost, sir, not a ghost. But all the flowers going on young Master Neill's grave. I see the man and the car he come in. I see him drive away. All yaller. Like light mustard in the distance."

"Do you hear what he says, Annesley? Neill Hillier's grave? I suppose he's just come from there."

Crispy Williams nodded enthusiastically and jerked his thumb over his shoulder in the direction of Lanrebel church. Keith Annesley half turned that he might see the square tower of it . . . a landmark from all points for many miles.

"Yes, sir," repeated the villager, "Master Neill Hillier's grave . . . the new one in the churchyard. All yaller with flowers, like mustard on the side of a man's plate. I see the man what did it drive off. He went right fast, master . . . I ran straight up here to find somebody what I could tell it to. That's good for Crispy, isn't it?"

As he finished his statement, Williams leered cunningly at Anthony Bathurst. Anthony, unusually, and for some reason that was probably unknown to him, resented both the man and his manner. He spoke to him with sharp curtness. "You say that these flowers are all yellow? Like light mustard?"

"Yes, sir. That's how they be, indeed, sir. Just like a field of mustard. He-hee! Old Crispy was the first to see it. In front of the young 'uns even now. Crispy's always in the front row."

"What are these flowers, then? Have you any idea?"

Williams cocked his head in a gesture towards wisdom. "I've not been in the churchyard yet, master! I only go there on Sundays. And Sundays, thank the Lord, only come once in a week. I've only seen they flowers in the distance, I say."

Anthony realized that little further assistance could be reasonably expected from Crispy Williams. He turned to Keith Annesley. "It seems to me we'd better walk up there and have a look for ourselves. Shan't get any more from this fellow. That's pretty evident."

Annesley assented. Anthony and he left Crispy Williams and walked towards the church. Strange, thought Annesley, that this should be the second journey of this kind. First to Jacqueline Hillier's grave to view the blanket of blue violets, and now to Neill Hillier's to view—what? Crispy Williams' field of light mustard? They came to the road again which leads to Bonallack Ferry and stood again under the shadow of Lanrebel church tower. Once more since he had come to Glebeshire on holiday, Keith Annesley put his hand through the iron gate that led to the churchyard and pulled back the unwieldy latch. Once again, he and Anthony Bathurst travelled the path which passed the church and made its way into the burial ground. Neill Hillier's grave was next to his mother's. The Hilliers, as comparative newcomers to the district of Liskerry, had no family grave within the churchyard, so that next to the blue blanket, now withered and faded, Anthony and Annesley could see the light yellow covering which Crispy Williams had already described to them. They turned towards the slope in the right-hand corner of the churchyard.

"Roses this time," said Anthony as soon as they had taken a few paces—"yellow roses." They came to the two newly dug graves, and directly he reached them Keith Annesley saw that Anthony was right. Neill Hillier's grave had been covered with yellow roses. In the same prodigal profusion as Jacqueline's had been with the violets.

"Amazing," murmured Mr. Bathurst. "It never occurred to me that I should live to see two sights of this kind. What a feast of colour! Beautiful, and yet to me—caught in crime contact as I am so repeatedly—there is something else about it besides beauty. What is it, Annesley? Can you help me?"

Annesley shook his head. "I don't think I can. I don't think I know quite what you mean. Perhaps I haven't caught your essential mood."

"I know what I mean all right. To me there is something sinister about all this, in addition to the beautiful."

Annesley nodded. "Yes. I think I understand you. To me, it seems as though I were passing through a bad but fantastic dream. When I decided to come to Lanrebel for my holiday I little knew to what an extraordinary chain of events I was coming. Sometimes I even find myself assuring myself that I *haven't* come, and that it is all a dream from which I shall wake before very long." There was a curiously attractive shyness about him as he spoke. Anthony recognized and respected it.

"We shall need Lysbeth Paske again. To tell us of the flower language and the meaning therein of the yellow rose. She educated us, if you remember, with regard to the violet. It seems that your education and mine have been neglected." Anthony went on: "You know, Annesley, you as a successful novelist should know these things."

Annesley smiled. "I'm no hand at the love story, Bathurst. So I must remain a disappointment to you."

"H'm! Pity. I shall have to fall back upon the little lady Lysbeth again. And the sooner the better."

Annesley gazed at the yellow roses.

"What is the matter, Annesley? Anything struck you?"

"No—but I feel a sense of intrusion very deeply. I feel that I am trespassing on a private grief. I didn't feel that before. Now—I do! I can't explain what it is that has suddenly changed me. So it's no use your asking me. But I feel that I am staring with great eyes and laughing with alien lips. Sorry—and all that!"

Anthony thought hard before he nodded. He saw that his companion spoke with sincerity. "I don't know that I agree with you . . . all the way . . . but I'm in your debt. You've given me an idea. You imply that these flowers have been put here by a mourner? By a special—I don't like the word, but I can't think of another at the present moment—mourner?"

"Yes. They look to me . . . don't laugh at me . . . like the expression of a broken and contrite heart. You know—something like the spikenard, the box of precious ointment which Mary of Magdala used on the Christ."

Anthony nodded a second time. "I'm beginning to follow you. You're on a different viewpoint from me. Entirely. I've thought all along that these 'floral tributes', as the journalists call them, have come from the murderer—or, shall I say—from the evil influence behind these happenings. Something akin to the very prevalent idea that the murderer will often mingle with the crowds at his victim's funeral."

Annesley shook his head vigorously. "I disagree with you, Bathurst. I disagree *in toto*."

Anthony persisted. "If I am right in my theory they could still be . . . in a way . . . the expression of what you have just described as 'a broken and a contrite heart'—couldn't they?"

Annesley again shook his head in vigorous disclaimer.

"No. Of course not. Take a murderer who is touched by repentance. It's quite within the realms of probability. Real repentance, I mean. Not an ephemeral transient sorrow that dies as quickly as it is born, but something real—permanent. He would not repent . . . to murder again at an absurdly short interval . . . and then find this condition of immediate repentance again! To me, at any rate, such a condition is unthinkable. It's neither common sense nor even elementary psychology."

Anthony stooped and picked up one of the yellow roses. It was almost perfect in shape and colour. "I have two answers to you, Annesley, with regard to that. Two answers that have come to me at once."

"And what are they?"

"One—that it's quite possible that we are dealing with two causes of death—which fact may even postulate two murderers; and a second— that one may be dealing with a person of unbalanced mind. Certainly unbalanced if not actually diseased! If you prefer to have it in ordinary everyday language—with a madman!"

"In that you may be right, of course, Bathurst. But I feel convinced that I'm right and you're wrong. These flowers here are emblems of sorrow. I'm positive of it. They're not the cunning track-covering of a homicidal maniac."

Anthony conceded ground. "Well, it's an idea, as I said before, and I must thank you for presenting it to me."

Annesley smiled at his companion's concession. "Glad I haven't been wasting my time."

Anthony returned to more practical issues. "If that oaf's story is a true one, we're better off in the matter of these roses than we were in respect of the tribute of violets. Nobody, it seems, has the slightest idea how they came to Mrs. Hillier's grave, but our recent yokel acquaintance gives us chapter and verse for the coming of these yellow roses. He says that he actually saw a man place them on the grave! Moreover, a man who came in a car. Cars, my dear Annesley, are traceable. *N'est-ce pas?*"

"Sometimes," returned Keith Annesley. "I should think, however, it would be a fairly easy matter to trace this one. Of course, it *would* be something like a half-wit who had the luck to see it!"

"That's the roll of the ball, Annesley. I've an idea. That car must have stayed outside the church gate for some little time. Those blooms couldn't possibly have been placed here in a few seconds, could they? The job must have meant minutes—surely?"

"I should imagine so. They had to be carried in here, for one thing. But what do you intend to do?"

"Try to find somebody who saw the vehicle, in addition to our country bumpkin. It seems to me that there must have been somebody. Let's come on to the village at once."

They made their way out of the churchyard of the blue and yellow. When they came to the gate, Anthony turned straight into the street and walked in the direction of the "Salvation". Annesley found himself wondering how he would set about his task. As they came close to the inn they saw that Lysbeth Paske was standing at the side of the wooden gates—sunning herself. She waved to these two guests of hers as they approached her. They happened to be, both of them, in Lysbeth's good books. For one thing, they not only appreciated her cooking—but in addition they were also eloquent with regard to that appreciation. Anthony smiled as they drew up in front of her. Lysbeth smiled back.

"The sun is love-ly. Aren't you luck-y to have such lovely weather for your holiday?"

Anthony nodded. "We aren't the only lucky ones. What about yourself? You haven't been doing too badly. How long have you been standing in the sunshine idling your time away?"

Lysbeth laughed gaily at the taunt. Her eyes flashed.

"Why do you ask me that? Are you going to tease me again? You are always teasing me about something."

"That only goes to show how much we like you, Mrs. Paske. No—I'm perfectly serious this time. No teasing at all. How long have you been out here?"

Lysbeth Paske laughed again. "This last time, do you mean only, or since—"

"This last time only."

"Well, then, you have nothing on me, as they say! Because I have only just come out here. See? This time you cannot tease me and say that I am idling. You are like Frank, my husband. Every time I stop my work, for just a little minute, he says, 'Come, now, Lysbeth, this won't get the baby a new frock!' Just as though there was a baby." Lysbeth blushed at the admission.

"Then it's no good my asking you a question. I was going to ask you if you had seen a car near the churchyard. Have you, Mrs. Paske?"

"No, I have not. I have not seen any car."

"That settles it, then."

"Perhaps it may not." Lysbeth looked roguish.

"How do you mean?" Anthony's eyes searched her. "Because if I have not seen a car I have seen a motor-van. Ah—you did not think of that, did you? I saw it stop by the gate of the churchyard about half an hour ago. Indeed—I wondered why it was stopping there. I had come out here to the front for just a moment or two. The sun was so nice and warm. Does that answer your question, Mr. Curiosity?"

Anthony smiled with satisfaction. "Mrs. Paske," he said, "you're *the* diamond from Amsterdam—you are really! Until I met you my life was absolutely incomplete. A motor-van—eh? That makes it better still!"

"Makes what better still?" Lysbeth plainly was puzzled at his statement.

"I want to know where that motor-van came from—will you be able to tell me?—that's all."

"You need have no worry about that. Because I can tell you. I am clever." Lysbeth looked more demure than ever.

"What? You can? Then please tell me, Lysbeth. For I'm dying to know."

A smile played round the corners of her mouth. "The van belonged to Clutterbuck's. I saw the name on the side of it. I knew the name. They're the big florists in Liskerry. There—are you satisfied now, Mr. Bathurst?"

Anthony smiled at her. "Almost, Mrs. Paske. Now I expect that answer has disappointed you. Am I right?"

Lysbeth laughed gaily. "Of course I'm disappointed. I thought you would have been pleased with me and praised me. 'Almost', indeed! Why do you say only—almost?"

"Because I'm on the point of asking you something else. Do you remember telling Mr. Annesley and me at breakfast the other morning of the meaning of the violet in the language of flowers?"

Lysbeth's gaiety departed. Gravity reigned in its stead. "Why— yes! Of course I do."

"Then I'm here for some more information of a similar kind. What does the yellow rose signify in the same tongue?"

Lysbeth looked frightened at Mr. Bathurst's question. She began to shake her head. "Why do you ask me that, sir? Has there been another—"

Anthony gravely nodded. "Yes, Mrs. Lysbeth. There are yellow roses on Neill Hillier's grave—yellow roses in profusion . . . in the same way as there were violets on his mother's. That is why I asked you the question I did. Do you understand?"

Lysbeth's eyes showed fear and a strained look came over her face. "I don't like it," she half whispered. The words were almost to herself. Anthony attempted to reassure her.

"We don't understand yet . . . why these flowers have been placed on the graves . . . do we?"

Lysbeth shook her head. The fear which had shown in her eyes had given place to tears. "Well, then, until we do understand . . . properly . . . there is no reason why we should upset ourselves . . . is there?"

"I suppose not, Mr. Bathurst. Looking at it like that. But all the same—"

Anthony checked what she had been about to say. "You know—you haven't told me yet what I asked you. What is the meaning of the yellow rose?"

"There are so many different kinds of roses," said Lysbeth almost rapturously. "And they all, naturally, have different meanings. So that I shall have to think it out very seriously." She closed her eyes in an evident effort to stimulate thought and remembrance. "Most of them," she said after a time, "are to do with Love in some way or the other. The yellow rose signifies what you call infidelity. You know—to be false in love—unfaithfulness!" She nodded as she finished. "Yes . . . that is so, Mr. Bathurst. I am sure of that."

"Infidelity—eh?" murmured Anthony Bathurst. "That gives me an idea. Do you hear that, Annesley? What do you make of it?"

"I think, perhaps," returned Keith Annesley, "that you're looking for too much. Deliberately trying to find something that isn't there. That you're attaching special significances to circumstances which possess only commonplace meanings. I may be wrong."

"I think you are," responded Mr. Bathurst.

"It won't be the first time," returned Annesley good-humouredly.

"THAT shop opposite," said Mr. Bathurst, "is my objective for this afternoon. You will observe that the name is Clutterbuck, and its business is the selling of flowers, in the town of Liskerry and its vicinity. Ask Miss Hillier if she'll pull up there, will you, Annesley? Thank you." Keith Annesley leant forward in Ann's car. "Bathurst wants you to stop at Clutterbuck's, Miss Hillier. Do you mind?"

Ann, pale-faced and fine-drawn, seared and scarred by successive sorrows, nodded quickly and obeyed Anthony's request. Mr. Bathurst alighted. Keith Annesley joined him on the pavement. Anthony walked round at once to the front of the car. "I should like you to come in with me, Miss Hillier, if you would. Run the car round somewhere and park, will you?"

Ann nodded again. "I know where I can park it. In the street at the side of the Roundhouse. You stay here and I'll rejoin you in a few moments."

Ann drove off. Anthony and Annesley stood on the edge of the pavement and awaited her return. As good as her word, she was back with them in less than five minutes. "Why do you want me to come in?"

"I should like you to hear what these people have to say. That's one thing. Another is that you represent your family. In that way you establish, as it were, the *bona fides* of our call. Please don't be distressed at . . . well, at anything."

"I am past that, I think," said Ann coldly.

They entered the florist's shop. Anthony saw at once that its trade was first class from every point of view. A girl, trim, neat, and well schooled, came to meet them.

Anthony smiled. "May I have a word with the manager . . . or perhaps manageress?"

The girl bowed. "Certainly, sir. I'll call Mr. Tomlinson for you. Will you wait a moment, please?"

They waited, Ann, Anthony, and Annesley. A murmur of approaching voices reached them. It came from no great distance. The heavy scent of many blooms began to be apparent. A man came towards them. Tall, thin, and stooping-shouldered. "I am the manager here," he said, almost with an air of apology. "What can I do for you?"

"Good afternoon," said Anthony. He indicated the proximity of Ann Hillier. "This lady is Miss Hillier. From 'Hillearys', Lanrebel. The address, I take it, is familiar to you."

Mr. Tomlinson furrowed his brows in an attempt to remember. "I don't really know—do you mean that I should know the address?"

"I am not altogether sure of that," returned Mr. Bathurst, "but I fancy that you should. In the matter of a recent order—shall we say? I suggest that either the name 'Hillier' or the address 'Hillearys' should be known to you."

The manager murmured a polite "Excuse me for a moment," and faded away. Again a murmur of voices came to the ears of the three people who were waiting in the shop. The manager of Clutterbuck's, florists of Liskerry, was in consultation with two of his young lady assistants. Anthony could see that a book was being brought into reference. There was more discussion before Mr. Tomlinson broke away from his auxiliaries and came down the shop again. He carried a book in his hands.

"I am sorry to have kept you waiting, sir. But you will understand that I was checking up on your statement. It was necessary. Anyhow, you are quite right, sir. We executed an order this morning, sir, at Lanrebel. An unusually—er—large order, sir. For two hundred yellow roses."

Anthony checked a movement on the part of Ann. It seemed to him that she was on the point of saying something. "Would it be convenient," said Anthony, "to let us know the exact terms of this . . . er . . . unusual order? You will realize that it closely concerns Miss Hillier here."

"Certainly," replied Mr. Tomlinson. "I will do that for you with pleasure." He flicked the pages of the order book. "The order to which I referred was for two hundred yellow roses . . . as I previously indicated. They were to be delivered this morning to the churchyard of Lanrebel church. To be placed on a fresh, a newly dug, grave. Full directions were given as to the position of this grave—er—geographically, that is. We were informed that the grave was the grave of the late Mr. Neill Hillier. The order was duly carried out by our representative. We have the reputation of always executing our orders with the utmost promptitude. The firm has been in the flower business for several generations. Now, sir, may I ask what lies behind your inquiries?"

"Just a moment," Anthony cut in. Annesley and Ann listened eagerly for what was to come. "When was this order given?"

Tomlinson referred to the book. "Yesterday morning."

"Was it a written order or did somebody call here and deliver it?"

Tomlinson shook his head. "Neither, sir. We received the order by the medium of the telephone."

Anthony nodded. "Of course. I might have known it. I wasted our time when I asked the question. But what about the cash side of it? Surely you safeguard the firm's interests in that direction? Who's to pay for the order?"

Mr. Tomlinson looked hurt beyond measure. "If you will pardon my saying so, sir, my worst enemies could not accuse me—that is, justifiably—of want of discretion or even a lack of business acumen."

Unhappily (for Mr. Bathurst's ear) he emphasized the first syllable of the last word. "Well?" said Mr. Bathurst quietly—"do you mean by that, that your intending purchaser who used the telephone to send his order satisfied you fully as to the soundness of his credentials?"

"Quite so, sir. He must have done, otherwise the order wouldn't have been executed."

Anthony regarded him curiously. "Please remember that this lady is Miss Hillier. The late Mr. Neill Hillier was her brother. That is our only excuse for bothering you as we are. You will pardon me, I'm sure, if I ask you questions that must sound like an impertinence? Is the account in respect of the yellow roses paid?"

Tomlinson moved a shoulder a trifle uneasily. "As a matter of fact, no, sir. Not at the moment."

Up went Mr. Bathurst's eyebrows. Ann moved forward impulsively. Annesley felt that he was on the fringe of something like a comedy which was about to turn sharply and suddenly into drama. Tomlinson hastened to amplify his statement. "But there isn't the slightest cause, sir, to think that it won't be paid. As I said, I am not in the habit of making business errors."

Anthony shook his head. "I'm very much afraid you've made one this time. Very much afraid. But tell me—we'll leave that part for a moment—what was the name of the purchaser—and to what address are you required to deliver the account?"

Tomlinson looked up as he replied to Anthony's question. "To Mr. Paul Hillier, sir. At the address which you mentioned a moment or so ago. 'Hillearys', Lanrebel."

Tomlinson looked his blandest. He imagined that he had put the ace on Mr. Bathurst's king. He had the satisfaction, too, of seeing the surprise registered on Mr. Bathurst's face. Anthony recovered, however, from what had been an undoubted shock and turned to Ann Hillier. "Well, Miss Hillier, what are your reactions to that piece of information?"

"It's absurd!" Ann exclaimed hotly—and then Anthony and Keith Annesley saw her stop. Stop suddenly in her stride, as it were. Her eyes held something like doubt . . . or was it possibly fear? Anthony wasn't sure. He waited for her to continue. "It's all wrong," she said, much more quietly this time, "it's a hoax. The whole thing. Somebody taking my father's name. Pretending to be him. It must be so."

She turned impetuously to Anthony Bathurst. "You must realize that, Mr. Bathurst."

Anthony nodded. He felt it would be wiser if further revelations were kept away from the excellent Tomlinson and his equally excellent staff of young ladies. He thanked Tomlinson therefore for his attention and courtesy. "I will see that Mr. Paul Hillier communicates with you with regard to this," he promised. "Thank you again." Tomlinson led the way and bowed his three visitors from the shop. Anthony waited until the car was well under way before he tackled Ann.

"Miss Ann," he said gravely, "I consider that this news is definitely disturbing. We can't dismiss it before looking more closely at it."

Ann looked both petulant and turbulent. "I can tell you my father knows nothing about the flowers—if that's what you mean, Mr. Bathurst. When I told him they were on Neill's grave . . . he was in a dreadful state and terribly upset."

"Who told you about it?"

"Mowbray."

"Where did he hear it?"

"From Dr. Pakenham."

"Where did Mowbray meet Dr. Pakenham?"

"He was crossing the drive at the front of the house when Dr. Pakenham went by in his car. The doctor saw Mowbray standing there and stopped his car. When Mowbray went up to him the doctor told him the news about Neill's grave. At least, that's what Mowbray says. Any more questions?"

Anthony looked at her—whimsically critical. Ann thought that she knew the meaning of the glance. "I'm sorry," she said spontaneously. "Please forgive me."

"I understand," returned Anthony: "don't worry about that."

"Thank you."

"You've no idea, I suppose, who told Pakenham?"

"Not the foggiest."

"And your father's response to the news—was definitely antagonistic?"

"Very definitely. There was not only antagonism, to use your word, but annoyance as well. To say that he lost his temper would be putting it but mildly."

"Pardon a personal question . . . or rather a more personal one. What was the name of your great-uncle from whom your father inherited his money?"

Ann stared at him in surprise. "George Rice," she answered eventually. "He was one of the cotton millionaires. Lancashire born and bred. My father's mother was a Miss Rice. George's only niece."

"Do you know of any other members of the family?"

"The Rice family, do you mean?"

"Yes, the Lancashire family."

Ann puckered her brows. "I have never actually met any. But I believe that father's Uncle George had a son. He disappeared. Got into trouble and then there was the usual row with his father. He cleared out. Abroad somewhere. I don't think he's been heard of since. I think it was Australia he went to—but I'm not sure of that. From what I've heard from my people, the Rices were always quarrelling. Generally with one another. They were never happy unless they were thoroughly miserable."

"I see. So there *was* another Rice. That's interesting."

"That 'phone call we've been told about this afternoon, Mr. Bathurst—that could be traced, couldn't it?"

"Oh, easily. I'm afraid, though, that knowing from where it came will help us but little. It's bound to have been put through from a call-box somewhere near at hand. Either Lanrebel, Laran, or Liskerry, I should say. Possibly as far away as Frayne or Bonallack, but certainly no farther than that."

"Why no farther than that?" queried Annesley quietly, from the back of the car.

"Well, it isn't likely, as I'm seeing things," replied Mr. Bathurst. "I am certain that the person we're looking for is in our midst. Right amongst us. All that has come to me out of the case so far confirms that opinion." Ann stopped the car outside "Hillearys". "Will you come in and see my father?"

Anthony stood in the road with Keith Annesley. "I don't think I'll come in now, Miss Hillier, if you don't mind. Forgive me, won't you? But I should like you to tell your father what we have discovered at Liskerry this afternoon. Tell him all that we heard. In your own words. Every bit of it. Will you, please?"

"And after that?" questioned Ann Hillier doubtfully.

"I'm not sure," said Mr. Bathurst. "I'll let you know about that tomorrow. Good-bye till then, Miss Hillier."

He and Annesley saluted her. Ann waved a hand and turned the car towards the house.

"What's your plan now?" asked Annesley.

"I'm going back to the 'Salvation'," responded Mr. Bathurst, "to start all over again. I'm going to reassemble the pieces."

"Why that?"

"Why that, Annesley? I'll tell you why that. I've a feeling in my bones that I've missed something. Something that's vitally important. In fact I'm certain I have, Annesley."

Keith Annesley shook his head. "I can't see why you should say that."

"Can't you?" Anthony grinned. "Perhaps you're missing the same point that I was."

CHAPTER XVIII
MOWBRAY IS UNEASY

MOWBRAY, the butler of "Hillearys", stood outside the post office in the main street of Laran. It was his evening out. The particular night was hot and oppressive. The air was almost still. There was anxiety in the eyes of Mowbray. Anxiety of more than one kind. Firstly, he feared the approach of a thunderstorm, and repeatedly his upturned eyes sought the heavy clouds as he endeavoured to read their intentions. Secondly, the time was five minutes past six, and the big picture at the "Laurel" cinema started, according to the announcement on the bill, at six-seventeen. That is to say within another twelve minutes. The cinema was situated between the fire station and the Laran public offices and was at least five minutes' walk from where Mowbray waited outside the post office. Thirdly, his eyes inspected the various passengers as they alighted from the red-coloured bus that travels at half-hourly intervals between Lanrebel and Laran with eager and unconcealed anticipation. It will be deduced from these statements that Mowbray was waiting for somebody who was behind time. That deduction would be sound. It must be admitted that Mowbray was waiting for a woman!

He paced up and down with a frown settled heavily on his face. Several times he compared the time shown by his own rather imposing silver watch with that announced by the clock in front of the public offices. None of these comparisons seemed to afford him any comfort. The truth was gradually borne in upon him that he would be compelled to wait for at least one more bus-load from Lanrebel. There was nothing else for it. Mowbray resumed his monotonous promenade. As far as the "Duke's Head" and then back again to the post office. Many more minutes passed. Mowbray knew now with a sickening feeling that whatever the next bus might bring, the big picture had inevitably already started on its way. He resigned himself to the loss and glanced anxiously across the bridge to the road along which the Lanrebel bus must come. There was one thing he had decided—he would give Jennifer a piece of his mind when she did arrive. If a girl can't meet a man at the proper time she ought to be jolly well told about it. "Some men wouldn't stand for it. Besides— women liked a man who knew his own mind." Mowbray gradually worked up a large-sized grievance. Suddenly his mood softened. After all, Jennifer wasn't an ordinary girl. Jennifer's circumstances and Jennifer's conditions weren't ordinary either! Jennifer wasn't able to walk out of her house when the whim took her. Even to meet him, who happened to be Mr. Paul Hillier's butler! For Jennifer, alas, was married to another, and her meetings with Mowbray were therefore clandestine.

The cinema at Laran made an excellent rendezvous for them as it did for other pairs of lovers. Surely she wouldn't be very long now? Mowbray, with an increasing anxiety, consulted his watch again. The next bus from Lanrebel should be in within five minutes. If Jennifer wasn't on that, it would mean that she wasn't going to keep the appointment. There must be a vital reason for this, because Jennifer was always reliable. And her habit of punctuality was an unique part of this quality of reliability. Mowbray admired reliability, especially when he encountered it in a woman.

When he had been in the service of Colonel Todhunter, before he came to the Hilliers, the Colonel himself had made much of his butler's reliability. Mowbray had held this with pride ever since. As he paced up and down waiting for Jennifer, he surrendered to the temptation of reminiscence. Colonel Todhunter! What a man he had been! To have satisfied and to have received encomiums from him was indeed an achievement! For the Colonel was satisfied with only the best. The merely very good had assuredly not been enough. When he had died he had left Mowbray the sum of one hundred pounds and an enduring testimonial. Mowbray, tactful and dour, had saved the former and conscientiously used the latter. Paul Hillier, when it had been presented to him in faithful anticipation, had been suitably impressed and had taken almost joyfully the same Charles Mowbray into his service. Mowbray always remembered what Mr. Hillier had said to him on that morning of his engagement. "If Colonel Todhunter were as satisfied with you as he implies he was in this reference . . ."

At that precise moment, Mowbray's thoughts in this direction were abruptly dismissed. The red bus from Lanrebel was coming across the bridge that spans the Lar. As he looked in that direction Mowbray's eyes caught it, and having caught it, did not leave it. It turned the corner of the bridge and rapidly approached him. It stopped by the kerb—almost exactly where he was standing. Mowbray's heart gave a little leap, for there was Jennifer Hillman on the platform smiling at him, all ready and eager to alight. Trim and neat she looked to Mowbray's eye, as trim and as neat as ever. "As smart as paint," he murmured. Jennifer Treglown had been the village beauty in Lanrebel for at least three years before she married Ralph Hillman, the smart young gardener employed by the Rev. Septimus Aylmer at the Vicarage. Unhappily, the marriage had been a failure. Hillman's only attraction for her had been his physique, and very soon after the ceremony Jennifer found herself sighing for the open admiration of the many swains which had been hers for the asking prior to her alliance with Ralph Hillman.

Mowbray, always with a shrewd eye for "an affair", especially of an attractive nature, had quickly sensed the conditions existing in the Hillman home and had made hay while the sun shone, and after a time Jennifer had cast discretion to the winds and entered upon a flirtation. So much so, and so openly, that the tongues of Lanrebel had begun to wag. After a time they wagged so vigorously that Jennifer and her middle-aged beau had been forced to forsake the isolated lanes of Lanrebel for the more thickly crowded streets of Laran. In Laran, the "Laurel" cinema had offered a satisfactory sanctuary, and away from the prying eyes and chattering tongues of Lanrebel Jennifer's love affair had progressed until a critical stage had been reached and she had come to contemplate what she termed to herself "the parting of the ways". As she stepped from the conductor's platform, almost into the arms of the waiting Mowbray, she knew that he was expecting an immediate explanation of her lateness. There was question in his eyes. There was question even in his stance. "Not now, Charles," she said almost in a whisper, and with a shake of her pretty head, "not until we're inside the pictures."

Charles made a slight movement of the head, which might mean anything. But all he said was, "The big picture's been going nearly half an hour." He piloted Jennifer to the pay-box, found the necessary silver, and escorted her up the flight of steps that led to the auditorium. An attendant took them to the seats they wanted. Mowbray and Jennifer liked the back row. It was convenient to them from all standpoints. Mowbray slipped his arm round Jennifer's waist.

"What's the trouble?" he said rather uneasily. "Why were you so late?"

"I couldn't get out," she whispered. "Ralph's at the village flower show. But he didn't go out until half past five, so I was stopped. He said he was going out at five o'clock. That put me all out. I'm so sorry to have kept you waiting, Charles. Forgive me!"

He patted her on the cheek with his disengaged hand, and as he did so looked more like her uncle than ever.

"That's nice of you," she whispered. She put her lips up to Mowbray. Mowbray, true to form, improved the shining hour. His displeasure quickly passed. He bent his head towards Jennifer . . . to draw back again and regard her intently.

"What's the matter, Jennifer? What's worrying you? You're hiding something from me. I can see that, plainly."

She shook her head, but Mowbray was not convinced by the denial. "You *are*, Jennifer. I'm certain of it. What is it? Tell me."

Jennifer, thus challenged, gave in. She always did when Mowbray became peremptory and dominated her. "I didn't mean to tell you," she said. "I wasn't going to. I didn't mean to worry you with it." She stopped, and Mowbray saw that she was on the verge of tears.

"S'sh," he said quietly, "whisper. Don't talk so loudly. Those people in front will hear if you aren't careful. What's the matter, my lovely?"

"The police have been," she whispered fearfully.

"The police? Do you mean to your place?"

Jennifer nodded. Mowbray frowned.

"Which of the police?"

"That fool of an inspector from Liskerry. The big fellow—Rock-ingham, I think his name is."

"Rocking-horse," returned the butler from "Hillearys" with appropriate scorn in his voice. "What the hell did he want with you?"

Jennifer hesitated. Mowbray instantly detected the hesitation. "He came and asked me questions."

"When?"

"Yesterday afternoon. Soon after dinner."

"Who did he ask the questions of?"

"Me, of course! I *said* he asked me. I was the only one in the house. Ralph was up at the Vicar's. Working in the kitchen garden."

"Did he know that?"

"Expect so. Expect that was why he chose his time to come. There's no doubt it was me he wanted to ask the questions of."

"Why? What makes you so certain of that?"

Again Jennifer Hillman showed signs of hesitation. Mowbray pressed her for an answer. By now, all his interest in the screen and in what the screen was portraying had vanished. "Why was it, Jennifer?"

"Because . . . because he asked me questions about *you*." There were real tears now in Jennifer's eyes. Mowbray caught his breath. The news came as a shattering blow to him.

"About me? Blasted effrontery! What did you tell him?"

"Nothing, Charles. Not a thing. Absolutely nothing at all."

Mowbray's mind was beginning to function properly again. Jennifer's announcement had put it temporarily out of gear.

"Just a minute, Jennifer. Let me get this straight and all in order. What right's he got to come and worry you with questions about *me*?"

"I thought it was funny. I couldn't understand it at all. But I suppose people have been talking of *us* again. I hope none of it gets to Ralph's ears."

Mowbray grew impatient with her. "That doesn't matter—now. I mean this other business is much more important. Can't you see that? It's murder. And not merely one murder! Two murders. And I must know about it. What questions did he ask you? You must tell me everything."

"Questions about the night Mrs. Hillier died. The 8th of June, wasn't it?"

"It was. But what were the questions? Good Lord, Jennifer! Don't keep putting me off, my girl. Surely you can see it's a most serious matter for me?"

Jennifer nodded uneasily. She could already visualize her portly lover standing on the gallows with his arms pinioned and the noose round his ample neck. They put black bags over their heads as well . . . she had seen pictures of executions in lurid weeklies which her husband upon occasions had brought home to her as an extra special treat. She steeled herself to the task of telling her companion what he demanded to know.

"First of all he asked me if I had been out that night. I said 'Yes'. I think I did right to tell the truth, don't you?"

"Depends on how much and what else you told him," grunted Mowbray. "But go on."

Jennifer exhibited reluctance. "Well—after that—he asked me if I had seen you that night."

"Yes," cut in the butler sharply, "and what did you say?"

"I told a lie, Charles. I said 'No'. I did it for your sake. I don't see how those few minutes we spent together that evening could harm anybody, do you? Or matter in any way?"

Mowbray was cold consideration. "Don't know," he said eventually. "Can't tell, unless you know where the interfering busybody's leading up to. But what was his reply when you told him that?"

"Well . . . he seemed—as far as I could judge—to be satisfied. To accept it. Then he asked me if you had seemed at all worried lately.

Mowbray swore roundly and heartily. "I like their methods, I must say! Crawling round behind people's backs. No business to do such a thing. For two pins I'd show him up. I wasn't with you more than five minutes all told—that night. And that was after Dr. Pakenham had been and gone and it was all over. What did you tell him about my being worried? Did you choke the swine off?"

"You reckon I did! He didn't get much change out of me. Don't see that our private business is any concern of his. Or anything to do with Mrs. Hillier being killed, either! What about young Mr. Neill too? Have they forgotten about him?"

"Quite likely," replied Mowbray, "for all the real good they ever are. Their proper place is at football matches or sticking up their great fat hands to stop the traffic. Well, I'm blessed! I reckon all this beats the band."

"Do you know what I really think?" whispered Jennifer into his coat collar.

"No. What?"

"Why, I think that I know the persons in Lanrebel who've been doin' the talking. They very likely went to this Rockingham man and told him a lot of lies about us."

"Who?"

"Josh Toft and that long-tongued wife of his. Rotten old cat that woman is. Don't you remember we thought he saw us one night? When we were in the lane between the 'Salvation' and 'Woodruffs'?"

Mowbray shook his head violently.

"No. You're wrong. I told you so at the time. He didn't see us. I'm certain of that. Only you're that scared always that shadows frighten you. Toft wasn't spying on us. He had his eye on that motor-car which was standing at the top of the crossroads."

Directly he had spoken, Mowbray was annoyed with himself. He knew that he had said more than it had been his intention to say. He hoped against hope, however, that Jennifer would miss the point of what he had said and that the farther issue would be glossed over. He remembered that on the night in question he had found it difficult to divert the distinctly pertinent inquiries which had come from her. His hope on this last occasion was dashed to the ground. The remark he had made had revived the memory which was stored in Jennifer's brain. "That car, Charles! I remember now. That car at the top of the crossroads that night. I asked you about it on the night we saw it. But you wouldn't tell me. I'm sure that you did know, though, and were deliberately putting me off. Whose was it, Charles? Tell me—you must."

Mowbray cursed inwardly at the turn affairs had taken. As he had feared, he had pushed the fat into the fire. He thought hastily and came to a quick decision. There were some matters which Jennifer would do well not to know. Come what may, he felt confident that Jennifer would never be disloyal to him. Mowbray, the "gentleman's gentleman", was certain of that, but he wouldn't rate her discretion at anything like the same standard as he would assess her loyalty. He must find a way out. A *via media* which would satisfy her curiosity and at the same time lead her nowhere along a road which might prove unpleasant for him. "Look here, Jennifer. You must be careful. You've got to be. And I must be careful. We both must say as little as possible when interfering people come round asking questions. That's the plan we must adopt. You can see the truth of that as well as I can."

She nodded—a little mystified at what Mowbray was about to say next. In a way—which she couldn't have explained even had she been taxed—she was just a little afraid of what was coming. To her surprise, Mowbray's next remark was in the form of a question.

"You ask me whose the car was. I'll ask you something. Whose did you think it was yourself?"

Her apprehension increased. Mowbray always worried her when he retreated into one of these moods. But she faced the problem he had presented to her with courage and resolution. "I thought the car belonged to Mrs. Hillier. You know I thought that on the very evening, and it was only about a week, too, before the actual murder. You can't get away from that. There you are, I've made a clean breast of my thoughts." She half laughed—nervously.

Mowbray looked befittingly grave and judicial. "Well—you were quite right. I'll admit it to you now, although I didn't intend to. It was Madam's car. I didn't tell you at the time because I considered it the best policy not to. Even now, Jennifer, you must regard the information I have given you as given in the very strictest confidence."

Jennifer Hillman clutched at the arm which wasn't round her waist. "Charles," she said, "I wouldn't dream of telling a single soul. You know that you can trust me, don't you?" She shook his arm in her impatience. "You do know that, don't you, Charles?"

As Charles didn't immediately answer, Jennifer followed up with a second question. A second and much more vital one.

"Who was she waiting for, Charles? You must know, living in the same house with her. Do tell me, Charles. I'll keep it ever so secret."

Mowbray frowned again and shook his head, thereby making Jennifer feel all the more uncomfortable. For a moment she wished that she hadn't asked this second question.

"I cannot tell you," said Mowbray. "If the matter concerned me alone, it would make a difference. But it doesn't: it concerns others also. And because of that fact I cannot tell you. It would not be the right thing for me to do. To some people, it might appear to be a trifle. I am different, however. I pride myself on knowing what is right. And when I know the right thing to do—there is only one course for me to pursue—I try to do it." Mowbray coughed discreetly behind his own idle hand.

Despite her fears and vague apprehensions, Jennifer contrived to pout petulantly. "You might tell me, Charles. Just as though! I thought you said you trusted me. Only the other day you said that you'd do anything for me."

Mowbray quoted the time-honoured words of Lovelace, although he remained unaware of the fact. Jennifer affected to be unconvinced. "That's old-fashioned talk. All early Victorian. It might have been all right in my grandmother's time. Things are different now, and what's more you know they are. Please tell me, Charles."

"No, my dear, I cannot. Please don't persist in asking me. You put me in an unfair position. Do try to see my point of view."

Jennifer resorted to the traditional practice of the inordinately curious. She put a pointed question. "Do I know the man, Charles?"

Mowbray cleared his throat. "I didn't say it was a man."

"Mrs. Hillier wouldn't wait at that time of night for a woman. Not if I know her properly. She wasn't the kind."

"She was a very charming lady. One in a million."

"So she may have been. That's all the more reason, I should say, why she would have waited for a man." Jennifer projected this in triumphant challenge. Mowbray ignored it. Jennifer, however, followed it up. "Do I know him, Charles?"

"Perhaps."

"That means I do. Then he was a local man. Young or old, Charles?" She snuggled nearer to him, feminine and replete with temptation. Her face was upraised to his. Her lips were ripe and red. Mowbray fidgeted in his seat. What a mistake he had made when he had put Jennifer on the track again! Just because of a chance phrase. He endeavoured to pull himself together. He must assert his manhood and his proper domination over a merely curious female. Women were meant to be put in their proper place.

"I won't discuss the matter any further, Jennifer. Indeed, I refuse to. And I warn you that you will annoy me if you persist in this campaign of questioning me. You will annoy me seriously. In fact, my dear, you have already annoyed me." He caressed her with a gesture of proprietorship, bending down to whisper to her in a changed tone. "Don't let a miserable and paltry thing like this come between us,

Jennifer. Please! For both our sakes. Be guided by me. I've had more experience of the world than you. I'm older than you are."

The remark was unfortunate.

"You're telling me," snapped Jennifer, pushing his arm away ungenerously. Mowbray winced at the shrewdness of the thrust. It seemed to him that he could already see the writing on the wall. Writing that stood out in cold, clear characters. It was a pity in a way that he had never heard of the Rajah of Rukh or even of his philosophy.

CHAPTER XIX
MR. BATHURST AND ANALYSIS

IT WAS late. There was no denying that. But the June day, and the evening of it, had been so beautiful that the lateness of the hour mattered but little. Anthony Bathurst and Keith Annesley lay at length in deck-chairs in a remote corner of the garden of the "Salvation" inn. Full tankards (a repeat order) were on the grass beside them. The air was heavy scented. Gnats and mosquitoes and other winged things circled round unceasingly as the harbingers of an equally fine day on the morrow that was coming.

"Jove! what an evening!" said Annesley. "Superb. Reminds me of those we used to have years ago. I shall miss this when I'm back home tomorrow."

"What train are you catching in the morning?"

"The 11.11 from Liskerry. It's the only decent train there is. Uncle Arthur's running me over in the car. I shall have to be on the move soon after breakfast. Decent of him. He offered. I didn't ask him. He's a good scout and I'm glad I came here on the whole."

"Despite the tragedies in the midst?"

Annesley nodded gravely. "There's been only one tragedy during my stay. Don't forget that, Bathurst. The boy Neill. Pretty terrible, I know. Some people, I suppose, would have had their holiday spoiled by it . . . perhaps as a writer of books I react to occurrences of the kind you have had here, a little differently from the average person. I don't know. After all—any person's the worst judge of himself." Keith Annesley shrugged his shoulders as he concluded his attempt at self-introspection and smiled at Anthony. "Besides, you know," he continued, "look at the other side of the picture. If I hadn't come down here, I shouldn't have met you!" Anthony grinned at the compliment. "Lor' love us I Fancy that, now! Aren't you sweet?"

"No—I'm dead serious. Honest Injun. But I shall return with one regret."

"What's that, Annesley?"

"That the mystery—or mysteries—I suppose I had better say—haven't been solved. I should have liked to have been in at the death, as it were."

"That's mere vanity on your part." Mr. Bathurst drank.

Annesley disclaimed. "I don't think so. Honestly, I don't."

"Yes, it is. Desire for publicity. Not offensive, of course. I don't mean anything as bad as that."

"No, I disagree entirely. I won't have that. Call it rather just a genuine desire to understand. To know 'whys' and 'wherefores'. To me, the whole thing's like an unfinished story, without even a 'continued in our next' slogan to keep the reader's appetite whetted."

"You're trying to justify both yourself and your curiosity. And you can't even ascribe the latter to a quest for knowledge. What do *you* care if there's a fourth dimension? Not half a hoot. Well—deny it if you can."

"I don't. I'll be perfectly frank with regard to that. I wouldn't care if there were forty-four dimensions. Such things as dimensions don't interest me. Why should they? But the Hillier case does. I deal in flesh and blood. It makes contact with humanity. There are men and women in it. Men and women with beating hearts and blood in their veins. A charming lady dies in her car. Why? As far as one knows, there are no shadows in her life. I am desperately curious. A boy on the threshold of manhood is found dead in a lane. He has no enemies. His life is only just beginning. The victim of a savage attack. Again—why? My curiosity knows no bounds. To me it is all sheer drama." Keith Annesley picked up his tankard and drank from it. Anthony smiled at him. "Why do you smile like that?" queried Annesley. "Am I so terribly unusual?"

"No. I wouldn't level that accusation against you for a second. Still—I'll say this. Although you've admitted to your curiosity, I shall claim that you haven't entirely justified it."

Annesley emptied his tankard and then thrust back at him. "Well, then, it's your own fault. That is to say you're at least partly to blame."

"Meaning by that?"

"That if you had done your duty and solved the mystery, my curiosity would have been satisfied and I could have returned to my country home of Blackstock in Essex feeling that I had been something like an actor in a finished production. Whereas now, I feel that I've been present at a series of rehearsals and never come to grips with the real thing. I don't even turn up at the dress rehearsal. Hence these tears of disappointment. Does that fuller explanation clarify the position at all for you?"

The mood of Anthony Bathurst underwent a change. "Yes, I think it does. Because I realize the justice of the allegations."

"*Not* allegations."

"Well—in a way they are. If it comes to a show-down, I have made, I suppose, but little progress. I have so far failed to produce a prisoner and with appropriate drama click handcuffs on his guilty wrists. To which finale, naturally, you looked forward! I am not sure, though, that the blame for this deficiency is justly all mine. Bricks, you will remember, my dear Annesley, need for the purpose of their manufacture a certain supply of straw. And my supply of that estimable commodity has been strictly limited."

Annesley ventured upon further argument. "Agreed! But you are not entirely without straw, Bathurst."

"Taking you at your word, then—let us examine our straw. Before we do that, though—we'll get these tankards refilled again. Frank! Fra-ank!"

Frank Paske, passing through the greenhouse at the beginning of the garden, heard the call, turned his head, and hastened along to them. His smile, as he surveyed the two deck-chairs and the empty tankards, was broader than usual. He accepted Mr. Bathurst's order and promised that it would be executed with the utmost promptitude. He was as good as his word.

"Can't argue without beer, Annesley," announced Mr. Bathurst. "Even if we could, we wouldn't. Here's to you and the pleasantest of journeys in the morning."

Annesley suitably acknowledged the sentiment. "Now then," went on Anthony, "in the matter of that straw. Let's take joint stock of it. What have we, when all's said and done?"

Annesley looked at him. "Do you want me to collect it for examination? I thought that you—"

"All right. I don't mind in the least. I'll take on the job. Anthony Bathurst as a collector of straw. Straw in the wind and down wind. Listen to me carefully, Annesley. Because I shall probably want your help later on, when it comes to assessing straw values. Let's take case Number One. The death of Mrs. Hillier. What have we about that that needs close examination? In the way of what you would describe as clues? One—a letter which she crumples in her hand during the dinner that precedes her death. But note with regard to this, that we have only the word of the Vicar of Lanrebel in support of the statement. Nobody else saw this letter and, moreover, the letter hasn't been found since. Any remarks on that, Annesley?"

"No. Go ahead."

"Number Two, then. A few words spoken by the dying woman *in extremis*. A snatch of a sentence—no more. 'The Mile Cliff. Two—' This point, you will remember, you and I have discussed previously. Without getting any value particularly. Have you any further comments re our earlier conversation?"

Annesley shook his head again. "No, I've nothing to add to what I said before. Leave Mrs. Hillier's message and go on to the next point."

"All right. I will. I'll ignore the fact that she had slight physical injuries and soiled clothing. I'll pass on to one of our private clues. I refer, of course, to the fragment of cardboard which we found on the ledge at the Mile Cliff." Anthony stopped, as though he were deliberately awaiting Annesley's comment or criticism on this particular point. None came. Mr. Bathurst therefore continued. "So far, Annesley, I have done nothing with that curious corner of cardboard. But I have it safe here in my wallet." As he spoke, he touched his breast pocket. "And although I haven't moved very far in the matter up to the moment, that doesn't mean I shan't when the maggot bites me.

Now what else is there for our consideration? Very little, I fear. A continental holiday just before the tragedy? With the charming Miss Ann? Can we make anything of that? Yes? No? Candidly, Annesley, our collection of straw isn't very impressive, is it?"

"I'm afraid it isn't, when you arrange it as you have just done. My criticism seems unjust."

Anthony smiled. "Nary a bit. You say what you like, old son. And as often as you like. I can take it, don't you worry. Besides—it does me good to be criticized. Who am I that I should expect to be immune from the carpers? Suppose, though, that we now pass along to crime Number Two. The death of Neill Hillier. Here surely we have even less straw than we had in the case of Mrs. Hillier. Tell me this, Annesley—I'm interested. What straw did you yourself find round young Hillier?"

Keith Annesley answered immediately—"Only the rather pertinent question—why was he out on such a night? And what took him along that road?"

"Agreed on that. But there was one piece of straw there all the same. Which most of us missed. I missed it myself for a time. I say it was there. More correctly I should have said 'it wasn't very far away'. That would have been a truer statement. It certainly didn't stick out a mile."

Anthony held out his cigarette-case to Annesley. The latter accepted the invitation and lit a cigarette. "I am thinking of what you have just said. I certainly must have missed the point to which you refer. Because I can think of nothing that seems to fit. It's the natural difference, I suppose, which arises between the eye of the trained observer and that of the novice."

Anthony smiled again and shook his head at him.

"Not altogether, Annesley. You mustn't be too modest, you know. And I'm being a little unfair, perhaps—possibly trying you too highly. I found the particular piece of straw because I went over the ground again. Deliberately. Still—I'll give you the chance to retrieve your reputation."

"Such as it is," echoed Annesley semi-ruefully.

"More self-castigation?" mocked Anthony. "What a chap you are for crying *Mea culpa*! You'd never have made a successful Cabinet

Minister. I went over that particular piece of ground again, Annesley, because I wasn't satisfied with what I had seen. And, in a way, my persistence was rewarded. Now cast your mind back for a moment or so, will you? To the place where Neill Hillier's body was found. By a sergeant of police named Spiers. I mean to the actual place. Which was about a hundred yards from the crossroads. You will recall that the boy was lying in a ditch. You and I, Annesley, and Dr. Pakenham, who was with us when we were there, saw the place early on the next day. Yes?"

"Yes," contributed Annesley in agreement.

"Would it be correct for me to say that there were trees all round the spot?"

"It would."

"You noticed 'em?"

"I noticed 'em all right. Couldn't very well help it, could I?"

"What were they? Did you happen to notice that?"

Keith Annesley blew a puff of smoke from his cigarette.

"Elm—elm—definitely."

"All of 'em elm?"

"I think so. Why? What's your point?"

"Just this. Remember that patch of young foxgloves on the bank which I pointed out to you as we walked up that morning behind Pakenham's car?"

"Yes. Very well. I can see that clump of foxgloves now. What about 'em?"

"Just behind that foxglove clump was a big tree. A noble chap. Can you call it to mind?"

Annesley nodded confidently. "Easily. It was one of the first things I noticed."

"Good. Was that big fellow elm?"

"Undoubtedly. I know it was. Because as I stood there I took pains to satisfy myself." Annesley was emphatic.

Anthony smiled. "You're right about it. I'm not going to contradict you. Don't worry. But by your admission of that particular piece of observation on your part, you've brought me to my point. The storm that evening did a tremendous amount of damage. You saw it. I saw it. It was all around us, havoc and ruin on all sides. And underneath that huge elm, close by where Neill Hillier died, was a great branch of a tree. Lying at the foot of the trunk. As you looked at it and then at the tree itself you realized that only a giant divinity could have wrenched off such a limb of might and power and flung it there. Do you get me, Annesley?" Anthony regarded his companion grimly.

Annesley looked puzzled at the question.

"No. I *agree* with you, of course! The fury of that storm was unforgettable. Nobody could argue about it. So I don't quite see—"

"My real point? Well, my real point is this. I'll endeavour to explain it to you. That great bough beneath that majestic elm happened to be beech—that's all!" Anthony's mood changed and he grinned at the unfolding of his dénouement.

Annesley stared at him in amazement.

"Beech!" he exclaimed incredulously. "How is that possible? Not one of the trees by that bank is a beech! They're all elm—as I said, every one of 'em."

"That, my dear Annesley, is part of our problem. When we have settled it to our satisfaction I, for one, shall have a more complacent mind."

"Where is the nearest beech? Any idea?"

"Don't know. But I must find out. And that, I think, brings us to the last piece of our straw. Pretty thin consignment, isn't it?"

Annesley nodded. "Has the police chap been to see you at all since Neill was killed?"

Anthony smiled at him. "Not that you'd notice. Why?"

"I wondered, that's all. Wondered if the police had picked anything up that you don't know about."

"No. As far as I know, nothing doing. I'm still an outsider. Scotland Yard aren't moving down in these parts, you know." His mood changed. "By Jove! What a marvellous night! The air is still heavy with heat. Perfect!"

"Yes. It's grand. One can't say this evening with Villon, 'How cold this June air seems'. Although, very possibly, that will be the tale for me to-morrow evening. I shall be back home by that time, but I shall be with you in spirit, Bathurst." Annesley rose from his deckchair and shook his right trouser down to his ankle. "Drop me a line to Blackstock, will you? I'll leave the address. In the event of your wanting any help—you might, you know—I'll be only too pleased to come down again for a few days. I'd stay on now, but for the fact that contracts are contracts—and publishers won't wait."

"Meaning that holidays and 'such things' must stop?"

"You've said it, Bathurst. That's exactly what I do mean. Well, I'll leave you. But don't forget my offer. I must get off to Uncle Ned. Mustn't roll down to brekker too late in the morning. Night-night, Bathurst." Annesley stopped and looked across the wall of the garden.

"What's up?" inquired Anthony.

"I thought I saw a light. Across there."

"What sort of light?"

"A sudden light, that flickered. Not a big one. Tiny."

Anthony rose and stood at Annesley's side. He looked down towards the wall. "Where did you see it?"

"Down there. It seemed to move along."

"Let's go and explore, then. Come on. Your bed can wait for a few minutes."

They walked towards the low stone wall at the end of the garden. Anthony peered into the dusk. The silence was almost uncanny. Then he detected a slight movement. "Somebody there," he said tersely.

Keith Annesley strained his ears in an attempt to hear. The effort was ineffectual. Anthony spoke to him again.

"I'll tell you what. I can smell smoke. Can you?"

Annesley sniffed the night air. "Yes, I *think* . . . cigar smoke! Is that what you mean?"

"Yes. Now who is it that lurks at the bottom of the 'Salvation' garden and smokes cigars at this time of night?"

"Search me," replied Annesley. "'Whoever it was, he's well away by now."

"I'm afraid that's only too true," returned Mr. Bathurst. They turned away and walked slowly back. Anthony went to his deck-chair again for a final pipe. Keith Annesley went to bed.

Chapter XX
THE THIRD BLOW

ALMOST exactly twenty-two hours after Anthony Bathurst had smelt cigar smoke in the lane that runs at the back of the wall at the bottom of the "Salvation" garden, Ann Hillier drove the Bentley into the garage at "Hillearys". The night was as gloriously beautiful as its immediate predecessor had been. Ann Hillier put the car away and then looked at her wrist-watch. The time showed twelve minutes to ten. She walked round the side of the garage and on to the large stretch of grass at the back of the house. As she walked towards the lounge, she saw, to her surprise, that one of the french doors was open. Ann, as she realized this, instinctively quickened her pace. She knew that it was Mowbray's night off . . . but all the same . . .

As she hastened, the many June-wafted scents assailed her and she heard the soft murmur of the gentle June breeze through the branches of the big trees all round the garden of "Hillearys". For some reason which she couldn't altogether explain, Ann felt exceedingly afraid. Influences affected her. Most unusually! Sinister influences. Strange influences. Her walk, which she had instinctively quickened, became a rapid run.

As she came close to the lounge of "Hillearys" she saw, or rather she realized, for she had actually seen it before without proper understanding, that the room was in complete darkness. Ann's hand went to her throat. If Neill had been there with her . . . Then the thought, swift-dying as it had been quick-born, told her that Neill could not be there, could not be anywhere, for Neill was dead. Ann came to the intimacy of the open french door. Two paces from actual entrance, she paused irresolutely and half turned.

The moonlight shining on the glass of the window laid a silver band across the dark carpet of the lounge. Ann's fear increased. Her heart began to beat with a strange fierceness. All inside the room was eerily still and silent. The effect of the moon made it even more ghostly and ethereal. Ann walked to the glass of the doors and peered into the room. She could see or hear no sign of life or movement. She took one step forward and called in a voice that to her ears sounded absolutely unlike her own—"Paul! Father!"

There was no reply. Just dead, white-banded silence. Ann took another pace forward and put her hand on the edge of the door that was open. This move gave her a clear view of the entire room. She saw that it was empty. She felt an emotion of relief. Her father was not here. She felt thankful for that. But where was he, then, and why was the one door open? If her father had walked into the garden, as he might reasonably do at this time on such a lovely night, he would have been walking on the grass, or be at least near at hand somewhere. She would have seen him by now. Still—there might well be a multitude of reasons which would account intelligently for his absence.

He might be elsewhere in the house—and yet . . . this open door! It disturbed her. There was something wrong about it. Why was it open? Who had opened it? She stood there and thought hard for about a minute before she arrived at a decision. She would go in. She was being absurd—behaving like a child . . . frightened at the dark and at being alone. But Jacqueline was dead . . . and Neill was dead . . . and Life had become a vastly different proposition from what it had been for her but a few weeks ago. There was, after all, an excuse for her inclination towards panic. She was human, and very nearly alone.

She stepped over the threshold and put her hand across one of the curtains to feel for the electric light switch. She must have friendly light as an auxiliary. Not this semi-spectral hostile moonlight which seemed to hint at ghastly happenings, and to come from another world. Ann found the switch, moved it, and flooded the room with warm, hospitable light. She looked round with quick nervous glances, and, although she fought bravely against it, apprehension came to her as her eyes searched the room. Again, however, relief companioned her. Not only was the room most certainly empty, but, in addition, there were no indications of disturbance or of anything that might cause her alarm.

The chairs were all in place. The tables had not been moved in any way. Her father's special chair was still in its usual place by the big standard lamp . . . everything, everywhere, was in order. What an idiot she had been to have worked herself up to that ridiculous state of nervousness! She decided to go back and to close the open door. It was getting late and the air wasn't as warm as it had been. Ann walked back to the french door and shut it. She now had her back to the rear door of the lounge. It was at that precise moment that the thought came to her that all was *not* well.

More than the thought—the definite knowledge! By an instinct, or by an intuitive quality, Ann knew—beyond doubt—as her right hand closed that door, that there was something wrong—something hideously wrong—in that room in which she was standing. She turned and steeled herself to the urgent need of the moment. She came back into the middle of the room and looked round. She was scared—but by now she had schooled herself and had herself under control.

She looked across at the settee that covered the space from the corner of the big open fireplace to the middle of the wall directly opposite to the french doors. Something prompted her. A sixth sense. She advanced towards the settee. The cushions on it looked unusual, as though they had been recently pulled about. Almost untidy. She stood close to the settee—and then, in a ghastly flash—she knew! The body of Paul Hillier, her father, lay on the carpet behind the settee.

Ann's first impulse was to scream, but she quickly mastered it. She bent over and looked down at her father lying there. The sight was not pleasant. Paul Hillier lay on his back with his arms extended. His features were twisted and contorted with pain. His collar was crumpled and his hair disarrayed. His eyes had a most horribly glassy stare. Ann had no doubt whatever that her father was dead. She knew that it would be futile for her to call for assistance. She backed away from the settee with slow halting steps and wondered what she—the last of the Paul Hilliers—had best do.

Where was Uncle Maurice? Surely he must be near at hand. Then she remembered that he and her aunt had gone to the cinema in Laran. Why had she herself gone out . . . and Mowbray . . . and Uncle Maurice with Aunt Belle? If she had only stayed with her father . . . if but one of them had stayed . . . !

Then Ann Hillier threw self-castigation to the winds, made up her mind, and decided on her course of action. She went out of the lounge, by way of the window, which was standing open, locked it behind her, and took the key with her. She didn't care if she were disturbing the conditions . . . the police would have to take her word for everything . . . she would be able to reconstruct it all for them when the time came. . . . Besides—there was Anthony Bathurst close at hand . . . he would understand what she told him and would help her again. Ann walked to the telephone in the hall and put a call through to Dr. Pakenham. Fortune was with her. The doctor was at home and eventually came to the telephone.

She told him quietly what had occurred and what she wanted him to do. He seemed agitated, she thought, when he answered her.

"You were lucky to catch me, Miss Hillier. As a matter of fact, I've been in all the evening, but was just thinking of going out for a run in the car. Such a glorious night—too good to miss by far—but this news of yours is terrible. I'll be right over to you at once. Leave all the police business to me when I come. Don't you worry about any of that. I'll see to that for you . . . if I find that it's necessary."

Thoughtfully, Ann replaced the receiver. Then she realized for the first time that she wasn't alone in the house. She should have remembered before. The cook and the two maids were in the servants' quarters. Should she call them and tell them what had happened or wait until after Dr. Pakenham had been? She stood in the hall considering the problem. Indecision was not long with her. She decided that she would take no action until after the Divisional Surgeon had made his visit. The last things that she wanted near her at that moment were raised voices and fainting women. Although she was a woman herself, she had no sympathy with the peculiar frailties of her sex. So she stood by the large mirror in the hall and attempted to prepare herself for the coming of Dr. Pakenham. She must collect herself, control herself, and bring herself to her best.

Again she remembered that she was the last of her own family of Hilliers. What is gentility for—if it cannot stand fire? She put her hand to her hair and at that moment despair seized her. That sense of desperate loneliness which she had felt before almost engulfed her . . . but with rare courage she forced it back and mentally censured herself for having so nearly given way to her weakness. She held up her head, she squared her shoulders. There were the sounds of the wheels of a car stopping outside the main gate. Ann waited by the door, to open it quietly. Pakenham came quickly up the gravel path and entered. He looked tired and worn. Holding her hand for a second, he murmured, "I'm so sorry. More terribly sorry than I can possibly put into words. But you must be brave, Miss Hillier! Take me to him . . . will you, please?"

Ann nodded, took a grip upon herself, and led the way to the lounge. She found the key and unlocked the door.

"I locked this door," she explained to Pakenham, "when I came out to 'phone you . . . it was open. I didn't want to risk the room being disturbed. Couldn't bear to think of it."

He nodded as though he understood, and they entered the lounge. Ann saw the doctor raise his eyebrows. "Behind the settee—eh? Of course you've touched nothing inside the room, Miss Hillier?"

"Nothing—unless you count the doors. I had to use them." Ann pointed. "That one, of the french doors, was open, and so was this door through which we have just come. The one I told you that I locked. It was seeing the one french door open that first made me feel suspicious. I had just put the car away in the garage and was coming round by the garden. I came across the grass and saw the door open. There was bright moonlight, you see."

Pakenham nodded and walked across to the body of Paul Hillier. "I shall have to move the settee a little," he said, "otherwise I shan't be able to—Stand away, Miss Hillier, please."

Ann retreated a few paces as Pakenham pulled the settee a short distance from the wall. He went down on one knee at the side of the body. "Quite simple," he remarked almost at once; "your father's been strangled."

"Strangled?" repeated Ann after him. The idea seemed absurd to her as she first considered it. More than absurd. Completely incredible! But Pakenham's following words jerked her back to the credulity of reality.

"Yes, Miss Hillier. There's no doubt about it. This is death by strangulation, right enough. The murderer used his bare hands. I'm certain of it."

Pakenham paused, his eyes searched hers for her response. For a brief moment, he feared that she was on the verge of collapse, but once again Ann, with a supreme effort, pulled herself together and faced up to her trouble. She nodded vaguely at Pakenham's words. "Is there anything I can do for you, Miss Hillier, before I—er—get in touch with the police? I'm afraid that I must do that almost immediately, you know."

She shook her head aimlessly. "I don't think so. I don't know."

"Sit down, Miss Hillier. Please. Here—this chair." He spoke sharply—with a purpose.

Ann took the chair he indicated. "Who else is here besides yourself? Shall I get Mowbray?"

"He's out; my uncle and aunt are out, too. They've gone into Laran. They wanted to see a picture."

"I see. That's not so good, is it? Would you rather not stay in here? Would you rather come into another room?"

"No. I think that I would rather stay here, if you don't mind. Some of the servants in the house are here. The cook, Caldwell, is in, and two of the maids."

"I think I'll leave them to the police. If I get them in here they can't do anything, can they? Now I'll go and 'phone. You sit here quietly and . . ."

"Perhaps, on second thoughts, I'll come with you . . . if I may."

"Of course. But I know where your 'phone is, if that's what you're thinking of."

They went together. Ann stood at Dr. Pakenham's side as he picked up the telephone. He thought matters over with his brows knitted. "I'll get straight through to Rockingham . . . that's the Inspector at Liskerry. He's in charge of the . . . er . . . other case. That will be better than getting Spiers, the Lanrebel sergeant. You stop here for a moment or so."

Ann waited while Pakenham was 'phoning. When would this ghastly drama come to an end? She heard Pakenham speaking. His words meant nothing to her. They were mere sounds of vocalized breath without identification. "Yes, yes," said the doctor, "I'm at 'Hillearys' now. I was called here a few minutes ago by Miss Hillier. Good! All right, I'll wait for you." Pakenham replaced the receiver thoughtfully. "Rockingham's coming straight over, Miss Hillier. He shouldn't be too long. I told him we'd be waiting here for him. Don't worry too much." He gave her rather a sharp glance. "Come into the dining-room, Miss Hillier. Come and tell me all you can about to-night's business. Rockingham's bound to ask questions, so it will help you to talk to me. Get you ready, as it were, for a good many of his queries."

Ann accepted the suggestion with gratefulness. She took Dr. Pakenham into the dining-room. He asked many questions of her. She answered them. Half an hour must have passed in this fashion when Ann's ears again caught the sound of a car. Pakenham heard it too, and went to the door. Inspector Rockingham, who entered, was a tall, heavily built man. His face was fleshy and his nose prominent. His manner was abrupt and he was a strict economist with words. Pakenham, with but little preliminary explanation, took him to the place where Paul Hillier lay. Pakenham was suave and polished. Rockingham looked grim and savage. This Hillier case was already playing the very devil with his nerves, and here was a third dead body on his hands. Mother, son, and now the father. Pretty kettle of fish, to be sure. Inspector Rockingham bent down and examined the body.

"Strangled you say, Doctor?"

"Strangled. By a person with a most powerful grip."

"How long ago?"

"Say two to three hours. No more. Put it at the early part of the evening and you won't be far out."

Rockingham asked questions of Ann.

"I went out about half past eight. I got back before ten."

More questions to her.

"I went into Frayne by way of Bonallack. I called on Colonel Barrett by invitation. Daphne Barrett is a great friend of mine. The real reason I went over was that I've been helping her with her latest book."

Rockingham nodded repeatedly at her answers. Again more questions—questions that concerned the various other members of the household at "Hillearys". Ann answered them in the exact terms of her story to Dr. Pakenham.

"I see," said the Inspector, "so that's how it was. I suppose, as far as you know, Miss Hillier, that your father wasn't expecting anybody this evening?" He eyed her keenly as he waited for her reply.

Ann shook her head. "As far as I know, Inspector, my father expected to be alone this evening. If anybody were coming to see him, and he knew about it, he hadn't said a word of it to me."

Rockingham made certain notes before returning to the body of Paul Hillier. As Pakenham had done a short time previously, he knelt down on the carpet by the settee. Suddenly he gave a sharp exclamation. "Why, Doctor—what about this—eh?"

Pakenham turned with a look of alarmed surprise and went straight over to him. Ann held her breath . . . fearful of this new development . . . whatever it might be. Rockingham held something up to the doctor, who took it from him. Ann stared at it fascinated. It was a revolver.

"Tells a story, doesn't it?" remarked the Inspector drily.

Pakenham looked at Ann Hillier with an unspoken query in his eyes. She shook her head at him in a sort of hopeless resignation.

Rockingham was in again. "Is this your father's revolver, Miss Hillier?"

"I couldn't say, Inspector."

"Do you mean by that that you don't know?"

"Yes. That's exactly what I do mean. I don't know. I've never seen it before."

"Were you aware that he had a revolver?"

Ann paused before replying. "Again—I am not sure. Please don't misunderstand me, though. I believe that I've heard him say on occasion that he had a revolver somewhere—but where he actually kept it—I didn't know. I don't know, and therefore I don't know whether that one was his." Ann's words were lifeless, and from her eyes had gone every emotion except grief. In the meantime, Pakenham had handed the revolver back to Inspector Rockingham.

"As I said," declared the latter, "this little fellow tells us a great deal more than we previously knew. Fully loaded but not a shot fired. Didn't have a chance to use it, probably. Mr. Hillier expected somebody this evening and prepared himself accordingly. Not a doubt of it. Not an ordinary guest, either. You don't receive ordinary everyday guests with revolvers in your pockets—at least, it isn't usual."

Pakenham stared hard at Rockingham, who, in turn, was gazing intently at the body. "By the way, Miss Hillier," said Rockingham, "I see that your father's wearing a dinner-jacket. Was that—er—his habit of an evening?"

Ann shook her head. "No."

"Well . . . how is it that he's dressed like that—for this evening? It's hot, for one thing, and according to you, you dined alone. I mean you had no visitors . . . well, you see what I mean, don't you?"

At that precise moment, and, it must be admitted, quite unreasonably, Ann hated him.

"You asked me if it were my father's habit to dress for dinner, and I answered you truthfully. It wasn't. That isn't to say, though, he didn't dress upon occasion."

"Agreed," returned Rockingham heavily, "but surely you have just admitted that this evening wasn't an occasion?"

"Depends what you mean by the term 'occasion'." Ann's mouth grew hard and almost ugly. What blind fools most men were! They saw only the things that they wanted to see.

"Well"—Rockingham entered again, with little regard to the proverbial reluctance of angels—"you said yourself that nobody was here and also that nobody was expected—granted those conditions, then, how could it have been an occasion?"

"Inspector Rockingham," said Ann with thin-lipped sarcasm, "it's obvious that there are many matters you don't understand. But since you must interfere with what is purely private and intimate, I will tell you why I think my father dressed for dinner this evening. It happens to be the anniversary of my mother's birthday. He said nothing to me—seeing what has recently happened, that is quite understandable in the circumstances . . . and I asked no question of him. *You* doubtless would have done—but I *think* that was the reason. Amazing though it may seem, my father loved my mother. She died a little while ago, if you remember, and you, with your brilliant assistants, are still looking for her murderer." Ann stood there, white-faced and trembling. Directly she had spoken, she was sorry for what she had said. But if she imagined she had rattled Rockingham, she was mistaken. Utterly devoid of emotion, and with a hide like that of the elephant, he could take all that in daily doses and come up smiling for more.

"Sit down," he said curtly.

Ann choked back a sob and sat down. "Control yourself," he said sternly. "What good will you do by losing your temper and lashing out at me? Answer me that! I'm very sorry for you, Miss Hillier. Make no mistake about that. But try to help me and I'll try to help you."

Ann made no reply. Rockingham motioned to Pakenham. Ann failed to observe the motion. She was staring straight ahead of her. Pakenham crossed over to her and stood by her chair. "Don't upset yourself . . . any more," he said gently. "As the Inspector says, it won't do any good. Either to you or him. He has his duty to do, and he must—"

The bell rang. The bell at the front door. Voices were audible. Ann raised her head and listened.

"That's my uncle and aunt."

Pakenham raised his eyebrows as though about to ask a question. Ann shook her head. "Don't worry. One of the maids will go. That's why they've rung the bell."

Pakenham was fussy. "I'll have a word with Mrs. Belle before she comes in here. No need to make the shock a worse one. Just a moment." He bustled out of the room.

Ann watched him go. Rockingham watched Ann.

CHAPTER XXI
BELLE HILLIER SPEAKS HER MIND

As BELLE Hillier stood outside "Hillearys" on the night of Paul Hillier's murder, waiting to be admitted, she vented a certain amount of bad temper on her husband. She had done so, let it be said, ever since she and Maurice, her husband, had left the cinema at Laran.

Belle, in ordinary circumstances, was far from being a shrew, but she was no mean elocutionist, and possessed stamina to an amazing degree. And when she let Maurice "have it", the resonance of her vowel tone was fully equal to the maxillary precision of her consonantal attack. On this particular occasion, however, it must be conceded, in all fairness, that Maurice Hillier richly deserved most of what was coming his way. As his wife rang the bell which had interrupted Dr. Pakenham's reply to Ann, Maurice Hillier was endeavouring to remonstrate with her. "But my dear girl," he said, "after all—what harm did I do? Try to be reasonable. You saw the picture that you were so desirous of seeing. And it wasn't as though you didn't know where I'd gone. You knew perfectly well where I was. There was no need to worry about me. No need at all. And I came and picked you up when you came out. Exactly as I had promised you I would. Good God, Belle—have a heart!"

Belle continued to rage at him. "I call it downright discourteous and most disgustingly rude. Still—I'm only your wife—so it can't matter very much. Men can treat their wives as badly as they like— nobody cares." She flounced away from him. Maurice Hillier heard steps approaching. Steps that were very near to the door. "Pipe down a bit. Steady on, Belle. One of the maids is coming. She'll hear you if you raise your voice like that."

"Good job if she does, I don't care. It's time people knew how I'm treated by you. I'm sick of it."

Maurice Hillier quailed at the thrust. He had come to hate these scenes, which were now coming more frequently, and recoiled from even the thought of them. The door opened. "Thank you, Middleton," he said to the maid who admitted them. At that moment he noticed Pakenham standing close by. The surprise which he felt must have been visible in his eyes, but before he could say anything the doctor drew him and his wife to one side. Pakenham waited for Middleton to vanish again before he spoke.

"Oh . . . Mrs. Hillier . . . and you too, Hillier . . . I'd like a word with you quietly if you could spare a second."

Belle sensed something amiss, and flashed asperity at him. Here, before her, was another man, and therefore fair game. "Oh . . . cut the mystery. What is it?"

Pakenham gestured towards the dining-room. "Suppose we come in here for a moment." He ushered them into the room. As they passed him Maurice Hillier looked back at him anxiously and Belle indignantly. The doctor closed the door quietly behind them.

"What's the trouble?" half whispered Maurice as he stood irreso- lutely within the room.

Pakenham saw that Belle Hillier's lip was curling. He was surprised how much the fact annoyed him at a moment like this.

"I've bad news," he said. "It's your brother."

"What?" demanded Maurice. "What about my brother?"

"He's dead," returned Pakenham in a low voice . . . "we felt that you should know before you went into the other room."

The sneer had left the lips of Belle Hillier. Whitefaced, she caught Pakenham impulsively by the arm. "Paul dead? Is that all? Tell me—how did he die?" Maurice's face was trembling as he listened.

Pakenham went on with his story. "He has died a violent death. We fear that he has been strangled. Inspector Rockingham is in there now with your niece. She came home here and found her father dead."

Belle tottered towards a chair and sank on to it. Maurice Hillier was by now shaking all over. He found a handkerchief from his sleeve and nervously wiped his brow with it. "Strangled! I don't under-stand. Paul strangled! This is terrible! I can't think that—" He seized Pakenham suddenly by the wrist. The doctor noticed the strength of his grip. For a thin spare man it was abnormal. "Tell me, Pakenham, what does all this mean? Jacqueline, Neill, and now Paul? Who of us is next? That's what's beginning to worry me. Tell me, damn you—it's getting on my nerves—which one of us will be murdered next?" He dropped the doctor's wrist and stood there mouthing at him. Pakenham realized that Maurice Hillier was close to the edge of things.

"Pull yourself together, man. And stop thinking of your own skin. Look at your wife there. She's pretty well all in by the look of her."

Maurice Hillier shivered and turned towards his wife.

"Give her some brandy," said Pakenham curtly. "Or rather—if you'll tell me where it is, I'll get some myself."

Maurice gestured towards a sideboard. "You'll find some in there."

Pakenham stood and busied himself with a tantalus. He held brandy to Belle Hillier. She took the glass with shaking fingers.

"Give me a drop as well," muttered Maurice. He held out his hand.

"Where's Ann?" demanded Belle.

"With the Inspector."

"Poor kid!" Belle Hillier shook her head in an attempt at sympathy. Her husband gulped his brandy. He handed the glass back to the doctor. Pakenham indeed at that moment might have been Mowbray the perfect butler. In reality, Maurice's mind was incapable of recognizing the difference. "Strangled!" he muttered again. "Paul, my brother! . . . strangled! By the killer. First poison, then a lad's brains battered out . . . and now a strangling! It's ghastly, Pakenham, all of it! I tell you—I can't stand it! It is getting me down. I can't face it, I tell you. My nerves are all to pieces. Give me some more brandy."

Belle turned on him scathingly. "Be quiet, Maurice. And try to look something like a man. Think of Ann—poor kid—and what she's had to put up with. My God—it's a thin time for her these days!" As she spoke there came the sound of a raised voice. The voice was Rockingham's. He was calling from the other room to Dr. Pakenham. Belle Hillier looked more scared than before.

"The Inspector wants me in the other room. You must excuse me for a moment. You'll be all right in here, won't you?" Pakenham addressed the question to the lady, although he felt in his mind that, if anything, Maurice Hillier in his present condition needed his attendance more than she did. Belle expressed her willingness to be left, and Maurice, with shaking hands, went to the tantalus and sampled more brandy. Pakenham made his way to the Inspector and Ann Hillier.

"What's the trouble?" he asked when he reached the room.

Rockingham had the look of a man who was wrestling with Fate and beginning to realize at long last that his adversary was too formidable for him. "D'ye know, Doctor," he declared with aggression, "that there isn't a print in the whole of this damned room? Not the smell of one. I've been all over it . . . I've been hoping all the time that I should be able to pick something up, but the fairies won't smile on me."

The doctor frowned. "Is that all you wanted me for?"

"No. I'd like a word with one or two of the domestic staff, and I've a notion that I'd like you to be present while I'm having that word. You and Miss Hillier. You won't mind, will you, Doctor?"

"Not a bit. Go ahead."

Rockingham gestured to him. "I think I'll have a word with the cook first of all. She's the senior of the kitchen squad, I understood you to say. Will you see to that for me, Miss Hillier?"

Ann nodded. "Very well, Inspector."

Kate Caldwell might well be described as "fair, fat, and forty". Truthfully she was each one of these. The first rather effectively, the second undoubtedly, and the third exactly. Rockingham arranged the furniture of the room so that no shock came to Caldwell down the avenue of the sense of sight. The cook, entirely scared, looked to the Inspector as though she were the helpless victim of his fascination.

Ann took it upon herself to explain certain matters. Rockingham listened and approved. When he judged the time to be opportune, he took up the parable from Ann Hillier and addressed himself to Mrs. Caldwell.

"Mr. Hillier's had a rather severe accident this evening, and so far we're at a loss to make out what actually has happened. That's why I want to have just a few minutes' conversation with you, Mrs. Caldwell. Sit down, will you? Just there. That's right now."

The cook took the seat which Rockingham had indicated for her. "You've been in all the evening, I take it?"

"Yes, sir. All the evening. Been in the kitchen all the time. I haven't budged. Ada and Esther can vouch for that."

"The reference is to Ada Middleton and Esther Gamlin. Two of the maids." This amplification from Ann.

"I see," declared Rockingham. "So you've been in the kitchen ever since dinner?"

"Yes, sir, every minute."

"Have you heard anything suspicious? Any unusual noise, for instance?"

Caldwell shook her comely head. "No, sir. Nothing at all, sir. And certainly no noises. As far as we of the kitchen staff know, everything's been as quiet as the grave, sir."

"You heard nothing from Mr. Hillier—at any time during the evening?"

"No, sir. Not a word."

"And you heard nothing *of* Mr. Hillier?"

"No, sir. After dinner was finished and done with—there was the washing-up to be seen to. That took about half an hour, I should think. That's about the usual time. After that, we listened to the wireless— Esther's got a portable set—it was given to her on her birthday—and the master used to allow us to have it on when we liked. Well, what with washing-up and the wireless and chatting amongst ourselves afterwards—the evening passed pretty quickly, and we never heard no sound from any of these rooms. I know *I* didn't, and I'm positive that both Ada and Esther would tell you just the same if you asked them." Caldwell finished up in a state of recklessness after this somewhat lengthy effort. Rockingham nodded.

"Have the three of you been together all the time?"

"Oh yes, sir. The maids had done their work. They were quite free, as you might say, to please themselves. Which they did, and they stayed along of me. I can't recall that either of them went out at all—not for a single minute. Since you asked me, I've been thinking it all over again very carefully, and that's how it seems to me."

The Inspector thanked her for the information which she had given. "Ask Ada Middleton to come up, will you, Miss Hillier, please?"

Caldwell the cook, overjoyed that the interview was finished, rose to go, but Rockingham's hand restrained her. When Ann came back with Middleton in tow Rockingham released the cook, who, understanding the significance of the handwork, flounced from the room with a show of indignation. She had nothing to hide, and, what's more, this policeman ought to know it. The Inspector's questions to the maid were on the same lines as he had used with her colleague. But he achieved no more success with Middleton than he had with Caldwell, her predecessor.

The kitchen staff had done their work, had listened to various broadcasts from Esther's portable wireless, had talked amongst themselves, had had no call of any kind from Paul Hillier, had heard no sound that might be regarded as strange, and generally could offer no information likely to be of the slightest help to Inspector Rockingham. Finally Rockingham dismissed Ada to her kitchen again and informed Miss Hillier that he thought little purpose would be served by his interviewing the remaining member of the trio, Esther Gamlin. "She's bound to tell me exactly the same as the other two," he remarked.

"Nothing there, Doctor," he continued to Pakenham behind Middleton's retreating figure. "Nothing there for a copper to pin his teeth into. Not the shadow of a clue anywhere. Entertaining prospect, I must say. Three murders all in one family in the space of about three weeks and Bill Rockingham in the dirt looking for the murderer. A dog's life and no mistake. Anybody can have it for me. The sooner my retirement rolls on the better. Where's Miss Ann, Doctor?"

Pakenham turned round in evident surprise. "I think she's with her uncle and aunt, Mr. and Mrs. Maurice Hillier. She mentioned something about going in to them just as you were finishing up with that Middleton girl."

Rockingham appeared to be thinking things over. He put a further question to Pakenham. "These other Hilliers. This uncle and aunt you just mentioned. They've been out all the evening, haven't they?"

"I believe so. Into Laran. I understand that they've been to a 'flick'. But you can ask them yourself, if you want to. They're in the next room."

"I will. In a moment or so. I must make arrangements with my people with regard to that." He indicated the dead body of Paul Hillier lying there behind the settee. "I must use the telephone for a few minutes. You might inform Miss Hillier what I'm doing, will you, Doctor?"

Pakenham expressed his willingness to do this, and Rockingham went out to the telephone in the hall. Pakenham waited for him to return. His messages given, Rockingham requested the doctor to accompany him to the room where the three Hilliers waited. Pakenham introduced the Inspector. He noticed that Ann had become unnaturally silent. Belle Hillier was talking to her husband, who, however, was saying but little in return. Rockingham added to the explanation which Pakenham had already given.

"I'm afraid that we can tell you nothing, Inspector," said Belle. "Paul was all right when we went out . . . considering all that he's recently gone through, that is . . . and he told us that he didn't mind us going out at all. If he had minded, of course, we shouldn't have dreamt of going. That's perfectly true, isn't it, Maurice?"

Maurice gave unhesitating support. "Absolutely, Inspector. But, as I've told the doctor here, this business is playing merry hell with my nerves. It's a vendetta of some kind against the family, and you fellows simply must do something about it. Wholesale murder—there's no other word for it. We might be in America. Ann—you must tell the Inspector that you agree with me."

Ann shook her head. "I prefer to say nothing at all. If I'm to be murdered, I shall probably be murdered, and as things are I don't know that I'm terribly concerned."

Maurice threw up his hands in horror and resignation.

"Well—if you're not—I am. Another thing, I have my wife to think of."

Ann smiled. The smile was eloquent. Rockingham was unemotional. "Before I can help you, Mr. Hillier, you may be able to help me."

"I'll do my best, I'm sure."

"You had dinner with your brother before you went out this evening?"

"I did. I always do when I'm staying here. Why? What's the point in that?"

"Would you say that your brother was normal during the time you spent with him?"

Maurice hesitated. "Yes . . . if I may use the phrase that my wife used a little while ago—'considering all that he's recently been through'."

"He wasn't expecting anybody to visit him?"

"If he were, he had said nothing to me about it." Rockingham came back to the point he had raised originally with him. He rubbed his chin as he spoke. "I would point out that your brother was not only wearing a dinner-jacket, but also that he was carrying a revolver in one of his pockets. Does that latter statement surprise you, Mr. Hillier?"

Maurice started at the news. "It does . . . most certainly. I never knew Paul to do such a thing in all the years we've been together. Was the gun loaded?"

"It was, Mr. Hillier. Loaded in every chamber." Maurice came to the matter that was worrying him.

"Then . . . had the weapon been used . . . may I ask?"

"It had not," retorted Rockingham grimly.

"That's f-funny . . . isn't it?"

"Why—may I ask, Mr. Hillier?"

"Well, if a fellow puts a revolver in his pocket as a means of protection against somebody of whom he's afraid . . . or against some form of attack . . . that he's expecting . . . well, you'd think that he'd use it when the time came, wouldn't you? Especially as we know now that he was set upon by somebody. Seems to me all that makes cold sense . . . don't know what you think about it, Inspector."

The Inspector shook his head.

"That doesn't cut much ice—what you say. Suppose your brother was taken by surprise and didn't have time to use his revolver? What have you got to say about it then?"

Maurice Hillier shrugged his shoulders. "But surely—"

Rockingham cut in. "But surely what, Mr. Hillier?"

"I was going to say, surely Paul wasn't taken by surprise? Good Lord, man—look at it for yourself! If he *had* been surprised he wouldn't have had the revolver *in* his pocket, to begin with. The fact that he did provide himself with that revolver proves conclusively—to me at any rate—that he was definitely on his guard. This makes it plain that the man who murdered him couldn't have used the element of surprise. Otherwise the weapon would have been used."

"I'll go with you part of the way, Mr. Hillier—but not all the way. Let me put it to you like this. Supposing, for argument's sake, your brother was expecting a visitor. Somebody who was coming to see him after you and your good lady had gone out for the latter part of the evening. Well—then—what happens when that visitor arrives? Let me try my hand at a reconstruction of the crime. You don't mind, do you, Mr. Hillier?"

Maurice protested fiercely that by this time he was past minding and more or less prepared for anything.

"Oh, very well, then—have it your own way if you wish it. Go on."

Rockingham assented with grim readiness. "I was going to suggest that your brother, Mr. Hillier, expected a visitor this evening. Very probably the appointment was made with him by letter or even by telephone. We will have a look into those possibilities later on. This visitor your brother expected caused him apprehension. Even more than that perhaps. Fear! He took care to provide himself with a revolver in case it should be wanted. You said yourself just now that you had never known him carry one. The visitor arrived . . . the interview took place . . . unpleasantness developed . . . the quarrel . . . the anticipated quarrel . . . happened . . . but *before* your brother could use his revolver . . . he was set upon and strangled. His antagonist, I should say, was a much more powerful man that he himself was. That's the reason why the revolver is still fully loaded. Well, Mr. Hillier, what comments have you to make on that? Sounds pretty good to me."

Dr. Pakenham waited intently for Maurice Hillier's reply. It came. "I don't agree with you, Inspector. And I'll tell you why. If my wife and I hadn't decided to go into Laran to see a flick, we should have been in the house with my brother and his sinister guest. Paul knew nothing about our plans until we announced them during dinner. He couldn't possibly have done . . . because we weren't sure of them ourselves until just before we mentioned them. Where, then, does your idea of the previously arranged interview come in? Is it likely that it would have taken place if my wife and I had been here in the house?"

Maurice Hillier had made a good point, and the Inspector knew it.

Rockingham thought things over. "Tell me this, then—will you, Mr. Hillier? What was the exact time, or as near as you can remember it, when you told your brother you were going to the pictures?"

Maurice turned to his wife. "Could you answer that, Belle? You suggested it—if my memory serves me correctly."

Belle looked as though the milk of human kindness had turned sour within her. "Does it matter?"

"Well, you heard the Inspector here ask the question. There's no need to be stuffy about it." He gestured helplessly towards Rockingham.

The latter addressed himself to Belle. "I'm sure you will help me if you can, Mrs. Hillier." Rockingham made himself as gallant as he knew how.

"Certainly, Inspector. You should have asked me the question first. The time you're asking about—as nearly as possible—would be five minutes past seven. It was just after dinner started. I wanted to go to Laran, and naturally my husband agreed to take me."

Rockingham smiled. "Of course—that's what husbands are for."

"That—and other things," muttered Maurice ungraciously.

Belle frowned at him.

"H'm," said Rockingham, "just after seven o'clock. That would have just about given him plenty of time."

"Time for what?" inquired Pakenham, making his first contribution.

Ann bent forward to catch Rockingham's reply.

"Several things," returned Rockingham non-committally. "Amongst them he could have telephoned somebody."

There was a silence. "You can easily check up on that," said the doctor.

"You're tellin' me," answered Rockingham. "It's an idea of mine, and an attractive idea at that."

Belle laughed and looked significantly at her husband.

Ann Hillier was quick to intercept the look and wondered what it meant. But as she glanced round the circle she felt that Rockingham himself had missed it.

"You can't help me any more than that, I suppose, can you, Mrs. Hillier?"

"In what way, Inspector?"

"You didn't notice anything unusual about your brother-in-law—during dinner this evening or at any time recently?"

"I did not. I can't help you in that direction. I thought that I made that clear to you some little time ago."

"Ah well—that's a pity. Information from you might have been of great assistance to me. But if you can't—you can't—and that's all there is to it."

Rockingham made it evident that the interview, such as it was, might be regarded as over. The footsteps of maids, and after them other voices, could be heard outside. There was more police work to be done that evening in the house named "Hillearys".

Belle went across to Ann and put her arm round her shoulders. "Come, Ann dear. Come with me."

Maurice Hillier took a cigarette from his case and lit it with an unsteady hand. Dr. Pakenham went with Rockingham into that other room where the body of Paul Hillier still lay behind the settee. Rockingham at once commenced the work which he had still to do. Other men began to help him. The dead need attention.

CHAPTER XXII
THE DIARY OF JACQUELINE HILLIER

ON THE second day after the killing of Paul Hillier, Anthony Lotherington Bathurst sat in a field close to the spot where Neill Hillier's body had been found and read a letter. This letter had come to him from Keith Annesley. The postmark was Blackstock. The latter had caught the train which he had wanted on the morning of his departure from Lanrebel and was once again, as he himself put it, "back in harness" at his little place in Essex. As the letter made no reference to the third death in the Hillier family, Anthony presumed that the news of this had not yet reached Annesley in his country village. A glance at the date of the letter confirmed his impression.

Annesley wrote in glowing terms of the associations he had made in Lanrebel during his comparatively short stay there, hoped to see Anthony again "somewhere, somehow, and somewhen", and concluded a racy letter by saying that he would never forget his holiday at the "Salvation" and the kindness of "Uncle" Arthur Paske. He also requested that Mr. Bathurst, if he had time, would write him as soon as convenient and keep him more or less posted with the latest details of the Hillier problems.

Anthony, when he had read it, smiled to himself and put the letter back into his pocket. He liked Annesley as a companion and was glad that he had met him. He was good-tempered, an agreeable conversationalist, and intelligent. Also, for a novelist, surprisingly modest and by no means too full or too sure of himself. Anthony lay there in the sun on that wholly delightful June morning and once again pondered on the major issues of the Hillier case. The times he had gone over them in his mind!

Jacqueline Hillier poisoned in her car, Neill Hillier, her only son, struck down on the King's highway, and now Paul Hillier, her husband, strangled on a summer evening in his own apartment. Anthony's mind caught a shred of memory and toyed with the words of a former Anthony. "'Twas on a summer evening in his tent—that day he overcame the Nervii . . ." He thought of Caesar in his new mantle, of the daggers of the conspirators—of the rent the envious Casca made . . . of the forensic triumph of Marcus Antonius "and the end of the noblest Roman of them all". Strange how thoughts riot and run away with one.

Anthony turned over to ease himself into a more comfortable position, when, to his everlasting surprise, he heard a voice behind him. The voice was charming, and spoke his name. Anthony realized that the voice must come from the other side of the stone wall that bordered the field from the road. "May I come in there, Mr. Bath-urst?" said the voice.

Anthony scrambled to his feet, pushed back unruly hair from his forehead, and walked to the spot from which the voice appeared to be coming. He saw Ann Hillier standing there. "Now why did you do that? I didn't want you to move," she said, "you looked much too comfortable. Now I feel a beast to have disturbed you. But may I come in and talk to you?"

He smiled at her apology. "By all means, Miss Hillier. It's a beauti-ful field—the grass is delightful—and the sun is grand. Come in and share the pleasures with me."

Anthony walked round to the gate and held it open so that Ann might enter. "Come with me, Miss Hillier, you want the best field places—I have them."

She smiled at him, but there was no merriment in the smile. Ann sat on the grass at his side. "I wanted to see you specially," she said, "very specially. Now that my father's commission is a thing of the past I want you to think that *I* need you. Anyhow, you remember asking me questions about my mother, that day in the car when I called to see you? It's about her that I wanted to talk to you."

Mr. Bathurst found himself wondering what was coming next. No mention to him of her father's death or even of her brother's. Just her mother again. She had gone straight back to the first tragedy. Not by stages, not by an ordinary transition of thought, but with deliberate instancy.

"Tell me what you want," he answered her. He was surprised to find that he felt himself almost defensive.

"I have found something of my mother's," went on Ann with simple candour, "and because I think you will find it interesting I have brought it to you." Her face was half turned towards him. Anthony noticed that she was clasping something in her hand. "In my mother's bedroom there is a cabinet with a locked drawer. The police looked at it when they came investigating and it was opened. I was able to find the key for them. At the back of the drawer was this." She handed Anthony Bathurst a diary. A smallish pocket diary bound in a dark-green cover. "The police did not regard it as import-ant. I can, I think, understand that. It is, as you will see, her diary for last year. That means, of course, that the last entry in it is about six months old."

Anthony nodded. He appreciated the point she had made and again wondered at the worth of her discovery and why she had so deliberately brought it to him. "When I found it," went on Ann, "I hated reading it . . . it was like reading something so private as to be sacred . . . but I read it with an intention in my heart. You know well what I mean. I had in my mind what you had said to me. Try as I would, I couldn't rid myself of it. About Jacky's life 'being dedicated to a purpose'. I am using your words, you see. Well, Mr. Bathurst, what I have read in there"—she indicated the diary she had handed to him—"makes me think that your idea may be right. In fact, I almost feel sure it *is* right."

Anthony regarded her intently. "Yes. But let's get this straight. It wasn't my idea. In the first place, that is. It was suggested to me, and I handed on the suggestion to you. I wanted your opinion on it. I think that you ought to know that before we go any farther. You see—I don't want you to be under any misapprehensions. You knew your mother so well. I never knew her."

Ann opened her eyes. "Somebody else suggested it to you?"

Anthony nodded.

"Anybody I know?"

"Yes, you know the person well. At least, I should say that you do."

"Will you tell me if I ask you who it was?"

"Certainly. I can see no reason why it should be kept a secret. It was your doctor. Dr. Pakenham. From what I was able to gather, he has had unique opportunities of judging the members of your family. A doctor is often in that position."

"My family," she spoke sadly, "of whom I am the only one left. So it was Dr. Pakenham, was it? I should never have suspected it. He would have been almost the last person. If you had given me as many as six guesses I don't think that I should have picked on him." Anthony opened the diary of Jacqueline Hillier. Ann began to speak again. It seemed that she was endeavouring to direct him. "Just a moment, Mr. Bathurst. Before you look at that. Listen. She hasn't kept it like an ordinary diary. If you look at it right at the beginning you'll see what I mean. Take the first few days in January of last year for example. Look at them. She doesn't describe events as they are taking place. It's not a diary that records current events and happenings. It's been kept more like a remembrance book. I've not met the idea before. Are you following me, Mr. Bathurst?"

Anthony was quietly examining the first pages of the diary. He nodded again as Ann's eagerness touched him. "Yes, Miss Hillier—I can see what you mean. I think you're right and that your description—a remembrance book—is a happy one."

"Read some of it," prompted Ann.

Anthony needed no further bidding. "And remember that was written last year," urged Ann. "Only about eighteen months ago. Read it out to me, will you, please? I've read it, of course, but I'd like to hear you read it aloud to me. I don't think it will sound very different, but I must feel sure about it. One's ear will often give a different impression of words from one's eye."

Anthony read the opening remarks of Jacqueline's year-old diary.

"Time moves on. I begin with a cliché. Within a few months I shall add yet another unit to the tale of my age. Awful! That means I shall soon be what is politely called 'passée'. Another way of saying 'almost a hag'. But I have never forgotten and I shall never forget. Because of that, I always remember to keep to my heart's intention. To adhere to my self-appointed discipline. Not only do I feel young—but to my own supreme joy my mirror tells me that I also *look* young. It's pretty wonderful—but it's true. Constantly is it said to me, 'It's incredible that you are as old as that,' or even 'My dear Jacqueline, nobody who didn't know would ever *dream* that you were Ann's mother. You look so utterly and so absurdly juvenile.' If the people who say these things to me only knew the joy that comes in my heart when I hear them they would go on saying them to me for ever. The dear people! My heart's intention! Also—my heart's delight! I am striving to keep young for you, my darling of the dear days long ago. This is the least I can do for you, you to whom I owe so much. I wonder— shall I ever hear you say again—'my Jacqueline'. Somehow I don't think I ever shall."

Anthony paused. He looked across at the girl who now sat on the grass in front of him. "This is most significant, Miss Hillier. Here we have a very definite inclination towards the condition which I myself discussed with you. Dr. Pakenham was undoubtedly right. Here, surely, is the romantic attachment which I attempted to visualize. You remember, don't you?"

Ann nodded impatiently.

"I know—but I still don't understand. It's nothing that I know about. But read some more, Mr. Bathurst. I want to hear you. Go to—I think it's April 18th. Something about 'an unlucky day'. I remember it made a great impression on me. Find it and read it out to me, will you?"

Anthony turned to the page containing the 18th of April. He began to read again.

"I wonder where you are to-day, my angel. And whether you are thinking of to-day in the same terms as I am. How many years is it since Mavis followed me . . . and our hearts were so torn? And then the year after, with Oakley—remember? And here am I now, with Paul, and Neill and Ann, my dear children, still thinking of you, still loving you and really living for you, and yet without the slightest idea as to where you are or even whether you are still alive. I have paid the bill and yet I go on paying it . . . until I pay it twenty-twofold. But that is what I deserve, and in a way I welcome the punishment. Funny Jacky? Listen, darling—I can still crinkle my nose. And I can still crow—gurgle. S'true as s'true can be. Good-night, my own dear sweetheart. I love you! *Toujours!*"

Again Anthony paused and nodded. "Yes, Miss Hillier. It all rings true."

She nodded as he had done.

"Now look at the entry under the date of July 8th Read it to me as you have the others."

Anthony obeyed her again.

"July the 8th. To-day is your birthday—my heart has been singing to you all day. Have you heard it, I wonder? I have tried to make it reach you wherever you are. I will tell you what I have done to-day. You want to know, don't you? I have done this on every one of your birthdays since the dear days died. I have kept my eyes on the calendar—all day. The calendar on my wall with a big July and a perfectly enormous 8 underneath it. I have tried to think that there is a little photograph of you between the month and the date. There is, lover-boy, but only in my imagination. You used to tell me that imagination was always one of my strongest points. Now listen to this! At 12.22 this morning I turned on my radio quite by chance! I hadn't the slightest idea what was coming. And what do you think *did* come? A string orchestra was playing 'The Spring Song'. Honest Injun—angel! I believe you *knew*! You may even have told them to. Or aren't you as clever as I think you are? Of course you're not! You couldn't be. It wouldn't be possible for any human being. Goodnight, darling. Remember the pride of High Helvellyn?

> 'Nature, once in mood capricious,
> Sets herself a task delicious.
> How she might achieve perfection'!"

Ann stared ahead of her. Anthony shook his head in grave consideration of the words he had been reading.

"Well?" inquired Ann, with a little touch of defiance. "What are you thinking now?"

"Frankly, Miss Hillier, I'm not sure—I'm puzzled."

Ann wrinkled her brows. "I am too—but I don't know that I follow you. Tell me exactly."

"I'm not surprised to hear you say that you are puzzled. But my contention is this. We seem to have established the fact that there had been a romance in your mother's life some years ago—a tremendous one at that—and also I feel bound to point out that you, who have been so close to her for so many years now, had no knowledge of it. More than that even—because knowledge is an exact thing—you had no hint or inkling of it. You admit that?"

Ann nodded vigorously. "Yes—certainly."

"Proceeding from there, then—it gives us no reason why your mother should have been murdered—does it? In other words, we are finding love, affection, wonderful comradeship, and sympathetic understanding—not hate or enmity."

"Couldn't the hate, and with the hate the desire for revenge, have come from something else? Have you considered that as a probability?"

"From a third party, you mean?"

"Yes. One of the oldest of all old stories. It's feasible, Mr. Bathurst, isn't it?"

Anthony pulled doubtfully at his upper lip. "I'm going to speak frankly, Miss Hillier. You must promise me your forgiveness in advance if I hurt your feelings. But are you referring now by any chance to your father?"

Anthony was amazed at the sudden transformation that came over the girl. A sudden flame burned in her eyes.

"No," she said fiercely, "no—no—certainly not! My father was a gentleman." Her hands were clenched tight. The knuckles showed white on each of them.

"Miss Hillier," he urged—"forget the personal side of it. You must! I know that I'm asking you something that's frightfully difficult—but try to, please. It's imperative that you should. Think of the people whom we're discussing not as flesh and blood but as mere numbers—symbols only, if you'd like that description better. Who else is there to fit the equation you've just produced—except your father?"

Ann remained the spitfire. "I can't answer—I don't know—but that isn't to say there isn't anybody—or couldn't be anybody."

Anthony considered the terms of her reply. "No—I suppose that's a perfectly fair answer." There was still a dangerous glint in Ann's eye which, frankly, Anthony wasn't altogether able to understand. He tacked, however. "I'm going back into the past, Miss Hillier. Back into family history—and I'm going to ask you to come with me. Yes?"

She nodded her acquiescence but said no word.

"Where did your mother live before she married your father?"

"At Trinket, in Berkshire."

The name of the place surprised him.

"At Trinket? Nothing to do with the school, I suppose?"

She smiled—it was a pale, weary smile. "No—Jacky hadn't. But my father had. He was a master there. But why do you ask—do you know the school particularly well?"

"I had a nephew there. But that's nothing. So your father was a master at Trinket, was he?"

"Yes. For five years. He was the languages master. Modern languages, French and German."

"And he met your mother while he was there, I suppose?"

"Yes. At a dance I believe. On the eve of one of the annual matches with Brooch. Jacky did tell me. Sometimes she used to talk to me a lot about the time when she was a girl."

"How old was your father . . . when he died?"

"He would have been fifty-five in November—Armistice Day."

"How long had they been married?"

"Nearly twenty-two years. I am twenty, and Neill was a year younger. Jacky was only about eighteen when she married my father. He would have been between thirty-two and thirty-three. He left Trinket—you see—soon after the marriage. Before I was born."

"Why was that, Miss Hillier?"

"He got fed up with the life . . . so I've always understood and been told . . . and started a private school on his own, you know—preparatory. He really wasn't the kind of man who gave his best working for other people. That was at Dance, near Hove. I was born at Dance. So was Neill. It's a lovely little spot. We lived there for five years . . . until we came to Lanrebel, in fact."

"That was a big change for you, wasn't it?"

Anthony was thinking hard and with intense concentration. Ann nodded her head briskly. "Oh, I should say so. Though of course Neill and I were at school for some years. He was at Repton—father preferred him not to go to Trinket, which was natural in a way, I suppose, seeing he'd been on the staff there, and I was sent to Hartdene. You see, my father came into a lot of money . . . he went to America with Mother for a year while we were at school . . . he had always wanted to go, and—well—the money made a tremendous difference to us in every way. It changed our lives altogether. I shall never forget how excited Neill and I were when the first news came to us of Father's legacy."

Anthony was still thinking hard. Jacqueline Hillier's adult life had been spent at Trinket, Dance, and Lanrebel. With the exception of the time that she had spent in the States . . . he supposed it was the States . . . her romantic contact, therefore, should have been made at one of these three places. With the odds, he thought, distinctly on Dance. She had been unusually young when Hillier married her at Trinket. Unless . . . and Mr. Bathurst realized that this was a possibility . . . she had met somebody whilst on holiday somewhere . . . away from the normal circle and apart from ordinary routine conditions. If this latter contingency were indeed the case the probability was that he would never strike the right track. The outlook was black indeed!

"Do you mind," he asked Ann, "if I keep this diary for just a little while? I think it might help me if I could look through it carefully. You know—when I'm alone. Tell me you won't mind."

Ann looked a trifle dubious at the request.

"It will be quite safe with me, Miss Hillier. I'll promise you that. And you know I shall treat it all as confidential."

Her face cleared a little. "It wasn't that I was worrying about. It was that—oh, it's so dreadfully hard to explain."

"Try," urged Anthony. "You won't find me unreasonable or unsympathetic."

"Well, I shouldn't like any unhappiness to come to anybody because of it. Any *more* unhappiness I suppose I ought to say. I shouldn't like to think that I had been the cause of it. Through finding that little book and showing it to you. Frightfully silly of me?" She looked up at him.

He shook his head at her question. "No, Miss Hillier. Not a bit of it. Look here—I understand perfectly—I promise you I'll do nothing whatever without consulting you first. That is, if I *should* run across anything that has a bearing on the case. Agree?"

"All right, then. But you will see me first about anything—won't you?"

Anthony nodded. "Look at me, Miss Hillier. No action unless I tell you first—see my finger wet . . ."

She smiled at him, but he saw that her eyes were brimming with tears. A thought struck him. "Miss Hillier, when you and Jacqueline went abroad recently, did your mother suffer from sea-sickness?"

"On the way across . . . terribly . . . but why do you ask?"

"It was just an idea of mine," replied Mr. Bathurst.

Chapter XXIII
PAGES OF THE PAST

ANTHONY watched Ann make her way back to the lane where she had left her car. When she reached it, she turned and gave him a wave of her hand. He heard the car start and then the noise of it recede into the distance. He lay on his back and mused. How much, he thought, had she really known of her mother and, conversely, how much actually had her mother known of her? He looked again at the diary of Jacqueline as it lay there on the grass beside him. He picked it up and examined it carefully. It was of quite ordinary type and had cost, he calculated, when new, something between one and two shillings. *Collingridge's Emerald Diary.*

He turned it over in his hand before opening it again. That it had been in the constant, almost daily use of Jacqueline, was fairly obvious. Every feature of it was an indication of this regular usage. He opened it. As he did so, he observed that before the space allotted to the 1st day of January there were several pages described under the heading of "Memoranda". On the last of these Jacqueline had written something. He read the written words carefully.

"December the 31st. Midnight once again, my angel, and I have performed the last task of each year that comes and goes. The task which has been self-appointed for so long. I have burnt the record of the year which has just gone. Given it back to time from whence it came. As I write, I can hear all the noises outside that are welcoming the year which is just being born. My only thought as I hear them is that every year which is born and dies adds one to the tale of my age and one to the tale of yours. Kiss me, sweetheart, and wish me a Happy New Year. Like you did three times . . . just fancy . . . only three times. No more than that, and yet my entire Life seems to have been yours and yours only. I would swear that we have been together since Life began. When you were a King in Babylon and I was a Christian slave! I know why I think as I do—I didn't begin to live until I met you! Of course that must be the explanation! It's the only one. I'm going to drink a toast to you . . . remember our old understanding of the dear days . . . 'every time we raise a glass . . . every hour the clock strikes . . . tell me you do . . . *always*'!"

Anthony read and reflected upon what he had read. Was there anything hidden or buried here that might help him? Yes. There was! Of course—and he had nearly missed it. Jacqueline's acquaintanceship with the man to whom she wrote had been of about *three years' duration*. "Like you did three times . . . only three times." Not much—but something. Anthony read on with increased interest. The entries were, as Ann and he had previously seen, almost entirely reminiscent. Occasionally, however, there came snatches of poems. On the 22nd of January, for example, he came across the following:

> "'Lost Adventurers, watching ever, over the toss of the green-
> tipped foam.
> Many a foreign port and city, never the harbour lights of Home.'

"Lost Adventurers! How true that is! That's you and I, my darling . . . and that's all I can think of to-day." There were no entries of any kind, Anthony noted, with reference to anything that she did from day to day. The diary was just an intimate communion, as it were, between Jacqueline and this unknown other. It seemed to Anthony, as he read these pages of the past, that the key to this particular matter *must* lie somewhere in Dance. Then he found something else to attract both his interest and attention. It was as follows. Certain words he had read before were clearly repeated.

> "'Nature once in mood capricious,
> Set herself a task delicious.
> How she might achieve Perfection,
> Therefore I must follow gladly,
> And probably extremely badly,
> To demonstrate just sheer—affection.'

"So here goes.

> "'My song's of the charming Miss Parr,
> With eyes like the shine of a Star,
> Alluring, mysterious—sweetly imperious.
> I'm enthralled and enraptured—*ma foi!*

> So here's a Toast to the charming Miss Parr,
> To fling to the world—near and far,
> Were the lovely Miss Parr mine.
> On her lips of rich carmine
> I'd taste Paradise Perfect—*n'est-ce pas*'?

"How many years since you wrote that to me, my darling? I know—but I dare not whisper it . . . even to the trees outside my window—I'm the only person who does know. Some memories, darling—never die. They can't—Love wouldn't let them. It frightens me—the thought of all those lost years. They never come back to us. God sends them to us only once. How wrong and sinful it is to wish them away, yet if I thought you would come to me at the age of threescore years and ten, I'd wish the intervening time away—in a flaming flash. That shows how much I love you. Good-night once again, my heart's delight . . . let me kiss you just behind the ear. That spot I've always loved so much. Sleep well, wherever you are—oh, if my songs were only winged!"

Anthony thought hard over this last-mentioned entry. Here at last was something extremely valuable. "My song's of the charming Miss Parr!" This allusion was presumably to Jacqueline Hillier herself. In her maiden state. He could confirm that fact with Ann, of course, directly he wanted to. If, therefore, Jacqueline had been Miss Parr when the lines had been dedicated to her, *the romance must have been* born when she was at Trinket, and his previous ideas with regard to Dance must have been wrong! This was about the first piece of really good fortune that had come his way, and he was grateful to the Gods of Chance and their agent, Ann Hillier, for having sent it to him.

Then he realized that he must ask Ann many more questions concerning her mother and father in the hope that she would be able to answer them. He remembered she had told him that when she and Neill had been at school her father and mother had gone to America for a time. Why was that?—Anthony wondered. Why had they gone there? Was it the desire of Paul Hillier for travel as Ann had hinted to him, or was it, possibly, the fulfilment of a wish of his wife? Mr. Bathurst would have given much to have known which for certain.

He returned to the perusal of Jacqueline's diary. He combed it thoroughly for a tangible reference. There was none. Not a definite name of a person or of a place—anywhere within its pages. Then a further thought occurred to him, a vital thought. This was the diary which Jacqueline had written *during the previous year*. Two questions were born at once. Why hadn't she destroyed it as had been her yearly habit (*vide* her own written words), and where was the diary for the current year? Anthony went back to intensive thought.

Suddenly he began to shake his head. Things were going to be excessively difficult for him after all. He wasn't able to answer the first part of the question but he imagined that he could find the correct answer to the second. From many points of view he was compelled to consider the case as the most intricate of all the many problems that had so far come his way. Three deaths touching one family and each one so different in character and in design from the other two. For whatever might be said concerning the death of Jacqueline, and even of Neill, the son, this strangling of Paul Hillier was altogether different—so clear-cut and direct. Much more to the ordinary pattern of crime than its two predecessors had been. A revolver in the dead man's pocket and the marks of murderous fingers round his throat.

Anthony reviewed the personal circle round the three dead people. From the standpoint of one killer and one killer only. The "inner ring" possibles. There were so few of them. He considered them one by one. Ann herself, Maurice Hillier, Belle Hillier . . . not much beyond these in all conscience . . . but perhaps Mowbray, the butler at "Hillearys" . . . and the Vicar of Lanrebel (Heaven forbid!) . . . these names, to all intents and purposes, exhausted the list. They had one thing in common. They had all been present at the dinner on the 8th of June, the evening that Jacqueline died. He then contemplated those whom he termed to himself the "outer ring" possibles. Again the list showed an appalling paucity. He had to drag the names almost from the recesses of his brain. Even then they were meagre in the extreme.

Pakenham . . . he felt that he must include the doctor on the list . . . and in addition to him there were certain others who had been in the district during the time that covered all the three deaths. The names of the people at the "Salvation" inn occurred to him first of all. Arthur Paske, Frank Paske . . . several guests there . . . some of whose names he knew and some of whose names he didn't. Small satisfaction to be obtained from this second list. Mr. Bathurst, it must be admitted, cursed softly under his breath. He realized with a tinge of annoyance that he was getting nowhere. Except perhaps in the all-important matter of this diary which Jacqueline had left behind her. He felt somewhat in a dilemma.

At the moment he was torn between two strong desires. One—to visit Trinket as soon as he conveniently could—and the second, which was perhaps more of an instinct than a desire—to stay rooted to this spot of Lanrebel so that he might watch unceasingly and with a vigilance that must never be relaxed, in case something vital should turn up.

The inquest on the body of Paul Hillier was to be opened that afternoon. He knew very well what would happen after that. The same procedure would take place that had taken place before. There would be three inquests left in a state of adjournment. He had ascertained all that he could with regard to Paul Hillier's death . . . from more than one source, but chiefly from Ann herself . . . and as a result of these inquiries had formed the opinion that attendance at the inquest would almost certainly bring him nothing of value. He felt that he was far more interested in the funeral than in the inquest. For this reason. There would be a third Hillier grave in the churchyard at Lanrebel. Judging from previous interments, this third Hillier grave might well be garlanded with flowers before the week was out.

Anthony clung persistently to the idea that the truth of the problem might come to him down this particular avenue. He had already made a second contact with Clutterbuck's, the florists at Liskerry, and they had promised him faithfully as a result of this second visit he had made to their establishment that they would adhere to certain arrangements which he had suggested to them. He knew all the time, though, that it would be a mistake for him to foster anything like optimism with regard to this particular point. There might be a break in his direction—on the other hand, the break might well go right the other way and leave him high and dry again. All the same, it was a definite chance, and he must try to take any chance that was offered to him. Mr. Bathurst placed Jacqueline's diary in his pocket and made his way from the field of his repose back to the inn bearing the sign of "Salvation". As he came abreast of the big wooden gates he was surprised to see Pereira come out. The man seemed in a bad temper about something, and, for once in a while, for a man usually so genial, nodded rather curtly to Anthony.

"It's not often I'm riled, Mr. Bathurst," he said venomously, "no, sir—but things have happened to me this morning—in this little burg, that have jest about got my goat. It's a punishment to me. There's no doubt about that. I took the place too much to my heart in the first place and now the bill's being sent in to me, I guess. Things have a way of pannin' out like that in life. I figure it out like this here. I've got my own ideas of things. If you put too much ribbon round the cat's neck—well, be careful you don't lose the darned cat, ribbon and all."

Anthony's face registered surprise. "Don't tell me you're going away from us, Mr. Pereira."

The man addressed shook his head slowly. "Mr. Bathurst," he said solemnly, "you've got me all wrong. I'm that soft-hearted that Angora rabbits seem like Bengal tigers to me."

Anthony smiled. "I'm sure you are, Mr. Pereira. Nothing I've ever heard about you would persuade me otherwise."

Mr. Pereira blew out his cheeks and snorted. He was such a good-natured man that he could find no words for an adequate reply. Anthony passed into the inn and went upstairs to his bedroom. He must go to Trinket, in Berkshire—but the question was—when?

Chapter XXIV
FRESH FIELDS

Before Mr. Bathurst did eventually start on his journey to Trinket there were four important points which should be recorded and noted. The first of these points concerns the inquest that took place on the body of Paul Hillier. Contrary to his first intentions, Anthony decided at the last moment to go to Liskerry and be present at the proceedings. He gained little, however, as a direct consequence of the action. Ann Hillier; her uncle, Maurice Hillier; Mowbray, the butler; and Dr. Pakenham were questioned by the Coroner in turn, and then at a suitable time during the hearing the Coroner made the anticipated announcement to the effect that at the request of the police an adjournment would be made.

Anthony watched both Mowbray and Dr. Pakenham very closely as they took the stand, and he listened to their statements with every possible attention. The crowd filed out of the Court when the Coroner announced the adjournment in the usual listless manner of such crowds, and Anthony was just about to turn towards Lanrebel, when he felt a light touch on his arm. Turning quickly, he saw a man standing at his side. The man's face seemed familiar to him. In an instant Anthony knew who the man was. It was the man who had been foreman of the Coroner's jury at the three inquests which had so far been held and who had asked several questions of the witnesses at the first inquest, that on the body of Jacqueline Hillier. The man was a farmer, Anthony remembered that, but at the moment he wasn't able to recall the man's name.

"Excuse me, sir," said the farmer, "but would you be good enough to let me have just a word with you?" He seemed a trifle nervous and embarrassed.

Something prompted Mr. Bathurst to accept the invitation.

"Only too pleased," he murmured cordially. "Where do you suggest?"

"Come with me, sir," replied Joshua Toft. "I know a nice little place just up the road."

Anthony smiled at the familiar phrase and thought of Harris in *Three Men in a Boat*. "How far?"

"A matter of about two hundred yards, sir. No more." Toft led the way. On the short journey to the haven of Toft's desire, Anthony contributed commonplace conversation. His companion, however, seemed to have retired into his shell. Anthony recognized the signs and respected them. Toft stopped in front of a luxurious-looking hotel which bore the name of "Bristow's Bar". Toft motioned to Mr. Bathurst to enter with him. Anthony accepted. Toft pushed open the big revolving doors and soon found a convenient table. Anthony Bathurst looked round and was surprised at the quality of all the appointments around him. They approximated luxury. Toft bought drinks.

"I observe," remarked Mr. Bathurst, "that you have chosen a quiet corner where we may gossip in peace."

Toft nodded. "I did so on purpose."

Anthony waited for him to open the ball. "I'd better explain first of all," said the farmer who had also been foreman, "that my name's Toft. Joshua Toft. I'm a farmer in this district. Got a farm near Lanrebel. 'Woodruffs's the name of it. Dairy produce chiefly."

"Yes, I remember now. But I knew something about you when you first spoke to me. You have been the foreman on the jury at this tragic succession of inquests. And I think I've seen you at the inn where I'm staying. At the same time, though, I'm rather puzzled as to why you have spoken to me now. Suppose you explain that part of it to begin with?"

Joshua Toft looked a trifle uncomfortable. "It was a liberty, sir, I admit, but I'm hoping that you'll forgive me for it—when you hear what I've got to say." He leant across the table and with an air of exaggerated discretion lowered his tone. "Tell me if I'm wrong, sir—but haven't I the honour of addressing Mr. Anthony Bathurst?"

"Very true, Mr. Toft, but what of that?"

Toft brightened perceptibly. "Holding a watching brief, Mr. Bathurst? For the Yard?"

Anthony denied the soft impeachment. "No. Not exactly. Just trying to spend a few days' holiday in one of my favourite parts of England." Toft looked dubious and his eyes searched Anthony's face. "It's a fact, Mr. Toft. I assure you there's no deception."

The farmer's disappointment returned to his face. "In that case, sir, you must forgive me for approaching you and forget all about this little meeting. Then we'll drink up . . . shake hands . . . and call it a day."

"On the contrary, Mr. Toft, we'll drink up. After we've drunk I'll order another round and you shall tell me everything that you're wanting to. How does the offer suit you?"

Toft radiated enthusiasm at the suggestion. "Dang me, but that's rare good hearing. Because I want to get something off my chest." He drank his beer right down—with the smooth and eloquent ripple movement round the Adam's apple which distinguishes the true artist. Anthony called the waiter over to the table and gave that second order he had promised. Toft, warmed by his reception, drew his chair closer to the table. "No doubt you're wonderin' a bit as to how I knew who you were." Toft chuckled at a remembrance. "It's not always those what live longest who see the most. My old grandfather used to tell me that, and I know now the truth of the words he spoke.

"But I was glancing through some old *Illustrateds* last Sunday afternoon. It was rare hot and sultry, if you remember—and I was takin' things nice and easy—I like to do myself well sometimes—and dang me if I didn't run across your photo! I knew it was you directly I clapped my eyes on it. I'll tell you what the connection was. It was to do with that murder you was mixed up with down at Chalke. You remember—what the papers all called the 'Ebony Stag' murder. A bloke was found with a harpoon through his chest. Well—I calls to my missus and I shows this photograph to her. 'Dang me,' I says to her, 'but if this ain't that gentleman what's stoppin' up at the 'Salvation' along of Arthur Paske, you can put me down a Dutchman.' They were my very words."

Toft paused in his recital and eyed Anthony expectantly. The latter nodded encouragingly. Toft proceeded with renewed exuberance. "Well, then I began to put two and two together. I can do that as well as the next man. You were down in these parts, I says to myself, investigatin' these murders in Lanrebel. Sort of secret police inquiry. And then things generally began to come home to me, most plain like. I remembered the first inquest here on Mrs. Hillier when I asked a few questions of some of the witnesses. Of the doctor and so on. You were present in the County Hall that day. I saw you there— caught sight of your face more than once. That set me off wonderin', and when I spotted you at the inquest to-day, well—my two and two made five and I felt more certain about everything than ever. Felt I was on a sure thing, so to speak. Have I made myself clear, sir?"

"Quite, Toft. Now go on with your good news. You've aroused my curiosity."

"I'm none so sure you can call it good news, sir. It certainly won't be good for everybody."

"What does that matter? Is anything—ever?"

Toft looked gloomy. "I suppose not, sir. In a manner of speaking. When you come to weigh it all up." He looked carefully round the bar before he put his next question. "Now I'd like to know this, sir. Have you formed any very definite opinion with regard to the murders,

Mr. Bathurst? I feel that I must know that before I get right down to my own little matter."

Anthony took his time with regard to replying. "Yes, Toft—and no. All the same, though, I think I know who killed Mrs. Hillier." He paused deliberately to observe the effect of his words. Toft gasped in astonishment and spilt some of his beer. Anthony went on serenely. "But until I'm sure—and I want you to understand me, Mr. Toft—you realize that I must keep that opinion to myself."

Toft nodded blankly.

"And I think, too, that I know how Neill Hillier came to be removed. But with regard to the third killing—that of Paul Hillier himself—well, I must confess I haven't yet finally made up my mind."

Toft leant over to Anthony with a strange expression in his eyes. "Surely—one person killed all three of 'em?"

To Toft's surprise, Mr. Bathurst did not immediately agree. When his answer did come, it was a guarded answer. "I don't think that I'm certain about that."

"Not certain, sir? Why—surely—"

Anthony checked what the farmer was on the point of saying. Although he had no clarified intention of confiding in Toft, he felt that, to extract from Toft all that he wanted to say, he must on his own part cultivate, as it were, Toft's complete confidence. "I don't want you to jump at conclusions. Especially when the leap itself is being taken more or less in the dark. You said just now, 'Surely one person killed the three victims.' I replied to you. My reply was perhaps a little unexpected. I said in effect, 'Not one murderer, but three murderers.' But I might also have added, had I felt so disposed, 'and yet not three murderers, but one murderer'."

Toft looked confused. Mr. Bathurst could not find it in his heart to blame him for that. The Athanasian touch was probably beyond him.

"You mean," said Toft slowly, emerging from his condition of bewilderment, "that there's a connection between the three crimes . . . but not necessarily."

"Exactly," broke in Mr. Bathurst with deliberate interruption. "That's really what I do mean." Toft peered across at him and nodded. Anthony came to the point. "Now that we've cleared the air to some extent we can get down to what you wanted to tell me."

Toft, out of his depth, and by no means positive that the air *had* been cleared, surrendered to the double urge. "Perhaps you're right, sir. I don't know quite the best place to start. But I don't want you to think that I've just thought of all this. To tell the truth, it's been on my mind for some time. Fermenting like. I've actually talked it over with my missus. As much as you ever can discuss things with your own wife. You'd agree with me on that point I take it, sir?"

Anthony realized that Toft, a little slow possibly as to the more subtle understandings, was no fool. He smiled at the owner of "Woodruffs". "I happen, as a matter of fact, to be a bachelor," he returned.

"By choice, sir?"

"Partly, perhaps."

"You surprise me. A fine upstanding man like yourself. Still—that's neither here nor there. As I just said, I talked this little matter over with Mrs. Toft. You must understand that I'm going right back now to the death of Mrs. Hillier."

"I'm pleased at that."

"Why—if I may ask, sir?"

"Because that marks what we may reasonably call the beginning of events. I like beginning at the beginning. It's right. Proper. That's what I meant. Do you get me?"

Toft nodded.

"I'm going back to about a week before Mrs. Hillier was poisoned. The date was the 2nd of June. To be exact, sir, six days before the tragedy. It was in the evening. A lovely evening, too. You know what I mean—real June. Close on half past nine it was—the time. I'd been down to the 'Salvation' just to have my usual couple. They went down well. I don't think I saw you that evening, sir."

Mr. Bathurst smiled. "Let me get this straight. Are you asking me for an alibi?"

Toft let out a boisterous guffaw. "I left the 'Salvation' a bit earlier than I do most evenings, because I had a bit of booking to do that night when I got back to my place, and I made my usual road up to the farm. At the Laran crossroads—you know where I mean, sir—they're just before the turning that leads up to my place—Woodruffs—there was a car drawn up in the lee of the hedge. It wasn't dark, but duskish, as you might say. What some people 'ud call twilight. I couldn't see the number of the car, but I'm as certain as I can be that the car I saw was Mrs. Hillier's."

Anthony heard this story with pleasure. What else was coming?

Toft continued. He was well in his stride now. "I'll admit, sir, here and now, that I was curious about this car. Interested! Not nosey—I honestly think I can say that—but full of wonder as to why Mrs. Hillier—if it was her inside the car—was waitin' there at that time of the evening. You must remember that she hadn't long been back from her jaunt abroad—and we hadn't seen her runnin' round in her usual way. Then I saw something else. Something that made my curiosity red hot. I saw a man come up to the car and stand by the side of it."

"Just a moment, Mr. Toft. There's something here I'd like to know. How far were you away from the car when this happened?"

Toft thought over the question before he answered. "Call it a hundred yards and you won't be far out."

"Thank you, Mr. Toft. Go on, will you, please?"

"Well, this fellow, whoever he was, must have had a few words with the occupant of the car before he got in. When I was within about twenty-five yards of it he got in and the car moved away very quickly. Away from me, of course. As though they had seen me and wanted to clear off."

"In what particular direction did it go?"

"I should say towards 'Hillearys'—Mrs. Hillier's house. But it could also have been going towards Laran." Toft stopped abruptly.

"Now go on again," urged Mr. Bathurst, "and tell me exactly what you're thinking."

Toft leant back in his chair and fingered the rim of his glass. "You aren't the first person I've told about this. As I told you just now, I mentioned it to the wife some little time back. But I intend to tell you a little more than I told her. You're different."

"That's a sweeping statement, Mr. Toft." Anthony watched him carefully. He wondered, primarily, what had caused Mr. Toft to alter his tactics. He said nothing further, however, but waited for his companion to continue.

"I told my wife when she pressed me for further information that I didn't know who the man was. More than that. I told her I didn't even suspect anybody. That it was too dark for me to see and so on.

I had a bit of a task in putting her off—you know what Nosey Parkers women are—but I managed it. I didn't want her quacking round the village. They're all the same—the women in these parts—quack like a lot of blasted ducks."

"And all the time, I suppose, you did suspect somebody? Is that it, Mr. Toft?"

Toft beamed with satisfaction. "You've said it, sir. And that's why I'm talkin' to you as I am now."

"Let's have your suspicions, then. Pass them on to me. Even though there may be nothing in them."

Toft gave a heave of his broad shoulders. "I'm pretty positive in my own mind that the man I saw talking to Mrs. Hillier on the evening of June the 2nd and who drove off in the car with her was our friend Dr. Pakenham. The man was fairly tall and slim. I agree that I didn't see his face. But his build generally was the doctor's build, and I don't think you'd have to go any further than that to find him. Now, sir—what do you make of all that?"

If Anthony had been forced at that particular moment to make a secret admission it would have been that Toft's story had brought no great surprise to him. Because of the fact that the circle of acquaintanceship around Jacqueline Hillier had been so extremely limited as far as companionship of this kind had gone. He also, as he considered Toft's statement, remembered a vital something else. Pakenham's story that Jacqueline's life had been dedicated to a supreme cause. A story which had already through the pages of her own diary received such strong confirmation. Had Pakenham been in Jacqueline's confidence? Or had he made the statement as the result of his own powers of observation?

What had been the true relationship between him and Jacqueline? He was the family doctor, Mr. Bathurst knew that, but had he been more? This possibility must now be seriously considered. These thoughts ran through him as he sat there facing Toft, his present informant. It was borne in upon him, eventually, that Toft had demanded an answer to a specific question. Anthony brought himself to a reply.

"Well, Mr. Toft, your information is undoubtedly interesting. I can't deny that. And it may even prove to be of great value. But, after all, even if the man you saw that night *was* the man you think it was—you can't get away from the position that the action may have been quite an innocent one. You see that, don't you?"

Toft shook his head indignantly. All the malevolence of his morality reasserted itself. He wasn't accepting that possibility for a moment.

"Oh no, sir. I'm not havin' that! Not from you or from anybody else. I'm country bred—and I've lived in the country all my life. You can't throw dust in my eyes. People don't wait in cars down dark lanes at night-time to talk about politics or religion! You won't put that into me. Not on your life. They do those things for a spot of cuddle—it's slap and tickle every time with 'em—and it's no good shuttin' your eyes to it."

Anthony smiled.

"I should have thought that would have been the best course to adopt! It certainly seems to me indicated."

He suddenly changed his tone.

"But seriously, Mr. Toft, let me point out one or two things. I'll take your story at its face value. In the first place, you admit that you aren't certain as to who was inside the car, and in the second place the car wasn't waiting down a dark lane. That is to say in the accepted sense of the term. You yourself were in the lane, for instance. The car was at the crossroads, which fact alone, I submit, immediately makes your story a somewhat different proposition from the one that you have put forward."

Toft was annoyed. He shrugged his shoulders with a gesture of impatience and spoke darkly into his glass. "There's an old saying— 'There's none so deaf as those that won't hear.'"

"That's true—but again to a degree only. If I hear a bell ringing I am not bound to describe the sound as that of angel voices. It may merely herald the anticipated sale of muffins and crumpets."

"Angel voices," repeated Toft with an unexpected sourness—"they haven't been sounding in these parts of late. Far from it, indeed! I should say that what most people have been hearing has come from the other place."

Anthony rose from his seat. "Perhaps you're right, Mr. Toft. But places, you know, don't matter of themselves. People matter so much more. If you were in hell, that fact alone might make it heaven for somebody else. Because it's people who make places. Ever thought of that?"

"Can't say that I have," retorted the master of "Woodruffs"—a trifle uncertain as to Mr. Bathurst's real meaning.

"Well," replied Anthony Bathurst with a smile that gilded the pill, "suppose you start thinking of it now."

Chapter XXV
IT NEVER RAINS BUT IT POURS

NOT more than half an hour after the conversation which has just been described, Anthony Bathurst stood outside the post office at Laran. That same post office in front of which Mowbray, the butler at "Hillearys", was in the habit of waiting for his light-o'-love, Jennifer. On the present occasion Mowbray was there again. In these days, with the Hillier family dying one by one, Mowbray found many more opportunities than usual for his absence from both the trivial round and the common task, which had always furnished very much less than his natural demands. He was by no means surprised to see Mr. Bathurst standing at his side. Mainly for the reason that he had been hoping to see him either there or close at hand in the Lanrebel vicinity. To tell the truth, a strange story had recently reached Mowbray's ears. A story which had given him both anxiety and morbid sensation. A story which he had decided in his own mind he would rather tell to this rather attractive-looking Mr. Bathurst than to Inspector Rockingham of the regular police. When he saw Anthony standing there, obviously waiting for the local bus into Lanrebel, Mowbray grasped the opportunity, sidled up to him, and touched his hat. Mowbray always prided himself upon the excellence of his manners. "Good afternoon, sir."

Anthony, who had seen Mowbray at "Hillearys", returned his greeting. When Mowbray showed signs of conversational eagerness, Anthony, for a time, let him do all the talking. When Mowbray dropped his voice considerably and said suddenly, "And there's something I'd like to mention to you specially," Mr. Bathurst came to the conclusion that it must surely be an afternoon set apart by the saints for confidences.

Mowbray followed up his last remark. "That is, of course, sir, if you have a moment to spare. You should have, without any inconvenience. There won't be another bus, if it's any information to you, sir, for another quarter of an hour at least."

Anthony sensed that he must disregard no opportunity if it came his way. After Toft—Mowbray!

"In that case, then, Mowbray, we will stroll as far as the Roundhouse and back. I would rather talk walking than standing at the corner of the street. Count me as a devout lover of gentle exercise."

Mowbray smiled a studied smile. As a smile he would have described it himself to a man of his own calling as "just right".

"Very good, sir. I will accompany you as you suggest."

Anthony turned in the direction of the Roundhouse and Mowbray turned with him. They walked a few paces before the latter spoke again. Anthony purposely waited for him. Mowbray coughed. He had not seen Jennifer Hillman for over a week, and on that account was feeling rather more sure of himself than usual. When Mowbray was sick, it must be observed Mowbray a saint would be. When Mowbray was well . . .

"The fact is, Mr. Bathurst, I've been a little worried lately. That may sound strange to you, after all we've been through recently, but latterly this worry I mention has been a more personal matter."

Mr. Bathurst nodded sympathetically. Mowbray's confidence visibly increased. He felt instinctively that Mr. Bathurst, although a crime investigator, was by birth and breeding "a gentleman". Mowbray, in his literary taste, was a highbrow. Not by choice. But as the result of considered judgment. He had read in his time so much vindictive criticism of books wherein the investigation of crime played a prominent part that to find in Mr. Bathurst a gentleman not devoid of intelligence had surprised him tremendously and comforted him not a little. The surprise that had come to him was allied to a feeling of pleasure as well as to the sense of comfort. There had been, as is already known, in Mowbray's history, a certain Colonel Todhunter . . . "More personal," he continued, "because I happen to have certain information in my possession which I have reason to believe is definitely confined to my possession. This information I regard as so highly important that this personal possession of it has given rise to the anxiety I spoke of a moment or two ago."

"You are so anxious, I take it, that you desire to share the information? Do I understand you accurately?"

Mowbray beamed at Mr. Bathurst's ready acceptance of his statement. "That is exactly what I do desire, Mr. Bathurst."

"In that case, then," suggested Anthony, "perhaps you had better tell me all the trouble. I promise you that I shall listen with the greatest attention."

Mowbray gravely consulted his watch. "We have still ten minutes, sir, before the bus may be reasonably expected. Even if it runs to time, which is extremely improbable. Those ten minutes should be ample for my purpose."

"All the better. You may depend that I shall listen to your story with an entirely open mind."

"I would prefer that condition, sir. It will enable me to speak with more confidence. I want to take you back, sir, to the night on which my late master was murdered. You will doubtless remember the circumstances?"

"Very well indeed."

"You will remember, amongst other matters, that Mr. Hillier's brother, Mr. Maurice Hillier, accompanied by his good lady, came into Laran here for the purpose of an entertainment at the pictures. What is popularly known, sir, as a 'flick'."

"I do remember hearing that, Mowbray."

"Very good, sir. Having, as it were, established that starting point, sir, I will proceed." Mowbray coughed again. "Yesterday afternoon, sir, it was my unfortunate lot to overhear a conversation in the house where I am employed which quite frankly, sir, I would very much rather not have overheard! Don't construe from my words, sir, that I was engaged in anything like eavesdropping. Such an action is not, and I may say never has been, a habit of mine. I should inform you, sir, that I was with Colonel Todhunter before I came to Mr. Hillier. That fact alone will assist you to understand."

"Quite so," murmured Mr. Bathurst.

"The conversation to which I am referring, sir, took place between Mr. and Mrs. Hillier. With the exception of myself, sir, they were alone in the particular part of the house where we were. Miss Ann Hillier had gone out. I don't include the servants in my remarks, of course, sir. Mr. and Mrs. Maurice Hillier were in the lounge, sir, when the conversation to which I refer took place between them. It concerned the evening when Mr. Paul Hillier was murdered. Also it concerned Mr. Maurice Hillier's whereabouts on that evening. Unhappily, Mrs. Maurice Hillier's voice, when raised above the normal, approaches the shrill. One might almost employ the adjective 'strident'. It was impossible for me not to overhear what she was saying, sir. I give you my word of honour on that. She accused Mr. Maurice Hillier, her husband, *of not being at the cinema with her on the fatal evening*. You will realize, sir, the overwhelming importance of such an accusation, I am sure, sir." Mowbray paused. He was perilously close to breathlessness.

Anthony was puzzled in the extreme. There was something here in this statement which he wasn't able to understand. He broke in. "But I don't get you, Mowbray. Help me—will you? Surely Mr. Maurice Hillier accompanied his wife to the cinema on the evening his brother was killed? I have always understood so."

Mowbray shrugged excessively professional shoulders.

"From what I overheard, there seems to be a doubt about it, sir. I can assure you, sir, upon my personal integrity as a gentleman's gentleman, that I heard Mrs. H. say, 'You weren't with me. You know that! You were away over an hour. I was alone in that cinema as far as your companionship went. Where did you go? Whom did you meet? You were away over an hour. Where were you? You'll have to tell me, Maurice, so you may as well make up your mind and tell me now—before any mischief is done that can't be undone. And understand—I mean what I say.'"

Anthony was alert now. There was meat here at last. "And what was Mr. Maurice Hillier's reply to that barrage of questioning? Did you happen to overhear that as well?"

"I did, sir. As I said before, it was impossible for me not to hear. Before I could get away Mr. Hillier said, 'Don't be a damned fool, Belle, and keep your—er—blasted mouth shut. I went to meet Captain

Coster. He's in Laran every night about that time. You knew where I was—so don't deny it. It wasn't my fault that Coster didn't show up. You're making trouble for trouble's sake.' That was the reply, sir, and then Mrs. Hillier went on to say something else."

"What was that, Mowbray?"

"I was about to tell you, sir. 'Seems to me,' she said, 'that if I know anything you've a very good reason for telling me to keep my blasted mouth shut! A very good reason, indeed. Looks as though my mouth may be very closely concerned with your neck. One never knows.'" Mowbray paused, but continued again almost immediately. "When I heard that, sir, from Mrs. H. I was upset. Extremely upset. I came away."

"From the door?"

Mowbray looked hurt at the implication. "No, sir. Perhaps I have failed to make myself entirely clear. From the . . . er . . . area of audibility. Not to put too fine a point upon it, sir . . . I folded my tents like the Arabs . . . you understand my reference, sir?"

"Only too well," replied Anthony.

Mowbray became solicitous. "I trust that I have given you something to think about. I should deplore the fact that I had wasted your time."

"You have given me a great deal to think about. But not to talk about. You understand? And that applies to you as well, Mowbray. Got that?"

Mowbray coughed once more. "You may rely on me, sir. Implicitly. I pride myself upon an excess of tact. If you turn, sir, you will observe that the bus to Lanrebel is approaching. For once in a way it is on time."

"Thank you, Mowbray, for your information," said Mr. Bathurst. "I am indebted to you."

The bus drew up by the side of the road. Mr. Bathurst boarded it. Mowbray remained behind on the pavement. As he took his seat, Anthony found himself wondering what it was that took Mowbray to Laran and even kept him there when he might well be returning. But the wonder was short-lived, as Mr. Bathurst had more pressing problems to occupy his mind than the habits and idiosyncrasies of Charles Mowbray! These problems lasted him throughout the entire return journey to Lanrebel. Confusion was becoming even more confounded!

CHAPTER XXVI
STUDIO PORTRAIT

ANTHONY went straight to his room upon his arrival at the 'Salvation'. He had work to do. From his wallet he took the tiny piece of cardboard he had retrieved from the ledge on One Mile Cliff. He studied carefully again the faint lines that had been traced in the corner of the scrap of cardboard. At last he placed the fragment under his magnifying-glass. What he saw there only served to confirm his previous opinion. "Definitely 'Hea'," he murmured to himself. "The same opinion to which I came before. And I think from the position of the letters on the paper much more probably the end of a word than the beginning. Now, in the name of all things bright and beautiful, what word can possibly end in those three letters?" Anthony attempted to build words upon that termination. First of all—what letter could he reasonably place directly in front of H.E.A.?"

Mr. Bathurst packed a pipe with tobacco, lit the tobacco, and settled down once again to an exercise in intense thinking. The use of both "A" and "B" brought him nothing. "C" yielded him "Trachea", which, naturally, in this particular connection, he immediately discarded. He used the letters in alphabetical order one by one without arriving at any satisfactory conclusion until he came to "O". This gave him the word "Bohea". Anthony toyed with it for a time but eventually shook his head and passed on. Thus he continued the letters in order until he came to the letter "T". Here he paused. "Thea" held, it seemed to him, many intriguing possibilities. Names—of course! Feminine names at that.

"Alethea". Here he paused again. His first idea had been wrong. There weren't so many after all. He ransacked his brain for names and brought into play all the resources of his memory. Classical names, surely! He felt that there must be some that ended in "thea". He groped and after a time found another. One that pleased him. "Dorothea". Mr. Bathurst rubbed his hands. A sure sign of personal satisfaction. He recalled with feelings of thankfulness the modern tendency of certain shops to trade under single names similar to the two of which he had been able to think. He had noticed such names on shop fronts repeatedly—and in many different kinds of district. He inclined strongly towards his latter selection—"Dorothea". It was familiar, commonplace, and popular. There was one thing—he could test his new-found theory as soon as he liked. He constructed a message in telegram form. After some consideration, he decided to send this message to the Commissioner of Police at New Scotland Yard. Sir Austin Kemble would move in the matter for him as quickly as anybody, especially if he indicated to the Commissioner the urgency of its nature. Mr. Bathurst's telegram when completed ran as follows:

Please ascertain whether there is or has been within recent years a photographer in Trinket or near Trinket who traded under name of "Dorothea" or under any name at all similar which ends in the same four letters. Letter with fuller explanation following.

Anthony read what he had written, pushed the paper into his pocket, and set out for the post office at Lanrebel. As this happened to be but a few yards round the corner from the "Salvation", and on the Bonallack road, it will be seen that he hadn't far to travel. A noisy bell heralded his entrance into the shop. The ancient dame behind the counter welcomed him with a rather shrill effusiveness. She had already a soft corner in her heart for the tall gentleman from London with the grey eyes, for Mr. Bathurst had called upon her several times. She counted carefully the words of the wire that he handed to her and seemed a trifle shocked—first at the rather alarming address of the recipient and after that at what she considered most unintelligent extravagance with regard to the prodigality of word and phrase. She looked up at her customer as though she were about to censure him for this wanton waste of money. Money in these days was difficult enough to get in all conscience! But Mr. Bathurst's smile checked her intention. Funny a nice gentleman like this sending a telegram to Scotland Yard!

Well, well, you never do know, and that's a fact, and it's never safe to judge by appearances. She named the cost of the telegram. Mr. Bathurst smiled again and produced the required coin of the realm. He gestured towards the written message which lay on the counter. "You will forgive me, of course, for mentioning such a matter, but that is entirely between you and me." The old lady bridled at the insinuation.

"I am the postmistress, young man, of Lanrebel. I represent His Majesty's mails. I think I know my place . . . and my business. You understand me, I am sure, sir."

Anthony grinned at her cheerfully. "You bet I do, Mrs. Trevarth. Nobody could understand you better. That's all right, then, is it? You know your business and I know mine. We know exactly how we stand. Good afternoon, Mrs. Trevarth."

"Good afternoon to you, sir."

Mr. Bathurst raised his hat, left the post office, and returned to the quiet comfort of the "Salvation" inn. There he composed a letter to the Commissioner.

The reply, which Anthony awaited, was in his hands within a space of less than twenty-four hours. As he had anticipated. Sir Austin Kemble had moved immediately, and, which is more to the point, had moved successfully. Anthony opened the buff envelope which came to him with a certain amount of eagerness. A lot depended upon the Commissioner's information. He read as follows:

In reply to your wire of yesterday have obtained information for you as follows. Photographer business run under name of Dorothea at 22 Abingdon Crescent Trinket. Well known in Trinket and neighbouring district. Considerable trade with the school. Been established over forty years. Your supplementary letter just received. Expect answer later. Kemble.

Anthony refolded the flimsy sheet and replaced it within the official envelope with an emotion of satisfaction. Was there any real need now for him to visit Trinket? Before the funeral of Paul Hillier? After? Perhaps the latter. And yet—Mr. Bathurst was puzzled. He felt that his fingers were at last closing on the key to the problem, but he was still far from being entirely satisfied. He began to pace the room. If Neill Hillier had been killed, in the way he felt sure he had . . .

Chapter XXVII
AT THE VICARAGE

ON THE afternoon of the day which preceded the funeral of Paul Hillier a message was handed to Anthony by Frank Paske.

"There's a lad in the yard, sir—waiting. From what he said to me I rather think that he's waiting for an answer. He's from the Vicarage. Does a bit of gardening up there and runs errands. Helps Hillman, the regular gardener."

Anthony nodded and read the message. It ran thus:

Dear Mr. Bathurst,

I wasn't aware until a day or so ago that Lanrebel harboured such a celebrity in its midst. But I have since learned—and apologize for not having made myself known to you before. When you spoke to me—on that one occasion—I did not realize who you were. I should very much like to meet you and have a chat with you—particularly with regard to the terrible things that have been happening here. Will you therefore accept my invitation to dine at the Vicarage this evening with Mrs. Aylmer and me? We shall be alone. Time—7 o'clock. This messenger will bring back your answer. I know that the notice is short but I am trusting you not to disappoint me. I do not think that your time will be wasted.

Faithfully yours,

Septimus Aylmer.

Anthony read twice the sentence which the Vicar had underlined. What was behind this? Something—undoubtedly! Something, too, that he must on no account miss. He found a piece of writing-paper and scribbled an acceptance of the Vicar's invitation. Frank Paske was still waiting. Anthony handed him the reply and a coin.

"Give him this, Frank, will you, please? And tell him to get himself a drink."

Frank grinned and dashed off with Mr. Bathurst's note. Anthony sat down again to think. So the benevolent Vicar was desirous of entering the arena, was he? Now—why? What was inducing him to have a say in the matter? Did he know anything which so far he had kept to himself? It was certainly possible. He had lived in the

Hillier circle for some years—and better than that, he had been at the "Hillearys" dinner party on the evening when the tragedies had started. It was he who had seen the letter in Jacqueline's hand. Anthony's mind dwelt on the sentence which the Rev. Septimus had specially emphasized. "I do not think that your time will be wasted." Pregnant words! Mr. Bathurst settled himself to wait patiently for the hour of seven. Always a strict adherent of punctuality, he presented himself at the Vicarage of Lanrebel but a few minutes before the dock in the church tower struck the seventh hour of the afternoon. He was shown in to what was most obviously the Vicar's library. Almost immediately the Vicar joined him. His welcome could not have been more cordial. "Mr. Bathurst, need I say that I am delighted to have you with us? Mrs. Aylmer will join us in a moment or so."

Anthony murmured suitable commonplaces. The Vicar began to talk. He was fair, fat, and florid. Loquacious! In appearance far from spiritual. Of the earth, earthy. Anthony listened to him attentively. From time to time the Rev. Septimus smiled. These smiles were almost cherubic in quality. He was evidently striking a cheerful conversational note out of deliberate intention. There came a tap on the door. The Vicar answered it. He turned to Anthony. "Dinner is ready. Will you please come? Mrs. Aylmer is waiting for us in the dining-room."

Anthony bowed, and a moment later found himself shaking hands with Mildred Aylmer. "My wife," murmured the Vicar with benison in his voice, "Anthony Bathurst."

Mrs. Aylmer had a pleasant voice. The rest of her was different. Also her teeth were prominent. Anthony was on his best behaviour, wondering when the real business of the evening would commence. He had seen the Vicar but three times previously. At the inquests on Jacqueline and Paul Hillier and at Jacqueline's graveside when he and Annesley had looked at the violets. Soup was served, and suddenly the Vicar's mood changed. His cheerfulness, now clearly shown to have been assumed for the occasion, gave way to a note of studied gravity. "I expect you are wondering, Bathurst," he said, with one eye on his wife, "as to when I am coming to the matter that I . . . er . . . referred to in my little note to you this morning."

Anthony murmured a politeness. He, too, had a watching interest in Mrs. Aylmer. Reactions, to him, always held importance. The

Vicar proceeded. He waited for the service of the fish course, however, before he came to anything like definiteness.

"Mr. Bathurst," he said gravely, "three of my dearest friends, almost daily companions of mine, have been murdered in this village, of which I am the Vicar . . . within the last few days. That, to me, is an almost inexpressibly terrible thought."

"I can well understand that, sir."

"It has worried me intensely ever since that first night at 'Hillearys' when poor Jacqueline . . ."

"The Vicar hasn't slept properly for nights," prompted Mrs. Aylmer.

"That is very true, Bathurst, believe me. By the way, have you ever heard of a man-cat?" The Vicar leant across the table. His eyes searched Anthony's face.

"Only one, sir, and that merits little attention. A friend of mine dreamt of one once, but he assured me it was his wife's fault."

"Only a dream, eh? That's strange! But to get back to where we were. Will you pardon me if I carry your mind back to the time when you and I, with two others, stood by the side of Mrs. Hillier's newly dug grave? There were you and I, a friend of yours, and a gentleman named Pereira, if I remember correctly. An American gentleman who is staying with you at the 'Salvation'."

"You are right, sir. My friend was Keith Annesley, the novelist. I mentioned his name to you at the time."

"Ah yes, I do remember it now you come to mention it. I fear . . . er . . . Bathurst, that I was a little discourteous to you on that particular occasion."

Mrs. Aylmer contributed support. "I can't describe to you the extent to which the Vicar has grieved over it, Mr. Bathurst. Over what he has himself since called 'an unpardonable breach of good manners'."

Anthony realized that there was more in Mrs. Aylmer than merely offended the eye. He felt that a generous contribution of poured oil was called for from him. It was promptly forthcoming. The Vicar beamed his gratitude.

"To-morrow, Bathurst, there will fall to my lot the saddest duty, perhaps, of all. I shall be called upon to officiate at the funeral service on Paul Hillier, my dear friend. To a parish priest, you know, Bathurst, there come many trials. We are called upon to laugh with those who laugh, and to weep with them that weep, notwithstanding what our own feelings may be at the particular time. It is not always an easy or a comfortable matter . . . to be . . . er . . . adequate in the particular respect demanded. You follow me, Bathurst?"

"Entirely, sir."

The Vicar crumbled his bread on the white cloth, a procedure which his wife was viewing with evident disfavour. Suddenly the Vicar tangented. "Those violets, Bathurst—you remember how we stood there and looked at them—and then they were followed by the yellow roses. Perhaps we may see more flowers in the churchyard after Paul Hillier has been laid to rest. I wonder! I presume that you have not overlooked that last possibility?"

Anthony shook his head. "Not for a moment, sir. I am even cherishing a hope that it may lead us somewhere."

The Vicar looked startled. "Really? You attach as much importance to it as that, eh?" He turned towards his wife. "You hear what Mr. Bathurst says, my dear?"

She nodded to her husband. "Yes, I heard. And, of course, I'm terribly interested." Her teeth held centre stage.

"Well, then," remarked the Vicar, "that will bring me to my point. It gives me, as it were, an excellent 'jumping-off' point."

Anthony's mind tautened. What was coming? What was he about to hear?

"From what you said just now, Bathurst, I have formed the idea that you regard the tributes of the flowers as having a distinct bearing on the dreadful crimes that have taken place. Did I understand you aright?"

Anthony considered the terms of his answer. He felt uneasy. After all, Paul Hillier wasn't buried yet. He resolved to be as non-committal as possible. "In a way, I do. But the way may be indirect."

"I am not sure that I follow you. However, that doesn't matter." The Vicar was pompous. "I will develop my own idea after my own fashion."

"That will be better for all of us," Mildred contributed. Her voice was flat.

"Very likely. But I have given a considerable amount of attention to the incident of the flowers. Particularly the violets. And, Mr.

Bathurst, I have formed a very strange opinion with regard to them. I consider them, in the main, a projection of whimsicality. In that, I probably surprise you."

"No, sir. Not altogether."

"You don't regard whimsicality, then, as an impossible companion of murder?"

"No, sir. Certainly not in some murderers." Anthony watched the Vicar's face with keen interest. Geniality was there clearly portrayed for all to see. Anthony proceeded to amplify his last statement. "It depends almost entirely on the psychology of the murderer. You see, in the course of my career I have known so many murderers. All of them different. There was Skene, the sadist, to name but one of them. I feel sure that I shall never meet a replica of him. Skene, compared with Copeland, for instance, the criminal of the 'cold evil'—well, it would be absurd to attempt to compare them."

The Vicar frowned. He disliked the intensely practical turn which Anthony Bathurst had given to the conversation. "Well, without going into gruesome details, you are prepared to concede my point—whimsicality! That suits me! Now I am going to surprise you even further." The Vicar's eyes flashed.

"Be careful, Septimus," murmured Mildred. "Remember that you are not so young as you were. And Dr. Pakenham said . . ."

The Vicar paid her no heed. Her voice died away.

"Those violets, Bathurst, and those glorious roses, I believe that they are concerned with . . . *me*."

Anthony was certainly startled. This was the very last statement that he had expected to hear. What strange bee was buzzing in the Vicar's bonnet?

"Well, I have surprised you. You can't deny that, Bathurst. Come, now, admit the truth of it."

"You have, sir. And I should certainly like to hear more. Before I . . ."

The Vicar's tone was tinged with superiority. "Had you ever thought of the problem in the terms of my name, Bathurst? If you haven't, I recommend you to try that line of country."

Anthony thought. Aylmer—Septimus Aylmer. What was the Vicar driving at? Aylmer. Anthony tried again. Without success. He felt acute discomfort. His host was almost gloating over him. Strange old bird, this Glebeshire priest! He shook his head. "I'm sorry, sir, but you have the advantage of me."

"Ah ha! I thought I had. Try a poetic direction. No? I'll help you still further. Tennyson. Alfred, the Poet Laureate of Victoria. Do you know him, Bathurst—or is it that you are one of our moderns and only Rupert Brooke counts with you—or Sassoon?"

Anthony was still groping for the precise allusion. The Vicar could hold his literary secret no longer. "'Aylmer's Field,' Bathurst, 'Aylmer's Field'. What about it, eh? And what's more, I'm certain I'm on the right track! Well, are you there yet?"

"Aylmer's Field". Anthony did not know the poem well enough to discuss it. "I have heard of the poem, sir, but know little of it beyond its title."

"Then you must play the role of pupil. I will instruct you. It will be a change for you, no doubt, but no worse for you on that account. Listen. It won't take you long to grasp my point. Tennyson's poem tells of the Aylmers and the Averills. . . . 'When the red rose was redder than itself, and York's white rose as red as Lancaster's', and the poet's reference—with which we are primarily concerned—is to the supreme tyrant, the Emperor Nero. It is believed—you probably know this, Bathurst—that after Nero's death somebody went by night and strewed violets over his grave. Even a monster like Nero, you see, had someone who loved him. We are told, too, that at his death his statues were "owned with garlands of flowers. Now, mark you, Bathurst, in 'Aylmer's Field', Tennyson writes the line *'Pity, the violet on the Tyrant's grave'*. I feel that there must be in this something more than mere coincidence. I am the Vicar of Lanrebel. The churchyard is reverently spoken of as God's acre. My churchyard might reasonably be termed 'Aylmer's Field'. Have I interested you, my dear Bathurst?"

"You have, sir. Without a doubt."

"Have I convinced you—which is another matter?" Anthony finessed. "I feel that there must be some meaning behind what you have just told me, but I don't know that I can see the true meaning—yet awhile."

"Why not? What's troubling you?" The Reverend Septimus seemed a trifle impatient.

"Well, sir, the line you quoted from the poem to do with your namesake, 'the violet on the tyrant's grave'. How can we apply such a line to the memory of Jacqueline Hillier? She was no tyrant, surely?"

A strange far-away look came into the Vicar's eyes. He began to speak, as though communing with himself. "Tyranny! In how many different forms do we find it? Does it always translate itself into physical cruelty, plain and unvarnished? Or in mental oppression? Can it not be of subtler stuff? Are not many of us—even perhaps you and I—'hag-ridden' by a tyranny that is peculiarly personal? It may be petty, trivial, but we become its slaves. Do you know, my dear fellow, I was in Frayne a few days ago. I saw a book in a bookseller's window . . . the title of that book was *Love, the Tyrant*. Love! Perhaps the explanation of our little problem may even lie in that much-abused word."

"You mean in relation to Jacqueline Hillier?"

As Anthony spoke, Mrs. Aylmer gave a half-nod. It seemed of approbation. Her lips were prim and tight-pressed, as though she were anxious that her negative virtue should on no account escape her. Aylmer shrugged his shoulders. The gesture was eloquent of his opinion. Anthony realized that there might be truth in it, but still, despite all that he had heard, he was not satisfied. Those violets on the grave, that he had himself picked up and handled, those partly crushed violets . . . Anthony's mind almost stood still—if mental effort can ever be static.

He looked across at the Vicar, who, in his turn, was watching him intently. Of course! His mind rioted, it churned up fragments of truth that seemed to tumble out of their bewildered chaos and begin to form themselves into something like a sensible pattern of different and fierce-flashing colours. Jacqueline with the car, poisoned; Neill dead on the highway; and then Paul Hillier himself, strangled, but with a revolver (unfired) in the pocket of his dinner-jacket. The death of Jacqueline fitted . . . if he could but find the motive . . . the death of Neill was there for all to see, and Paul may well have followed, as a kind of natural sequence. Jacqueline—the motive behind her death? Where was this poetry-loving priest leading him? Love . . . the tyrant . . . but who could have filled the bill? . . . To his own utter surprise he observed that he had begun to address Aylmer again. "You have given me a wealth of ideas, sir. They are most welcome, because I am perfectly certain I should never have thought of 'Aylmer's Field'."

The Vicar's pleasure was visible. "I am delighted to think that I can play Gamaliel to one of our foremost investigators. I find the idea most refreshing—I'll candidly admit it. You must forgive me my little conceit, Mildred."

"I always do."

The Vicar looked sharply at her. The reply was not the one which he himself would have chosen. He resumed conversation with Mr. Bathurst in a slightly aggrieved tone of voice. "I promised you that if you accepted my invitation for this evening you wouldn't feel that your time with us had been wasted. When we've finished dinner you must come into the library and look at my books. I have several first editions. I've had to pay for them—pretty heavily, too. I don't regret that. When I make up my mind to get anything, I usually get it before I've finished."

"Usually?" queried Anthony. "Not always?"

Aylmer pursed his lips at Mr. Bathurst's second question. He might even have forgotten to answer it. Mildred, however, intervened. Dinner went on. In time Anthony handled some rare editions, thinking all the time that Paul Hillier would be buried in the morning. In the churchyard at Lanrebel, only a few yards from where Mr. Bathurst stood. Close to the bodies of his wife and son. In the midst of Life . . . Anthony came back to reply to the Vicar. It was half past eleven when he returned to the "Salvation", thinking now of the problem of "Aylmer's Field", and of the charming hospitality of the Reverend Aylmer himself.

Chapter XXVIII
INSIDE "HILLEARYS" AGAIN

Anthony Bathurst stood at his full height and faced Ann Hillier in her own home. "Going to do me a favour?" he asked, half smilingly.

"Of course. You have but to ask—you know that."

The black she wore suited her. "It's about your mother. The key to all this trouble will be found through her. That diary."

"Yes?" she said inquiringly.

"You found it amongst your mother's belongings. In her bedroom, I think you said."

"Yes," she said again, "in a drawer of a cabinet that's in the room."

"The drawer was locked, wasn't it?"

"Yes. The police were anxious for it to be opened. So it was opened. I rummaged about for them and was lucky enough to come across the diary. I knew where Jacqueline kept it because I had seen her use it on more than one occasion."

Mr. Bathurst nodded approvingly. "Now tell me, Miss Hillier, was there anything else in the drawer besides the diary? I am rather anxious to know that."

"Oh yes, Mr. Bathurst. A number of things. The drawer was full up with them."

"What were they, chiefly?"

"Trash," returned Ann with brutal candour, "personal junk. I don't think I can remember seeing a worse collection."

Anthony smiled at her description. "And by the term 'junk' you mean . . . ?"

"These foolish things," she replied with a tired smile. "Petty personal trifles that a woman hoards for a reason known to herself. Theatre programmes, powder-boxes, odd pieces of jewellery, trinkets—oh, you must know what I mean. If you haven't had a wife, you must have had a mother."

"I see. Your answer is the one that I was expecting. Now I'm coming to the favour I mentioned."

"What is it?"

"I want you to let me have a look at that drawer of your mother's. You can be there all the time, of course, while I'm looking at it. Do you mind?"

"No. Not a bit. Why should I mind? Will you come with me now?"

"Who's in the house?"

"Only the servants. The Inspector from Liskerry—Rockingham—has been here and gone. With a sergeant. They make a daily visit. The only finger-prints they could find on my father's revolver were my father's, Dr. Pakenham's, and the Inspector's own."

"What about your uncle?"

"He and Aunt Belle are out. So you can regard the coast as clear. Will you come with me?"

"I shall be only too pleased, Miss Hillier."

Ann led the way up by a broad winding staircase to the bedroom that had been her mother's. She entered on tiptoe with Anthony Bathurst following her. "That's the cabinet." She pointed to a corner of the room. "That's a corner of this little room," she murmured, "that will be for ever Jacqueline."

Anthony was silent. He knew the mood she was in, understood it completely, and surrendered it to her unconditionally. Ann went to the cabinet and opened the drawer. The drawer that Jacqueline had used for intimate associations. "Come and look for yourself, Mr. Bathurst. But it's all very 'feminine', I'm afraid." She contributed a running inventory as she turned over the contents of the drawer. "A box of air-floated face powder. Birch juice. Jacqueline was always frantically concerned to keep her youth, but you know all about that."

Anthony nodded. The pattern was still true to shape. "I know. Go on. Take the things one by one."

"A bundle of programmes. Theatre. Going back years."

Anthony noticed that the top one was of a performance of *Abraham Lincoln*, at the Lyric, Hammersmith. Ann went on. "A brooch. A cairngorm. A discarded wrist-watch. A tiny gold cigarette-case. Look. A farthing. And a Billiekin." Anthony saw a squat simian-like figure with its grotesque hands folded across its paunch. "An old season ticket—between Trinket and Paddington. A little pot of French mustard. A handkerchief. Initials—look."

"'What are they, Miss Hillier?"

"J.P.," replied Ann.

Anthony nodded again. "Jacqueline Parr."

"Yes, of course." Ann continued with the details. "A photo frame— no photo inside. It's been taken out." She remembered Mr. Bathurst's question on the day she had first driven to the "Salvation".

"Yes," said Anthony. "It would have been. It was a photograph, you see, of the murderer."

Ann gasped and turned to him, white-faced and shaken. "Mr. Bathurst! Do you really mean that? Are you absolutely sure?"

"Almost, Miss Hillier."

"But I don't understand. Why did he murder?"

"Because he loved your mother."

"Did she love him?"

"Worshipped him, I should say."

"Then why should he kill her?"

Anthony shrugged his shoulders. "I'll tell you the whole truth, Miss Hillier, if you don't mind, when the time comes. When I've got him and he's confessed. Go on with the things in the drawer, please."

Ann obeyed with unsteady fingers. "A bracelet. A bundle of old bus and tram tickets."

"Let me look at those, will you, please?"

She handed the bundle to Anthony Bathurst. He glanced through them in interested curiosity. They were of many different routes in various parts of the country. Some of the district round Trinket, some of well-known London journeys, some from the Dance district, and others over parts of Glebeshire, namely Laran, Lanrebel, Frayne, and Bonallack. From the cursory examination he gave to the little bundle, he gleaned nothing which seemed to him to be of the slightest importance. He handed the tickets back to Ann Hillier. She resumed her task. "Dance programmes. A scent bottle. Empty. Piver's Trèfle, bought in Paris. A newspaper cutting. Another bundle of something. Photos—look. Snapshots."

"May I look at them?" Anthony took this second bundle from her. The assortment was varied in the extreme. He could see as he went through them that Jacqueline herself figured in many. Also Ann, Neill, and Paul Hillier. These were the only faces which he was able to recognize. Judging from the age which Jacqueline looked to be in some of them, they covered a period of several years. As with the tickets, he handed back the little photographs.

"That seems to be about the lot," declared Ann, running her hand round the back of the drawer.

Anthony felt a sense of keen disappointment. The edifice of hope which he had begun to build appeared to have but little foundation, after all. "No letters of any kind?"

Ann shook her head. "None, I'm afraid. Were you expecting that I should find any?"

"I had hopes—of a kind." He thought things over. Of that day when he had walked with Keith Annesley to the Mile Cliff and he had lowered himself to the ledge to recover the scrap of paper he had seen there. Yes! That might well be the explanation.

"Seen enough?" said Ann, somewhat reluctantly.

For a moment or so Anthony did not reply. He went and stood close to his companion and looked at the miscellaneous contents of the drawer. He had the power of taking in many things with one sweepingly comprehensive glance. Suddenly, as he stood there, he thought of something. "What's that newspaper cutting lying there?" he asked.

Ann picked it from the heap and looked at it. "A local paper. *The* local paper, as far as we here in Lanrebel are concerned. It's a rag, of course, but everybody round here buys it. The *Laran Argus*. It's published twice a week. Wednesdays and Fridays. But that's twice too often."

"What's the date of that issue?" demanded Anthony.

"June the 8th," answered Ann, with a puckering of her brow.

"June the 8th," murmured Mr. Bathurst. "If I mistake not, that was the day on which your mother died."

"Yes," half whispered Ann. Fear began to show in her eyes. "But what do you mean? Again I don't think I understand."

"What's it all about? If we see that, it will help us. Read it, Miss Hillier, then we shall know the worst."

"It's nothing," announced Ann. "It's simply a list of the guests staying at the 'Salvation' on that particular day. Look! Oh, I feel so terribly relieved. Honestly I do. I was dreading what I should read there. Look!" She handed the newspaper cutting to Anthony Bathurst. He read the column carefully. It was exactly as she had described it to him. A list of people staying with the Paskes at the "Salvation" on the 8th of June. He read his own name in the list. He recognized some of the other names, of people who had been there with him. Ann took the cutting from him. "That's funny," she said. "Look what's underneath the 'Salvation' guest list. Perhaps that's why Jacky cut it out and kept it. It's much more likely."

Anthony looked over his shoulder at what she was reading. "St. Agnes's Cathedral, Sefton Hill, Lancashire. Stained-glass window dedicated by the Bishop of Light-pool to the memory of George Edmund Rice". Then followed a long account of the dedication ceremony and eulogy of the man commemorated. Anthony assimilated every word of it. He began to wonder more and more. If this new idea of his were true, it would mean that . . . He swung round to Ann with another question almost fiercely. "Tell me, Miss Hillier, your Rice cousins, if there really is more than one of them, was there any one of them at Trinket when your father was a master there?"

Ann shook her head blankly. "I never heard of it, but, of course, there may have been."

"I see." He handed the newspaper cutting back to her. Between her fingers and his, there came a mischance and the slip of paper fluttered to the ground. Anthony bent down at once to retrieve it for her. As he picked it up from the carpet, the sudden shock of realization came to him and he grasped completely, for the first time, the amazing truth. Ann Hillier noticed the excitement in his eyes. "What is it?" she exclaimed. "You have discovered something?"

"I think that I have discovered everything, Miss Hillier. And I'll tell you this. There will be no flowers, like the others, on your father's grave. Clutterbuck's won't be worried any more. For some time, that is, at least. He won't take the risk now—he'll never dare."

"What do you mean?" she cried. "Whom do you mean? Who is the man?"

"Give me until the end of the week, Miss Hillier, and I'll tell you all I know. Until then, you must wait in patience, please."

She held the newspaper cutting up to him. He took it from her and placed it in his wallet. "Is his name there?" she cried wildly.

"Yes," said Anthony, "but the name he goes by is not his real name. Don't forget that, it's important. Miss Hillier, I leave for Trinket to-morrow. I must. It will clinch everything. By the end of the week I hope to have the complete solution in my hands. The complete solution . . . and the murderer himself."

Ann watched him go, her eyes shining. Trinket . . . in the morning!

Chapter XXIX
THE "DEAR DAYS" OF JACQUELINE

WHEN Anthony Bathurst emerged from the train at the little Berkshire station of Trinket he knew that he had reached the penultimate stage of the Hillier murder case. For if his first string failed him he would still be able to employ his second. The platform bore the announcement. "Trinket. Alight here for Trinket School."

The day was glorious. June was departing in a blaze of sunshine. From the porter who took his ticket at the barrier he made inquiries as to direction. "Abingdon Crescent, sir, first right into the main street, turn round by the Roman Urn, then the second on your left."

Anthony thanked him suitably and strode forth for the right-hand turning that would take him into Trinket's main street. It proved to be farther away than the porter's indication suggested. Eventually, he came to the street called Abingdon Crescent. It was a mixed street of shops and private houses. Two or three of the houses, he observed as he passed them, had been converted into such offices as estate agents' and small branches of insurance companies. It was an easy matter to find the photographer's trading as "Dorothea". The name was on the front, artistically displayed for such as of the world who cared to see. Anthony entered. A tall, dark, entirely charming girl was there to greet him upon his entrance. She was immediately interested in the tall, grey-eyed, grey-flannel-suited stranger who said "Good afternoon" to her. "I'm afraid I may be giving you a great deal of trouble . . . I hope not . . . but I believe that you have been established here for many years. That is so, isn't it?"

She nodded brightly.

"Since 1892, sir . . . September, 1892. My grandfather started the business and the family has carried it on ever since. 'Dorothea' was my grandmother's name. It was my grandfather's idea to name the business after her. He set a fashion, I think . . . the idea has grown tremendously since."

Anthony took from his wallet the scrap he had salvaged from the ledge on the cliff at Lanrebel.

"Perhaps you could give me your own opinion. Is that fragment of writing on the corner there the tail-end of your trade signature?"

The girl looked a little dismayed at the question. "There's not very much to go on, is there?"

"Not a lot, I admit, but enough to give me high hope." The girl looked hard at the writing before looking up at Mr. Bathurst again. "Will you excuse me for a moment? I think there's someone in the studio who may be able to help me."

"Of course. Only too pleased."

The dark girl disappeared. Anthony waited patiently for her return. She was away for some minutes. When she came back, the dismay had left her face. "You've backed a winner," she said, smilingly. She handed him the scrap of cardboard. "One of the photographers has been with us many years. I have just shown that to him. He says he's confident it's from one of our photographs. He says he can tell by the 'flow' on the final 'A'. Tell me you're pleased," she added coquettishly.

He nodded. "Good. Now if you could do something else for me? Can you trace a customer for me—a Miss Jacqueline Parr?"

"I don't recall the name."

"It would be from twenty-two to twenty-five years ago. I was afraid you would recoil at the idea."

She shook her head doubtfully. "I'm afraid I do. There's no chance for you there. We never keep books or accounts longer than ten years. So I definitely can't help you."

"How about your ancient retainer in the studio who gave a helping hand just now?"

"Not a hope."

"None at all? Sure of it?"

"I'll try him. What was the name—Jacqueline Parr—but don't get all optimistic." She disappeared for the second time. But for the matter of a few moments only. "I was right," she said. "Not a hope. He doesn't know the name at all. Even he hasn't been here long enough for that. So I can't possibly help you."

"That's bad luck, then," returned Anthony gallantly. "Very many thanks for what you have been able to do. After all, my journey hasn't been entirely in vain. Thank you again." He raised his hat, and the dark girl's eyes followed him as he left the establishment of "Dorothea". His first string having failed him, Mr. Bathurst knew now that he must test the possibilities of his second. A taxi passed him, travelling in the direction of the studio. It showed its availability. Anthony hailed it. "To the school," he said, "as soon as you can get me there." The driver, who for some reason cultivated a moustache, wiped it with the back of his hand and grunted unintelligibly. The taxi started with an appalling jerk, but after a few moments produced a respectable speed. Trinket! Anthony's mind conjured up many memories of the famous school as he travelled towards it. Alderson, the Head at the time when Anthony's nephew Maurice Folliott had been there, would, of course, have gone by now. Yes, he had! Anthony remembered, when he came to consider it seriously, that Alderson had actually retired before Maurice Folliott had gone up to Oxford. Looking from the window of the taxi-cab, Anthony was able to see the school in the distance. He could see the row of big elms that lined the famous Dickon's Weald. Names of past Trinket giants floated into his brain and he marvelled at the strange touch of Fate which brought him here on this particular afternoon. He tried hard to think of the name of the present Head, but try as he would, it eluded him. The taxi turned, and Anthony saw that he was rapidly approaching the school. Yes, they were actually passing Dickon's Weald. Well, he must soon make up his mind. As the taxi commenced to slow down, the name of the Head came to him. Dallas! He had seen the announcement of his appointment in *The Times* a year or so previously. Anthony paid off the driver.

"Don't you want me to wait for you, sir?"

"No, thanks. You needn't trouble. I'll walk back. Besides, I may be here some little time."

The driver saluted and drove off. Anthony walked towards the main entrance of the school. A porter in a braided coat was in the hall. Anthony went straight to him. "The Head, sir? Yes, I've no doubt that can be arranged. Come with me, sir, will you, please?" Anthony followed the distinctive uniform. "Wait here, sir. Oh, have you a card, sir?"

Anthony had. It was transferred to the obliging porter. Anthony sat in a bare room. He could hear voices. They were not far away from him. His guide and friend the porter came back to him.

"Come this way, sir. The Headmaster will see you now."

Anthony was ushered into the Headmaster's study. A room of comfort, elegance, and distinction. The Head rose to greet him. A tall, spare intellectual, but a man, too, who had most obviously been an athlete.

"We are honoured," he remarked smoothly.

"The honour is mine, sir," replied Mr. Bathurst.

"Sit down, Bathurst." The Rev. Hugo Gascoigne Dallas, M.A. (Oxon), indicated a chair at the side of his desk. "Now tell me," he said, "whatever it is you want to tell me."

Anthony gratefully accepted the invitation. When he came to the name of Paul Hillier, Dallas stopped him.

"I was afraid that the murder of Hillier was behind your visit. Directly Waterson brought your card in to me. Terrible tragedy, indeed. I wasn't here, of course, when Hillier was on the staff. Before my time. Alderson was the Head in those days, so I never knew Hillier. Everybody, though, speaks most highly of him, and the Lanrebel affair has shocked the whole school."

Anthony made suitable and appropriate comment. Then he formulated a request. Dallas answered it at once. "That's comparatively easy. Pettigrew, the Maths. master, was here at the time. I'll send for him now." The Headmaster looked at his watch. "Yes. We shall catch him, it's just on the close of afternoon school. I'll ask him to come up." The Headmaster used his telephone. He stood up to it. Anthony calculated his height at six feet four inches. The Headmaster sat down again. He and Mr. Bathurst waited for the Pettigrew who had finished teaching mathematics for that afternoon. Pettigrew came in. Almost as tall as his chief, almost as thin, but woebegone and cadaverous. His gown trailed across his shoulders as though it might be even more tired of teaching than he himself was. The Head made the necessary introduction. He followed it up by an explanation. For once in a way Pettigrew's face showed interest. Like it did occasionally in the staff-room when the conversation turned to mountains and mountain-climbing. Then the Rev. Dallas put a question to him.

"Oh yes. I knew Hillier well. In fact, it was I who chiefly persuaded him to go to Dance and start on his own. That was soon after his marriage. I flatter myself to think that he rather valued my opinion." Anthony showed signs of complete understanding.

Pettigrew appreciated them. Decent fellow, Bathurst. Of course, he remembered, Uppingham and Oxford. By Jove, the old school tie does mean something, say what you like about it. The people who poke fun at it are always those that haven't one to wear!

"I suppose the school at Dance was a success, wasn't it?"

"Oh yes," responded Pettigrew. "Quite a success. The school developed splendidly. Hillier never regretted taking my advice. I know that. When he first went there, I had several letters from him. Then, of course, his uncle died and his fat legacy came to him. Lucky old devil. Not now, of course—I didn't mean that."

Pettigrew flushed as he mentally castigated himself. Like him to make a *faux pas*, but perhaps the others hadn't noticed it. The Headmaster turned to Anthony. "Perhaps you would like to put your particular questions now, Mr. Bathurst?"

"Thank you. Mr. Pettigrew, were you acquainted with the lady who became Mrs. Hillier?"

"Oh yes. I knew her well. She was Jacqueline Parr."

"She lived near here?"

"Oh yes, at 'The Tudors'. It was a big house between Trinket and Lokingham. The grandfather was a retired East India merchant. He died a few days after Jacqueline married Paul Hillier. Actually, I believe, when they were on their honeymoon."

"You may think my questions a little unusual, Mr. Pettigrew, but was the marriage of Miss Parr to—er—your colleague Hillier a particularly romantic one?"

The Rev. H.G. Dallas laughed. This inquiry was just a little . . .

Pettigrew commenced to reply. "Well, that's rather awkward to answer. Romantic, that was your word . . . well, it's difficult to say. It's a funny sort of word. Jacqueline was by way of being the beauty of Trinket. Hillier wasn't an obvious match for her, if it comes to that."

"You mean that Hillier wasn't her only admirer?"

"By Jove, I should say not. Jacqueline was a Trinket toast in those days, I can assure you. Why, there was actually another—" Pettigrew stopped abruptly as though he had said more than had been his intention. But Mr. Bathurst did not neglect the opportunity.

"Another? Were you alluding to another admirer of Miss Parr's?"

"Well, as a matter of fact, I was. Only I don't see much good in raking up old stories."

"Those stories sometimes assist an investigation, Mr. Pettigrew. They must—more often than not. You mentioned that the lady had many admirers, and then, almost in the same breath, you seemed to be on the point of a special reference. You will help me, I feel confident."

Pettigrew shrugged his shoulders. "Well, really, there's no reason why I shouldn't. As a matter of fact, I referred to another member of the staff here, at the time. His name was Paget. It was the general opinion in Trinket that Jacqueline Parr would become Mrs. Paget. But Hillier suddenly came on the scene and cut him out. The favourite went down. But eyebrows certainly went up when the news got round."

"Did she quarrel with Paget?"

"God knows—I don't. She seemed to drop him like a hot brick and teamed up with Hillier."

"What happened to Paget? Did he take it badly?"

"Like hell he did. I should say it nearly smashed him, if it didn't altogether."

"Why—don't you know?"

"No. He cleared out soon after the Hilliers were married. Went to America, I believe, or it may have been Australia. There was a rumour that he'd taken orders. I don't think any of us ever heard of him again. No news has ever come to me of him, from anywhere." Pettigrew looked a little sulky. He hated anything in the nature of gossiping and he felt that he had been guilty of something very much like it.

Anthony was conscious of a certain sense of bewilderment. He put a further question to Pettigrew. "Was Hillier a better match—at that time—than Paget?"

"Well, I suppose there were always expectations attached to him on account of his uncle. Rice—that was the name. Yes, Rice. I know the name, because several of the family have been to the school here, over many generations. That's all there was to it that I can see."

"So that Miss Parr may have been mercenary, shall we say?"

"Perhaps. But I don't think so, I don't really. I knew her."

Anthony nodded. "I can accept that. As you say, you knew the people concerned—that counts for more than anything."

"As I see it," said Pettigrew, "it's idle to conjecture or argue even about things like this. Something may have occurred between Jacqueline and Clifford Paget, although I admit they seemed terrifically attached to each other, and Hillier stepped in at the psychological moment, and there you are!"

Clifford Paget. Anthony put the name on the shelf of his brain. He looked at the Headmaster of Trinket School. "You've been extremely kind, sir. Do you think you could do one more thing for me, to clinch the position, as it were?"

The Reverend Dallas beamed at Mr. Bathurst. "Only too delighted, my dear Bathurst. Give a name to it and I'll see about it at once."

"Do you happen to have a photograph of Paget handy?"

The Headmaster gazed inquiringly at Pettigrew. "Is there one, Pettigrew? Do you happen to know?"

Pettigrew thought, and shook his head. "I'm afraid there isn't, on the premises, that is. Pity! No doubt there are photos existent, somewhere, if you only knew where to put your hand on them. But I'm afraid I can't help you."

"There you are, Bathurst," declared the Headmaster, "your ultimate lot is disappointment. I don't suppose it's the first time that it's come your way."

"You're right there, sir. But a good investigator learns to meet and treat disappointment as an impostor. Let me see now. How can I put it to you? If Mahomet won't go to the mountain, the mountain must come to Mahomet. Or, in other words, if you can't show me a photograph, I must be able to show you one." Anthony took his wallet from his breast pocket and found the cutting from the *Laran Argus* which Jacqueline had cut out and kept in her private drawer. "Have a look at this, and see if you can possibly recognize Paget."

Pettigrew took the cutting and looked at it blankly. Slowly, he began to shake his head. "Lord—no! Even allowing for the passage of the years, this is nothing like the Paget I used to know. Not a scrap like him. Differently shaped face, for one thing, nose all wrong. No, no."

Anthony bent forward towards him. "I fancy that you're looking at the wrong side, Mr. Pettigrew. Turn it over and have another look at it."

Pettigrew turned the paper over and at the same time muttered an apology for his mistake. Then instantaneously his eyes lit up. "This is Paget," he said simply . . . "not a doubt of it. He's much older, naturally, but I can recognize him at once. The nose, and the general expression on the face. Well, I'm blessed! After all these years, fancy running across Paget again like this. What a surprise!"

The Head held out his hand for the press cutting. Pettigrew passed it to him. The Head frowned. Pettigrew came to Anthony Bathurst again. "I say, Bathurst," he said. "Don't tell me that old Paget is a murderer. I can't . . ."

Anthony looked grave. "I'm not saying that, Mr. Pettigrew. I won't accuse him of that. Let me say, rather, that he's the last link in my chain. In other words, gentlemen, I can now regard my case as complete."

CHAPTER XXX
IN THE CHURCHYARD—MIDNIGHT

ANTHONY Lotherington Bathurst talked to Ann Hillier in the house called "Hillearys". She held her hand to him. "Thank you," she said simply, "for all you have done. And you say you have *not* told Inspector Rockingham?"

"Not a word, Miss Hillier. Remember that I hold no official connection with the case whatever. Until I have forced a confession—which I shall do at midnight to-night—I shall make no move. Now, one further question. No 'floral gesture' has been made so far in connection with your father's grave?"

"None at all. Before you went to Trinket you said that there would be no flowers like the others. You were right."

"Good! There's only one little matter that disturbs me. It concerns the Vicar. Before I left Trinket I sent him a note. Here's a copy of it."

Ann took the document Anthony offered to her.

Read's Hotel, Trinket.

Dear Vicar,

I am in Trinket now, as you will see from the above address. I hope to return to Lanrebel on Friday next. The information that you so kindly gave me last week has proved most valuable, and I hope to reach a complete and satisfactory solution of the Hillier case by Friday evening. Will you, therefore, kindly meet me in the churchyard of your own church a few minutes before midnight on that same evening? I rather fancy that, arising out of certain steps I have already taken, the murderer will be there to meet us.

Yours sincerely,

Anthony L. Bathurst.

Ann was shaken. "What is it, then, that disturbs you?"

"This. It seems that my cast is not going to be complete after all!"

Ann read the note for the second time. Anthony handed her another letter.

The Vicar of Lanrebel presents his compliments to Mr. Anthony L. Bathurst and thanks him for his letter, which came to hand to-day. Unhappily, however, he regrets that he is unable to accept Mr. Bathurst's invitation for Friday evening as, owing to slight indisposition, he will be away from Lanrebel for the next few days.

Anthony smiled at her as she read the second note.

"I suppose it can't be helped. All the same, I'm sorry. I should have liked the Vicar with us for the closing chapters of an extraordinary story." He chuckled. "One never likes to put on *Hamlet* without the Prince of Denmark. It simply isn't done."

"When shall I see you again?" asked Ann, a trifle dubiously.

"Early to-morrow, I hope, when I hope, too, to have in my hands the full facts of the case. Does that suit you, Miss Hillier?"

"Oh—absolutely. All right, then. Early to-morrow I shall be waiting here for you."

Anthony shook hands with her and departed. He looked at his watch. "Not long to go now," he whispered to himself. But as he made his way slowly to the "Salvation" he took himself severely to task and wondered if he were doing right. Just before he reached the inn, Dr. Pakenham flashed by in his car. Mr. Bathurst waved to him cheerfully.

The Paskes, Arthur, Frank, and Lysbeth, were talking to Pereira when Mr. Bathurst returned from "Hillearys". From the conversation Anthony could tell that Pereira had announced to them that the time had come for him to leave Lanrebel.

"I guess it's up to me to scram some time during the coming week, Uncle Arthur, and I can't tell you how genuinely sorry I shall be to have to go. I've kinda gotta like the little burg as though it were my home town. But there you are, the water flows along and we flow along with it. Human driftwood! Gee, what a swell title for a 'flick' . . . 'Human Driftwood'. Got a pull at the heartstrings directly it comes off your tongue." He spoke to Anthony as he came in. "Glad to see you back, sir!"

Anthony returned the salutation and Pereira bustled out. Arthur Paske sent his son on an errand before he looked across and spoke to Anthony. "While you were out, sir, we had a wire from Mr. Annesley. He'll be on the 7.10 train. Evidently he wanted you to know."

"Yes. I asked him to come. Thank you, Paske." Round about half past seven Keith Annesley arrived. Anthony was waiting for him. They shook hands cordially. "Tell me all about it," said Annesley . . . "tell me how you want me to help you."

"Remember what you said to me when you left here?"

"About dropping me a line, do you mean?"

"Yes, you said when you went away you would have liked to be in at the death. Well, you're going to be! I promised you, if you could help me, I'd let you know, towards the end of things, and as that end is pretty close to us now, I dropped you the appropriate line. Pleased?"

"Only too true, Bathurst. I should think I am. Am I permitted to ask questions?"

"Come into the corner, Annesley. I'll order some beer; you can ask as many questions as you please, and I will do my best to answer them—you've had some grub, of course?"

"Yes, in the train. So make it pint tankards." They migrated to their favourite corner of the lounge. Annesley leant forward eagerly. "Is it going to be a rough-house? I'd like to know that before everything else."

Anthony grinned at his enthusiasm. "Stout fellow! It depends. I'm not sure. He may take it quietly, if we can take him by surprise. So the old mind still hankers for the adventurous, eh, and spurns the commonplace?"

Keith Annesley grinned back. "Spill the facts, you old ruffian, and don't keep me in suspense."

Frank Paske put the filled tankards in front of them. Anthony began his story. Annesley listened to him with the keenest possible attention. Firstly to the details, previously unpublished, as far as he was concerned, of the murder of Paul Hillier. He made but one interruption. "It was Hillier's own revolver, you say?"

"Oh yes, that was established beyond any doubt. And I've been informed since that no finger-prints have been found anywhere in the room. I managed to get hold of that information through pulling a string at the Yard."

"That revolver business is significant, though, isn't it? Don't you consider it so?"

"Oh, undoubtedly. It proves that Hillier went in fear of something or somebody. But I'll go on."

Anthony went on with his story. He came to the invitation he had received from the Vicar of Lanrebel. Annesley's interest increased. "The Vicar, eh? That's a surprise to me, I must admit. Tell me what happened while you were there."

Again Anthony continued. To the end of the story, as far as he was able to enfold it. "Now I'll leave the details of the position as it is at the moment and come to my own plans."

"You have already made them, then?"

"Yes, I had to. I considered myself forced into the position. I knew that you would come directly I asked you, and so I was able to go ahead with confidence. I have made certain . . . well . . . I'll call them 'moves'. The word will do as well as any. Those 'moves' will cause the murderer to make at least one counter-move."

"I see. And what form do you expect that to take?"

Anthony drank from his tankard before replying. "He will come to Paul Hillier's grave at midnight tonight."

Annesley moved uneasily in his seat. "Going to be a bit eerie, isn't it? Are we in for a spot of churchyard larking? Is that the order?"

Anthony grinned. "Something like it. Why, don't you fancy it?"

"Can't say that I'm bursting with *joie de vivre* over it. Not being one of Nature's blinkin' heroes."

"Don't worry. I'll be with you—and, if you like, I'll hold your little hand when you get the jitters."

Keith Annesley grimaced at both prospects. Then his mood changed. "Are you absolutely certain that he will come? Suppose . . . just suppose . . . he didn't? What then?"

"He will come," replied Anthony gravely.

"With his flower tributes, or will he leave them out this time?"

"I'm not certain about that. All I say is he'll be there."

"Why are you so confoundedly certain about it?"

"Because of the steps that I have taken. I'm forcing his hand. If he doesn't come, you see, he gives himself away."

Annesley looked as though he were at a loss to understand. "But, surely, if he does come, he gives himself away, just as completely? That's how I see it, from the way you've put it to me."

Anthony shook his head. "He won't be sure. He'll be in doubt about everything. At midnight to-night, you'll see how right I am. Drink up, and I'll order some more beer."

Annesley shrugged his shoulders. "'Wish I were as confident as you are. You must tell me before we go exactly what you want me to do. Thank you, Frank. That's Mr. Bathurst's tankard—the one on the right, with the hot handle!"

Frank Paske attended to what he had to do.

"I shall tell you, of course. But don't worry. I haven't the least fear of your letting me down. If I had, I assure you that you wouldn't be here now."

Annesley showed pleasure at Anthony's compliment.

When closing-time arrived, Anthony went and stood by the double doors that led to the yard of the inn. Talking loudly, in a crowd of men, was Joshua Toft. His voice, raised angrily, drowned the voices of the rest. A sharp argument was evidently in progress. Anthony was interested to see within the group, and smiling superciliously, no less a person than Charles Mowbray, one-time butler at "Hillearys". There was a young woman with him. Anthony didn't recognize her. After a time, the group began to break up. Anthony saw Toft look at his watch. Individuals drifted away one by one into the shadows of lanes and cross turnings. Mowbray and the girl who was with him strolled away in the direction of Laran. Annesley joined Anthony Bathurst at the entrance to the inn yard. "What time will you be setting out?"

"At half past eleven. Even then we shall have ample time. There is no distance to go."

"Do I bring anything?"

"A stout heart and a cheerful disposition."

Annesley looked dubious. "No weapon of any kind?"

"None at all. I'll deal with that part of the business—if there is any. But there won't be, you mark my words."

"As I said before, I wish I shared your confidence. A desperate man might—"

"Don't forget what 'desperate' really means. 'Without hope'!"

"I don't! Still, if you say so . . ."

Anthony smiled and patted him on the shoulder. "Meet me just outside here at half past eleven. I have a torch—in case we shall need more light than the moon will give us."

Punctually at the time arranged, Keith Annesley joined Mr. Bathurst outside the "Salvation". The place was deserted. The inhabitants of Lanrebel were in their beds, sleeping until the morrow. The only sound Anthony and Annesley heard, as they made their way to the churchyard, was of a motor-horn in the near distance. They travelled the path they had trodden before and came to the corner of the burial ground where lay the graves of the three Hilliers. Annesley shuddered as they picked their way across the grass and between the earthen mounds. The tombstones looked like white chair-backs in the moonlight. Anthony looked round, prospectingly. After a little while, he pointed to a big headstone, about a dozen yards from the Hillier graves.

"We'll get behind that, Annesley. I don't want to advertise our presence too much before that clock strikes twelve. That's the witching hour, you know. Come with me. We can park ourselves over there, and, I hope, make ourselves moderately comfortable."

Annesley followed him to the big stone and crouched there at his side.

"Don't talk loudly," whispered Anthony, "whisper if you want to say anything."

"What's the time?" returned Annesley.

"Five minutes to zero hour. We shan't have long to wait. Don't worry."

"Good," whispered Annesley. "The sooner the better, as far as I'm concerned."

They waited in the eerie, almost artificial silence. Suddenly the church clock of Lanrebel began to strike the midnight hour. Annesley felt his wrist clasped. "Don't move more than you can help. It may be any minute now." He nodded an assurance to his companion. The two men waited. Not a sound came to disturb the calm and tranquillity of the churchyard. The minutes went by, until the clock struck again, one stroke, a quarter past twelve. Then again, two strokes, half past twelve. Anthony and Annesley still waited. In vain. Nobody came.

"Lend me your torch," said Annesley. Anthony handed it to him. He walked over to the Hillier graves and shone the light of the torch across them. But only the ordinary wreaths showed upon the grave that was Paul Hillier's. "There's nothing there," he said as he returned. "And nobody will come now."

Anthony was silent, discomfited, and disturbed. At last he spoke. "No, nobody will come now. I feel annoyed at what must seem to you my stupidity. I'm sorry. It means that I was—we'll go back to the inn, Annesley."

They walked back. Anthony was silent again. He seemed to be absorbed in mental calculation. They came to the inn.

"Is it bed?" inquired Annesley. As he spoke a car passed the curve of the Bonallack road. Its headlights almost blinded them.

Anthony watched it as it straightened itself and roared by. He nodded as though in thought. "No," he said quietly, "we won't go up yet. The night isn't over. I know where I can get a drink. Come with me. While we're waiting, I'll attempt to justify myself. I'll tell you about 'Aylmer's Field' and Jacqueline Parr. In the light of what has happened to-night, I feel that I owe you a fuller story than I have so far told."

Chapter XXXI
IN THE "SALVATION". 1.15 A.M.

ANTHONY used a key, turned a door-handle, and found a room. Then he discovered a bottle and glasses. Annesley looked pale and tired.

"Drink up," said Mr. Bathurst. "It's not a bad whisky as proprietary brands go. What was that?" He went to the window. "Can't see anything."

"Probably the wind," remarked Annesley . . . "and what were you going to tell me?"

"Of 'Aylmer's Field' and Jacqueline Parr, and of the man who didn't come to the churchyard at midnight." Anthony held his glass to the light and spoke nonchalantly. "He *couldn't* come, very well, seeing that he was already there, could he, Paget?"

Annesley sat for a moment saying nothing. Then he looked up. "So you knew? I had my suspicions once or twice. Well, congratulations!" Bitterness and resentment tinged his voice. "Do I hold my wrists out . . . for the handcuffs? I presume that Rockingham lurks somewhere near at hand?"

Anthony Bathurst sat opposite him. "No. My interest in the case has been, and still is, entirely unofficial."

"I suppose I should be grateful for that. How long have you known?"

"Since I dined with the Vicar. The 'Aylmer's Field' clue almost clinched the issue. It magnified a mere suspicion. A newspaper cutting made me almost certain, and a visit to Trinket left me in no doubt."

"Whom did you see there?"

"Pettigrew, the Maths. master."

"Old Pettigrew? Is he still there? Good Lord!"

"Why did you kill Paul Hillier? Revenge, or self-defence?"

"Oh, self-defence! It was his life or mine. He drew a gun on me. There was a struggle. I got him by the throat. He suddenly collapsed. I was astounded when he crumpled up on the carpet. His heart must have been dicky. Shall I tell you the whole story, Bathurst?"

"Let me tell it to you. Where I go wrong, correct me. When I'm short of the truth, fill in the blanks. Agreed?"

"Yes, of course, if you'll allow me to interrupt when I want to."

"You and Hillier were on the staff at Trinket over twenty years ago?"

"How did you get on to that?"

"From the corner of the photograph which Mrs. Hillier burnt on the night she died. You remember we picked it up on the ledge of the cliff-face. The ending of the word on it was 'thea'. I deduced a photograph and a studio signature. I traced it to Trinket. 'Dorothea'. Miss Hillier told me of her mother's life in Trinket and Dance. Entries in a diary kept by Mrs. Hillier satisfied me that the photograph must have been taken at Trinket."

"You are right, of course. The photo was of me."

"I guessed as much. Well, to continue. You fell in love with Jacqueline Parr."

Annesley put his head in his hands. "Madly. Devotedly. Beautifully. Jacky and I were made for each other."

"Your affection was returned. Everybody knew of your entire devotion. But, suddenly, Jacqueline married Hillier, a colleague of yours on the staff at Trinket. I don't presume, or pretend, to know why she did this."

Annesley shook his head. "The shock nearly killed me. I believed in her, as I believed in Almighty God Himself. I learned afterwards that she feared she would handicap me, if we married, in my career. My career! Good God!" Torment and bitterness came back into his voice.

"We won't dwell on it. Women in love will often deceive themselves, and go almost gladly to an unnecessary self-sacrifice for the sake (as they think) of the loved one. She married Hillier. They went to Dance. You cleared off, began to write books, and shed Clifford Paget for Keith Annesley."

"Yes. All that is true."

"But Jacqueline's heart was yours always. The diaries prove it beyond a doubt. She cherished and clung to a rather pathetic belief that you and she would come together again. I know that."

Annesley's eyes shone. "Is that really true? It's pretty wonderful."

"It is truth itself."

"I never heard of her or from her. Not a word passed between us, from the day she married until the day she died. And yet you tell me this?"

"I do. You'll know it yourself one day. We will skip the years of pain, for you and Jacqueline, and come to the evening of the 8th of June last. The night of the Hilliers' dinner party. A most amazing incident occurred. Your American namesake died. The news of his death was published in the English newspapers."

Annesley nodded, but wonderment was in his eyes. "I know. I read it myself at Blackstock. It was a rather uncanny experience. I was in a pub at the time and had my leg pulled about it. But how did Jacqueline . . . ?"

"The local paper here made a bloomer. It published a short announcement of the death with a photograph of the deceased Keith Annesley. Unhappily, the Press Photography Bureau, which supplied it, sent one of you. I have known this mistake to happen before when two men have had identical names. The photograph had been taken from the wrong index. Easily done. In all probability the photographs were next to each other wherever they were kept."

"Go on," said Annesley hoarsely.

"This is the tragic part of it. Jacqueline saw the heading, 'Death of Keith Annesley', saw the photograph of you, jumped to an erroneous conclusion, and her life was over. Her dream, the dream that had sustained her, was shattered. The purpose to which she had so fervently dedicated her life no longer existed. She saw the name and the photograph, and the shock was so acute she didn't trouble to read any more. She went out. By her own hand. She had poison in her possession. It wasn't traced to her, because I fancy it was purchased on the Continent, where she was on holiday, as an antidote to sea-sickness, which she dreaded."

Annesley was close to breaking down. Anthony Bathurst saw it, and paused for a moment. After a time he went on again. "She took with her her treasured memories of you, Annesley. Letters. The last letter you ever wrote to her was the one she had in her hand, I suggest, during dinner. Your photograph. She burnt them before she took the poison that was to kill her, driving the car, homeward, until the time came. Her last words were, I suggest, 'My Cliff! *Toujours!*' Cliff being the abbreviated form of your Christian name, Clifford. Neill, who found her, interpreted them, quite reasonably, in the way he did. Do you think I'm right in my surmise, Annesley?"

Annesley just moved his head as his hands covered his face. Shaking sobs began to come from him. Anthony waited. Annesley pulled himself together. "I'm sorry," he said quietly. "I loved her. I have always loved her, and this realization of her faithfulness to me has knocked me over. When I heard, as I thought, of her murder, and came down here to find out what I could, I didn't suffer much. I thought she had forgotten me years ago, but now it's different."

"Yes. You came down here. And I met Ann and Neill Hillier. The latter had been the last person to see his mother alive. His sister knew her mother much better than he did. He was certain that his mother had been murdered. When I went to 'Hillearys' first of all, Neill came in. I was introduced to him. He was coming to see me the night he died. You know now how he died, Annesley, don't you?"

Annesley shook his head. "I haven't the slightest idea. I can't think of anybody who had a motive to kill him."

"There was nobody. Neill Hillier died, as the insurance policies put it, by an 'act of God'. You remember the storm, Annesley?"

Annesley nodded.

"He was killed, poor lad, by the flying branch of a tree. No human hand could have smashed a skull as his was smashed."

"Are you sure of that, Bathurst?"

"Don't you remember my discussing it with you on your last evening at the inn? I put the solution in front of you then. Neill was killed by a branch of flying beech . . . I told you of it. But there wasn't a beech tree anywhere near the spot where his body was found. The nearest beech was just over a hundred yards away across the meadow. I located it and saw the place from which that mighty branch had come. So there we were, you see. I was already contemplating the fact that two 'murders' had not been murders at all. The first had been a suicide. The second had been an accident. But then, right on the heels of my forming this opinion, I was brought up with a jerk. Paul Hillier was found dead, and in this third instance there wasn't the slightest doubt that he had been killed by some person or persons unknown. Then I began to think in terms of *you*. The violets. The yellow roses. Can you recall what I pointed out to you at Mrs. Hillier's grave? With regard to the condition of the violets? That they were crushed?"

Annesley nodded again. "Yes, only too well."

"I deduced from that that they had been brought some distance, not purchased in the neighbourhood. They meant nothing, of course, beyond your tribute to a lady's memory?"

"Nothing beyond that. I brought them with me from town. I wanted to make a magnificent gesture, the last thing I could do for the girl I had loved. When you were asking Lysbeth about the language of flowers, I thought of 'Aylmer's Field', and the Vicar's name seemed so appropriate for the purpose. So I had the yellow roses put on Neill's grave when his turn came."

This time it was Anthony's turn to nod. "As I thought. I knew that you couldn't have killed Jacqueline. I knew that you didn't kill Neill, but I did suspect you as our floral expert. Why? I mean, why were you functioning thus? I was puzzled, frankly bewildered. The only chance was, as I could see it, that you had known Jacqueline before she had come to Lanrebel."

"But what made you suspect me in the beginning? I had only just arrived at the place."

"So had the flowers. The arrivals were coincident. In addition to which, you gave yourself away." Mr. Bathurst's tone was nonchalant, but the words were firm.

Annesley stared at him. "How on earth do you mean?"

"Remember when we went to look at the violets—your violets?"

"Yes."

"There's an iron gate that leads into the churchyard. You have to put your hand through the railings of it and find a most awkwardly placed latch. The first time I did it I thought how inconvenient it was. You push it up instead of down, which would be the customary method. Then I remembered that as we had come in, you had manipulated it with the greatest ease. I wondered then if you had been in the churchyard of Lanrebel before. It was an idea. I never relinquished that idea. You went back to Blackstock. I was content to wait; nobody had been murdered, but I was curious as to the reason of it all happening. You called on Hillier, I suppose, that day you left?"

"I broke my journey at Liskerry. Stayed there until the evening. I wanted to talk to him about Jacqueline. My mind was so full of her. He let me in himself. . . didn't recognize me at first. When he did—almost at once, when we got into his room there—he accused me of having murdered Neill . . . and her! The fact that I was in the district, I suppose, caused the suspicion to flash into his mind. I was amazed at his fury. He flew at me. I grappled with him. Then he drew his revolver. We struggled. I got him by the throat. Suddenly he dropped the gun and collapsed. His heart was not too good, I guess. You know the rest."

"Did he have the gun in his pocket?"

"Not at first. When he knew it was I he made an excuse to get away for a moment. When he returned you can guess he had it in his pocket."

"Yes, I see that."

"I tidied up after he died with my gloves on in case of fingerprints. There seemed nobody about. Cleared away all traces of the struggle, put the gun back in his pocket, shoved the body behind the settee, and caught the last bus into Laran. It was crowded. Nobody paid particular attention to me. Next day, I went back to Blackstock properly."

"Well, there I was when the Vicar sent for me and gave me the clue of 'Aylmer's Field'. Tennyson! You again. You had shown me you knew your Tennyson well. Not the trite quotations, but lines from such stuff as 'Vivien's Song'. Yes, you were the flower-giver, I felt certain. My visit to Trinket settled matters."

Annesley raised his head. It was evident where his thoughts still were.

"Bathurst, tell me, why were Jacqueline's clothes torn and mud-stained when she died?"

"She had wandered along the cliff in the half-light and knelt down on the grass. To burn her treasures. You know what it is when you do anything like that. Barbed wire, grass, earth. They are all destructive to clothing."

"You think it was that? I've worried over it."

"You know, Annesley, my luck has been in on this case. No investigator ever had more valuable help. Dr. Pakenham gave me the psychology of the affair, that Jacqueline had a secret dedication. Ann brought me the vital diaries, and the Vicar taught me about the Tennyson poem. Indeed, I have precious little myself to wave flags about."

"Pakenham," murmured Annesley reflectively. "I wonder how it was that he—"

"He was more than half in love with her, knowing all the time he had no chance. I think that she had probably told him a good deal of the truth. They were great friends. Sometimes, if he were walking, she would pick him up in her car and drop him where he wanted to be dropped. They were close pals—leave it at that, Annesley."

The latter rose. "It's late. Well, Bathurst, what do I do?"

"There's an early train in the morning. Why not catch it? I hate that sullen look on Rockingham's face."

Annesley moved to the door. "Thank you, Bathurst. I understand."

Anthony shook him by the hand.

Annesley pushed open the door.

Anthony called to him. "Oh, by the way, Annesley, here's something you might care to have. I'll fix it with Ann when I see her. Don't worry. It's that diary I mentioned to you."

Annesley's eyes shone with gratitude. "Oh, I say, how can I—"

"Don't try to. Good luck!"

Annesley closed the door behind him.

Mr. Bathurst communed with himself. "It was a lover and his lass that lost their way. Ah, well, it's time I was in bed." He lit a cigarette, and spoke aloud, whimsically.

"Good-night, Jacqueline."

THE END